MADLY

AMY ALWARD

SIMON & SCHUSTER BFYR

New York London Toronto Sydney New Delhi

SIMON & SCHUSTER BFYR

An imprint of Simon & Schuster Children's Publishing Division

1230 Avenue of the Americas, New York, New York 10020

Originally published in 2015 in Great Britain by Simon & Schuster UK Ltd.

First US edition September 2015

For information about special discounts for bulk purchases, please contact Simon & Schuster
Special Sales at 1-866-506-1949 or business@simonandschuster.com.

The Simon & Schuster Speakers Bureau can bring authors to your live event.

For more information or to book an event, contact the Simon & Schuster Speakers
Bureau at 1-866-248-3049 or visit our website at www.simonspeakers.com.

Jacket design and illustration by Greg Stadnyk

Interior design by Tom Daly

The text for this book is set in Goudy Oldstyle Std.

Manufactured in the United States of America

10 9 8 7 6 5 4 3 2 1

Library of Congress Cataloging-in-Publication Data

Alward, Amy.

Madly / Amy Alward.—First edition.

pages cm.— (The potion trilogy ; [1])

Summary: Samantha's ability to mix potions is needed when her family is summoned to take
part in an ancient quest to save Princess Evelyn from a potion gone awry, but will curing the
princess doom Samantha's chance at love?

ISBN 978-1-4814-4378-4 (hardback)—ISBN 978-1-4814-4380-7 (eBook)

[1. Alchemy—Fiction. 2. Magic—Fiction. 3. Love—Fiction. 4. Princesses—Fiction.] I. Title.

PZ7.1.A49Mad 2015

[Fic]—dc23

2015009955

To Juliet,

whose magical talent is to make things happen

Chapter One

Princess Evelyn

A TINY BEAD OF BLOOD BLOOMED WHERE the knifepoint pressed against the tip of her finger. She held it over the rim of a glass vial and watched as the droplet fell, turning the liquid in the bottom from pink to a dark, inky blue.

Strange.

She'd always expected a love potion to be red, not blue.

Chapter Two

Samantha

THE DIRT CAKED ONTO THE CURVED GLASS surface of the jar is so thick, not even a hint of a label is visible. I give it a quick scrub with the edge of my sleeve before remembering Mum's stern warning not to keep ruining my shop clothes. Instead, I grab the rag I shoved into my jeans pocket this morning. Another vigorous rub reveals my grandfather's spindly hand-writing, neat and precise except for where the ink has bled into cracks like fingers reaching out in the linen parchment.

Berd du Merlyn

"No way." The words slip out as a sudden swell of excitement wiggles its way up my spine. I have to put the jar back down onto the shelf and take a few deep breaths to calm myself before I can continue.

"What have you found?" My best friend Anita looks over at me from her perch a few shelves over.

The two of us are balancing on ladder rungs three stories and thirty-six shelves high. We have a deal. Anita helps me with my huge, mind-numbing task of doing an inventory on my family store's thousands of ingredients and mixes, potions, plants, and wotsits. In return, I agree to go with her to watch the princess's eighteenth birthday concert on one of the big screens by the castle, even though hearing about her life makes me cringe. I've secretly packed a book in my bag, just in case.

I grin widely and Anita drags her ladder toward me. The tracks are old and clogged with dust, and even with the drops of oil I use to lubricate the wheels they still won't run smoothly.

I turn the jar in her direction. She lets out a low whistle. "Do you think it's real?"

"Who knows," I say. My thumping heart betrays me. Every time I search these shelves, I feel like I'm digging deeper and deeper into a lost treasure trove, and one day I'm going to find something great. This could be it. "There's a plant I've read about in *Nature & Potion* that's known as wizard's beard. This could just be an old name for it." Uses for wizard's beard spring into my mind before I can stop them: A key ingredient in potions dealing with shock—brew for five minutes in hot (but not boiling) water to help ease the sharing of bad news.

It's a relatively common ingredient, and wouldn't be that exciting a find.

If, however, this turns out to be real Merlin's beard— from the man himself . . . well, I suddenly know how we're going to pay for the leak in the roof I found yesterday (the hard way, with a wet head) which is now temporarily taped over with duct tape.

I web my fingers over the top of the lid and twist with all my might. There's a brief tug of resistance and then the lid jumps off the jar, along with a great puff of dust that explodes right in my face.

A hacking cough and frantic arm-waving disperse the dust, but my heart sinks.

Empty.

Anita pats me on the arm. "Something else to add to Kirsty's list?"

"Looks like." I sigh, then take a pen out from behind my ear and jot down *wizard's beard* on my list of missing things to ask Kirsty, our Finder, to collect for us. And it looks like I'm going to have to find another way to fix that leak.

Sometimes, if I'm feeling romantic, I think about all the generations of Kemis that have stood on these rungs, how many great alchemists have studied these shelves.

But then reality hits: the store is falling apart, our supplies are diminishing, and we have no business coming in to change it.

It wasn't always this way. Kemi's Potion Shop was once one of the most prominent apothecaries in Kingstown. But no one needs apothecaries anymore. Not when they have the megapharmacies downtown selling synthetic versions of traditional potions for half the price. Now we're leftovers from a previous time. Relics.

Anita's dad also owns a potion store, specializing in mixing techniques from Bharat. When his apprentice left to retrain as an engineer, Mr. Patel decided not to hire another—even though Anita offered to give up her place at university to take over. When he retires in a couple of years, he's going to close his shop for good. Another apothecary bites the dust, while Kemi's Potion Shop clings on for dear life.

Mr. Patel is lucky. At least he's chosen to close his store, so he has some measure of control. A familiar pit opens in my stomach as I wonder what will happen to me when our time runs out.

Anita slides back along the shelves to where she'd last been working. I try to drum up some enthusiasm for the task again, but it's disappeared into the ether like the dust motes from the empty jar.

"Oh my god, Sam, look at this!"

"What?" I scramble my way across to her. What could she have found? Sphinx breath? Or maybe even a dragon's tooth?

She thrusts her phone in my face. Onscreen is Princess

Evelyn posing inside one of the grand palace ballrooms. "The Princess is wearing the same Prime Store dress to her eighteenth that I wanted to buy for the summer ball! Great, now it's going to be sold out everywhere," she pouts.

"I can't believe you're actually going to the summer ball."

"Yeah, well, not all of us shun boys for potions, like some people I know."

"Very funny. You don't have a date, though, do you?"

"I'm lining up my suitors like I'm Princess Evelyn herself, just waiting for my perfect match." Anita flicks her long glossy black hair, then sticks out her tongue.

I throw my cloth at her and she giggles.

"So who's your bet for her date tonight?" Anita asks.

"What do you mean?"

Anita rolls her eyes at me. "Come on, if you're going to force me to help with your inventory you have to make it a bit fun for me. I'll go first, I think it'll be Damian."

"No way. The royals would never let the princess marry a pop star. It'll be Prince Stefan from Gergon. It'd be good for diplomacy."

"Well, that's boring. Ooh, I know. Zain Aster."

"You think?"

"Why not? Arjun says all anyone at uni can talk about is how good friends he is with the princess." Arjun is

Anita's brother, two years older than we are. He and Zain had been in the same year at our school. "Have you seen Zain around lately?" Anita wiggles her eyebrows suggestively.

"That's all in your head, silly. Zain Aster has no idea who I am."

"If you say so."

Chapter Three

Princess Evelyn

HER HEART POUNDED AS RENEL, THE MOST senior advisor in the royal household, announced Zain's arrival. Around her neck was a silver heart-shaped locket, which she clutched tightly between her fingers. Yet the moment she saw him, she felt all her nerves and tension ease away. She even giggled as Zain strolled straight in as if he owned the place, bypassing her spluttering advisor.

"Evie!" He walked right up to her and wrapped her in his arms. He wore a musky, trendy cologne, with chemical undertones from the lab.

"You've dressed up for the occasion," she whispered, placing her fingers lightly on the textured shoulder of his dinner jacket.

He laughed. "Well, it's only the biggest party of the year, and I have to look good for the ladies." He started dancing on the spot and mimicked popping his collar.

"You scrub up okay, I suppose," she said in what she hoped was a normal tone, even though his words had been like miniature daggers to her heart.

"Renel, a moment?" she asked, and waited for the beak-nosed advisor to leave the room.

"You look insane!" Zain said, stepping back and holding her arm out to admire her.

She did look good. Her long blond hair was tied back from her face, a ribbon straining to contain the loose tumble of curls, and her stylist had embedded feather-light wisps of gold amongst the strands. Her floor-length dress, made of periwinkle blue sparkles, floated around her lithe frame. So many designers had begged for the commission to style her for her eighteenth birthday party. She'd chosen a local designer, stocked on the high street—a decision called "bold" and "courageous" by the media. She'd just liked the dress.

The locket was the only accessory that didn't match. But it had its own purpose. And now it was time.

"Drink?" she asked, cursing inwardly as her voice squeaked. She crossed to a small table by the window.

"Of course!" Zain replied.

She smiled, then turned her back on him to pour wine from a delicate crystal carafe into two of the finest goblets in Nova, with beautiful pewter bases polished to a mirror shine. With one swift movement, she opened the locket. Deep indigo powder fell into the bottom of his glass, dissolving into the dark red liquid.

She examined the glasses closely and breathed a sigh of relief—they looked identical. She waited for a beat, but he didn't question or confront her. All was going according to plan.

"To falling in love?" she proposed.

He took the glass from her outstretched hand and clinked it against hers, smiling.

"To you, Princess."

"To us." It came out as barely a whisper as she lifted the goblet to her lips and watched him do the same. Then she closed her eyes, threw back her head, and downed the wine in a single gulp. It slid down her throat as gently as honey. A warmth rushed through her body, coursing through her veins until it felt like her fingertips and toes were on fire and her heart would explode with happiness.

Her eyelashes fluttered open.

And staring into the cool blue eyes reflected in the silver base at the bottom of her goblet, she fell madly, deeply, and irrevocably in love.

Chapter Four

Samantha

THE BELL ATTACHED TO THE SHOP DOOR jingles, then abruptly snaps off its hinges and tumbles to the floor. I sigh, opening my notebook to another list: "Things to Repair." I scribble down *entrance bell* underneath *leaking roof.*

Looking down from the ladder, I spy the sweep of my mum's skirt as she comes out of the back room to greet the customer. My view is blocked by one of the big wooden beams that crisscross the higher levels of the store, supporting the vast expanse of shelves.

Snippets of conversation drift up from the shop floor, the sound bouncing off the hundreds of glass jars. "No trouble, Moira dear . . . pay us next week."

A groan escapes me before I can help it and I scramble down the series of ladders as fast as I can. Even so, I don't reach the ground floor until the door snaps shut on Moira's oversized behind.

"Mum, honestly!" I head over to where I've laid out the mixes due for pick-up that week. Sure enough, Moira's entire monthly prescription is missing. I bash the button that opens the till and all that's inside is the float: the pathetic array of coins left in the drawers every night and a dusty fiver so torn and faded I bet it isn't even legal tender anymore.

"Moira's seventy-three. You know she can be forgetful."

"What, so forgetful she leaves her purse behind every single time?" I mumble. It's no use bringing up this argument with Mum. She sees the good in everyone. The trouble is, at seventy-three, Moira is probably one of our youngest customers. No, really—the only people who choose us over one of the megapharmacies are the old folks who refuse to trust the synthetics. And I can tell from the way Moira stops just around the corner from the store to double- and triple-check her prescriptions that she knows exactly what she is doing whenever she comes into Kemi's Potion Shop.

The thought makes me angry again. "This is supposed to be a business."

"Sam! How many times do I have to tell you not to talk to your mother that way?" Dad strides in through the door in the shelving that leads to Granddad's lab, smoke billowing onto the shop floor before he manages to close it again. Granddad is concocting this week's mixes for our (admittedly very small) client base. A smidgeon of guilt tugs at me—I should be in there helping, like a good apprentice.

Dad wraps an arm around my mother's waist and kisses her on the cheek. I smile, unable to stay annoyed for too long about Moira. And it's nice to see my parents so happy: Mum in her bright lipstick, long skirt, and flower-print top, Dad staring at her like she is still a beautiful young woman way out of his league. And technically, she is way out of his league. She is Talented—a class of society with the ability to channel magic through an object. She's only got a low-grade ability, and her object—a divining rod—sits on top of her bedroom dresser gathering dust. But she's Talented all the same. She could have married into another Talented family and had lots of Talented babies. But instead, she fell in love with my dad, and Dad is ordinary—someone with no access to magic. Just like me.

Being ordinary is what makes us great alchemists. Our lack of magic means we can work with magical ingredients without risk of taint or contamination. But it's not the only factor. What makes the Kemi family special is our unrivalled skill in the alchemical arts—to know by feel the recipe of any potion, to tease out the properties of each ingredient, to understand the mysteries that go into building a cure.

In my dad's case, the gift of alchemy skipped a generation, so he could never become his father's apprentice.

But if he's ever felt any disappointment at not having potion-making skills, he tries not to show it. Instead, he works as a bus driver around town. Ordinaries dominate any job that requires interaction with technology—pilots and computer engineers are, for the most part, magicless. Mum works in the store but also took a second job teaching music at Molly's school, so we have a bit of extra income coming in. But despite both of them knowing how bad things are with the business, neither will let me do anything other than be an apprentice to my granddad.

Because when you have the Kemi gift, you have to use it.

When I can coax it out of him (and often only after I've scrubbed clean the lab), Granddad tells stories about how our ancestors were once the official potion-makers to the royal family. Now it's ZoroAster Corp., the top synth manufacturer in Nova, which holds that honor. They took it from us when the founder of ZA Corp., Zoro Aster himself, won the last Wilde Hunt to occur in Novaen history. Wilde Hunts were these intense competitions between alchemists, established by the first Novaen king, King Auden, to find the best cures whenever one of the royal family was in mortal danger. King Auden had a legendary hunting horn said to be made from a prehistoric creature that had its own form of Talent. The horn itself was definitely imbued with magic—it called alchemists to the hunt and determined the winner by turning gold if the correct potion was submitted.

The prize of winning a Wilde Hunt was a pot of gold crowns and, even more valuable, an immense share of the royal magic. For alchemists, who were almost exclusively ordinary, the dose of magic was invaluable. That didn't mean Talenteds didn't try to win the competition.

And Zoro was the first Talented to succeed. He used his winnings to set up the first ever synth lab, producing synthetic potions for every ache, pain, and ailment and changing our industry forever. In one fell swoop, he not only took the Kemi royal commission, but doomed the ancient art of potion-making in which we were expert.

Wilde Hunts are a thing of the past now. The royal family is so well protected—they have the best doctors, highly trained bodyguards, the Novaen secret service— that mortal danger is very hard for them to come by. They turn up at events, sure, to open hospitals and hand out honors, but not much else. Once it became clear the king and queen were only going to have one child, and Princess Evelyn was their sole heir to the throne of Nova, they did everything in their power to ensure nothing could ever happen to her.

Anita touches my arm; she's followed me down from the shelves. "If we don't get a move on, we're going to be late."

"Oh, sweetie, yes—you don't want to miss the start!" Mum is not-so-secretly in love with the royal family, and piles of glossy magazines are stuffed onto a ledge beneath the shop till. She keeps them out of sight from my grand-dad, who burns them in the lab's oven if he finds them. "You can tell me all about it when you get back."

"You know I'm not good with who's-wearing-what-designer and who's-arrived-with-whom and all that stuff."

"Take lots of pictures, then," she says with a smile. "Molly will want to see them."

"Molly will have a much better view than me," I say. Molly is my sister, and although she's only twelve, she's our family's hope. She is Talented, having inherited it against the odds from Mum's side of the family. When her Talent was first detected, I asked her what it felt like. In her cute, eight-year-old way she said it was like swim-ming in a stream of magic. Now that she's twelve, she'll soon be able to channel that magic through an object, like turning on a tap.

It's why my parents have been so happy lately. Molly's Talent test results came back sky-high. She's going to be strong. She can have a real future, one that's not dependent on a store that's going out of business. But to ensure that future, she needs to go to a special Talented school, and that costs money. Lots of money that we don't have, and won't have if Mum keeps giving away all our potions for free. Every spare penny goes toward Molly's education, making sure she has every opportunity. I could resent her for it, but I don't. She's a much better investment than me.

She is up at the castle already, on a day out with her Talented friends.

"Try to make sure Sam has a good time, won't you, Anita?" Mum shakes her head at me, her hands on her hips.

"I'll do my best, Mrs. Kemi."

Before Mum can delay us any more, I step out onto the street. The old wooden sign bearing the faded Kemi crest creaks above my head, and I skip out of its way on autopilot, convinced that one day soon it's going to come crashing down.

Anita links her arm in mine, and we follow Kemi Street out of the alchemist district. Kingstown is built on the remains of an extinct volcano, an imposing castle perched at the very top. Many of the oldest and most beautiful buildings in Kingstown stretch down the hill from the castle, along a wide high street known as the Royal Lane. The rest of the city spreads out around the hill, a sea of modernity around the island of old buildings.

The Royal Lane is already packed with people on their way up to watch the party. The normally bustling stores that line the street have closed early for the night, but large screens play a constant stream of advertising for everything from the newest fashion, to the finest wands, to the most advanced synths.

"Samantha Kemi," a voice says, deep and strangely familiar.

I spin around abruptly, bumping into a couple who had been walking hot on my heels. It clearly wasn't them calling me, and I mutter an apology. As they scurry away, I notice that the woman's dress morphs from rose pink to crimson and back again. Glamoured. I feel a stab of jealousy. I'll never be able to afford any glamoured clothing. I catch Anita's eye and we both roll our eyes as if on cue. "Talenteds," she mutters.

"Did you hear someone call my name?" I ask Anita.

She shakes her head, and when I don't hear it again, we keep walking.

We pass by a bus shelter, where an animated screen flashes an image of Princess Evelyn swirling in a glittering blue evening gown. TONIGHT: PRINCESS EVELYN TURNS EIGHTEEN! TUNE IN TO ATC FROM 7 P.M. Everyone who's not up at the castle with us will be glued to the cast, including my mum.

The crowds thicken, even though the party isn't due to start for another hour, and we're forced to stop by a small army of police on horseback.

"We should've left earlier," Anita says, craning her neck to try to see over the sea of people. "I heard most of our class got invites to the actual party in the palace."

"At the castle, you mean."

"No, I mean at the palace. Up there, somewhere," she waves her hand vaguely above our heads. The castle in Kingstown is the royal family's official residence. But their real home is Palace Great, a glamoured castle, rumored to be hidden in the skies above Kingstown, although even on a cloudless day there's nothing to be seen.

"Only the Talented people in our class, then."

"Okay, I'll give you that."

There's a great sound like a thousand trumpets blaring. I stop in my tracks and cover my ears with my hands. Has the concert started already?

"Are you okay?" Anita asks. She grabs one of my hands and I think she's afraid I'm going to run away back home and break my part of the bargain.

"Did you not hear that?" My ears are still ringing from the noise.

"Hear what?"

"Samantha Kemi," says the deep voice again.

"What? Who keeps saying my name?" I spin around, frustrated, as if someone is pulling my ponytail and then running away.

Anita frowns. "I didn't hear anything, Sam."

Then, out of the corner of my eye, I spy the bus stop ad. The Princess in her beautiful glittering dress is gone. In her place is the king of Nova.

And he's looking right at me.

Chapter Five

Samantha

THE KING SPEAKS. "SAMANTHA KEMI, AS the apprentice of registered alchemist Ostanes Kemi, you are Summoned to Palace Great immediately."

I blink, because anything requiring more rational thought is impossible right now. The king of Nova—a person I've only ever seen on television casts, in newspapers, and once very far away up on the balcony of the castle—is Summoning me to the palace.

Can he even Summon me to the palace? This has to be some kind of trick, because there's no way that the royal family want anything to do with some lowly apprentice alchemist . . . unless I did something wrong? But then it would be the police at my door, not the royal family. We have a government, politicians and laws like everywhere else. The royals are figureheads, not dictators.

They can't use their magic to stop someone in the street and Summon them to the palace.

This isn't real. It's a joke. "Anita, are you seeing this?" I ask.

"Sam, I have to go."

I tear my eyes from the king's face for a moment. Anita is staring wide-eyed at her phone. She looks scared. And if she can see the king's eyes narrowing every second I leave him hanging, she isn't showing any sign of it. It must be a private message just for me.

"My dad's been Summoned and Mum wants me to come home straightaway," she says, holding out her phone for me to see the text.

"You go," I say, and then I bite my bottom lip and swallow hard.

"What's happening?" she whispers. I guess we're both about to find out. She gives me a quick hug and then disappears into the crowd, heading in the direction of her home.

When I turn back to the screen, the king is gone—and for a brief moment I wonder if it's all been a dream. Now there's another man: one with a forked beard protruding from his chin.

"Samantha Kemi, I am Renel Landry, advisor to the royal family. Can you confirm that you have heard the Summons and are ready to travel to Palace Great immediately?"

I wonder what choice I have. What on earth can the royal family want with me? "Y-yes," I stammer.

I can't believe that no one has stopped to stare at this strange spectacle, but everyone flows past the bus shelter as if the entire structure doesn't exist. The power of the royals. The advisor shifts to one side, his hand beckoning me through the screen. "You have transported before, haven't you?" he asks.

Transported? The notion finally breaks my nerve and I almost laugh in the man's face. But I compose myself and shake my head. "No, sir." Then, my eyes finally focus and I see the opulent room behind him, one half of an immense gold chandelier behind his head, rich tapestries on the wall, and suddenly I'm overwhelmed by such an immense wave of curiosity that it converts into bravery. "But I've watched others do it and I'm confident I can do it too."

He gives me a withering look and I know he doesn't buy it for a second. "Such confidence is misplaced. The trip to Palace Great is long . . ."

Truth is, I'm not comfortable with the idea of transporting. I know a few of the basic rules: Hold tight. Keep your mouth closed. Never break eye contact. Any screen—or mirror—can be used to transport, although most Talented households have a designated screen known as a Summons. For long distances—or for travel overseas—most people use the kingstown Transport Terminal.

But doing it myself, from a bus stop in the middle of the street, is another thing entirely.

I can hear the king barking out an order. "Bring her. We're wasting time."

A grimace crosses Renel's face and he returns his gaze to me, eyes filled with determination. They don't lose their sheen of contempt, though. I hate the way snobby Talenteds look down on people like me. "All right, Miss Kemi. You say you can do it and it is a matter of urgency that you reach the palace as soon as possible." He holds his arms out, and the barriers between us break down. His fingertips push through the glass of the screen, which ripples like a pond disturbed by a stone.

"I'm coming," I say, with more determination than I feel. I reach out and grab his outstretched hands, stare into his eyes, and allow myself to be pulled into the glass.

The ground slips away from my feet, the crowds of people falling away from me even though I feel as if I'm not moving at all. His Talent is so strong; he guides me easily along the streams of magic to the palace. I'm pulled higher and higher, and in my peripheral vision I can see we're following the line of the rooftops as they slope abruptly upward. It's the strangest feeling—not like flying, since there's no wind, no rush of air passing by, just Renel's eyes locked on mine and the tug of his arms straining my shoulders.

It happens all too quickly. As we near the castle at the top of town, suddenly I'm being dragged directly upward, into the darkening sky. My heart rushes into my throat and although I know I don't have far to go, I feel an overwhelming urge to look down on the city. It's madness, it could mean my death, but the temptation is too much. I look down.

Renel grimaces, sweat breaking out on his forehead. "Don't break eye contact!" he shouts, but a moment too late.

I'm freefalling. Whatever magic had suspended me is gone. The first thing that strikes me is the cold. Blood of dragons, it's freezing! But then my stomach drops from my body and I scream as the wind roars in my ears.

Arms burst through the air, four strong hands gripping my shoulders. The wind and cold are shut out as abruptly as a slammed door, and with one final grunt of effort I am pulled through a screen and onto a polished marble floor.

I land with a thump I know will raise a blue-and-yellow bruise on my hip by morning.

Salve of Agata's hazel—to clear a bruise in less than twenty-four hours.

Renel waits for me as I scramble to my feet. A prickly wave of shame rises, the heat of it creeping up my neck to reach my cheeks. As if embarrassing myself in front of the king and his advisor could be any worse, the room is filled with people. I relax a little when I spot Mr. Patel in the crowd. His is the only face displaying a modicum of concern. I shuffle away from the large screen on the wall that I came in through, trying to blend into the crowd.

The king paces, and the sight of him is unnerving. He cuts a domineering silhouette in full military dress, every button bright and polished, obviously ready for a TV appearance. This is not an occasion for the likes of me, in my ripped jeans and the band T-shirt I was wearing out to the concert. I hug my arms around myself, wishing that I could crawl under the lovely oriental carpet and hide. Or at least put on a smarter shirt.

"Can we begin?" the king says, looking up from his pacing at Renel.

"We're still waiting for one more."

"Well, we can't wait any longer. Get started." He waves a gloved hand impatiently.

Renel draws a deep breath. "Princess Evelyn has been poisoned."

Shockwaves ripple through the room and my hand flies to my mouth. This is the last thing that I expected. The royal family is untouchable. The palace is one of the most secure buildings in Nova. Who could break down the magical barriers put up by one of the world's most powerful Talented families?

"Is she all right?" someone asks.

"We don't know. But we do know this . . ." Renel hesitates. He walks over to the center of the room, where there is a tall column of crimson velvet cloth. He pulls the cloth away, revealing an immense curved horn, as long as my arm and black as lacquered ebony.

Intricate hunting scenes are carved into the bone, and thin gold bands circle both ends. It floats in the center of the room, encased in a beam of golden light. It is breathtakingly beautiful. And it can only mean one thing. "Auden's Horn has awoken. The Princess's life is in mortal danger, and the horn has called you here to join in a Wilde Hunt for the cure."

A frisson of electricity runs through me. Can this really be happening? But I don't want to question it. Wilde Hunts create alchemy rock stars. My spine straightens, my arms fall by my sides, and I hold my head a little higher.

"Over my dead body." There's a growl from behind me that I recognize. My granddad enters the room, accompanied by two guards. The flat cap he always wears has been knocked askew; he looks like he's barely been able to button up his coat before they brought him in. They must have brought him here from the shop—my granddad would never transport. He shrugs off the guards, strides over to me in front of all the people, grabs me by the arm and yanks me away.

"Ostanes, stop," says the king. There's a collective intake of breath and the room falls silent. My granddad shakes with reluctance, but he stops and turns back to face the king.

"The Kemis don't participate in royal goose chases," he says through gritted teeth. "We don't need to be here, as we won't be participating." There is rage and defiance and even a touch of fear in my granddad's voice, and it sends chills down my spine.

"Let him leave," says a man's voice. The hairs on my arms rise as Zol steps forward. He's probably the richest man in Nova, CEO of ZA Corp., and close to the royals already. I suppress the urge to cower in his presence. "Your Highness, with respect, why didn't you come straight to us? We have the best mixers in the business. We can cure anything. Create any potion. I have a hundred graduate interns that could beat anyone in this room. But a Wilde Hunt? Is that really necessary?"

"I'm sure you would rather send one of your interns than risk it yourself," my grandfather says.

"Be quiet, old man!" Zol snaps.

"Are you suggesting we ignore the call of Auden's Horn and endanger my daughter's life?" the king asks.

"No, of course not, Your Highness." Zol bows.

The king slumps into his throne. "Believe me, if we could avoid this, we would. But the Wilde Hunts have protected my family for centuries. If the hunt has been called, then we have no choice but to obey."

Chapter Six

Samantha

"CAN WE SEE HER?" THE WORDS ARE OUT OF my mouth before I remember the company I'm in. But the whole crowd tilts forward slightly toward the king and Renel, as if they were waiting to ask the same question.

Renel's mouth is set in a firm line, but he walks over to a darkened window on the opposite side of the room and touches it with his staff, and it becomes clear glass. "For the moment, the princess is residing in these chambers, looked after by palace doctors."

We edge forward, desperate to see what on earth can have happened to one of the richest and most powerful people in the world. Granddad mutters to himself, although I can tell he's still intrigued. But there's nothing to see. In fact, if Renel hadn't told us that something was wrong, I wouldn't have suspected a thing.

Princess Evelyn is sitting quietly, her hands in her lap. The room is sparsely furnished, just a simple desk, the chair she's sitting on, and a mirror hanging on the far wall.

She's just as pretty as in the casts. Prettier, actually. She's wearing the super-cool dress that Anita loves, all light-blue sparkle and sequins but still somehow lighter than air. It floats around her body, almost as if it's suspended in water. I wonder if any of it is glamoured, but if it is, it's the most natural one I've seen.

Sitting there, surrounded by the gray stone walls, she looks so vulnerable, like an exotic bird trapped in a cage. Occasionally she looks up, but not at us. The window must be one-way, as she doesn't seem to notice the people peering at her through the glass.

"I'm confused, I thought you said she had been poisoned?" asks someone.

Renel nods. "She has."

"Then let ZoroAster Corp. be the first to agree to join the hunt," says Zol, from the back of the room. He doesn't step forward to look at the princess.

There's a crackle of electricity and a shrill voice fills the air. In the center of the room, a frail form emerges, swathed in a long purple gown. The Queen Mother. "Why should we trust you when it was likely your son who administered the potion!" she says accusingly.

Shockwave number two—and I don't think some of the older folk in the room are going to be able to handle any more bombshells. Zol's son . . . Zain? He's here too, cringing behind his dad, his face pale. He's in a tuxedo, but he looks disheveled—his bow tie hanging loose around his neck, the top buttons of his shirt undone. He must've been on his way to the princess's party when he . . . I can't even bring myself to think it. I don't know Zain well, but what I do know about him makes me skeptical that he'd poison the princess. Top of his class in basically everything, most popular boy in school, captain of the Talented rugby team, apprentice to his father, and heir apparent to ZoroAster Corp.—not to mention incredibly hot. Not someone who needs to resort to potions to solve his problems.

I want to disappear into a hole in the ground, but I relax as I doubt Zain will recognize me.

Anita might refute that statement. Zain has this weird habit of showing up wherever we are—at the coffee shop where Anita and I order our sugar-laden frappuccinos, at Molly's school piano recital, and, most recently, he came back to our high school just to judge our annual potions competition. I chalk it up to coincidence, but Anita is convinced it's somehow because of me. I deny it every time, but once, at the coffee shop, I caught his eye and we ended up staring at each other for longer was normal. He broke off first, his friends noticing, pointing at me and laughing. Except he had looked at me first. I was sure of it.

It didn't matter, anyway. The potions fair was the only thing that annoyed me. That competition was my one chance to show off my skills somewhere other than in my granddad's lab. Of course, what I learned in potions class at school could never compare to the training I was getting as my granddad's apprentice, so I knew it wasn't a fair game. But I'd never seen the girls in my class throw so much effort into a potions fair before. Now that he was judging, suddenly it was mixing this, and potions that.

I'd thrown my all into my project, but I'd done that every year. This time I'd decided to experiment with mixing rosemary oil and Sphinx breath to try and come up with a formula to help sharpen focus. The problem was, it worked even better than I intended. I tried a tiny sample, and before I knew it I was up all night, my mind racing a million miles an hour, drinking up information from textbooks like it was water. I kept waiting for the inevitable crash, but it never came.

It was kind of genius. I knew if I took more of my potion, I'd be able to study for hours on end, without needing a break. I'd probably pass all my exams with flying colors. This was high-level stuff, well beyond my current grade. But I also knew it was insanely dangerous. It had been all over the news last year when two kids desperate to pass their exams OD'd on a synth version of the potion that was meant to counteract hyperactivity disorder.

But before the big day I noticed some of the potion had gone missing. Only about half of it remained in the container. As soon as I realized that, I pushed the mix into the sink, the glass smashing into a million pieces, the liquid swirling down the drain.

So instead, my competition entry was a simple tonic to cure a sore throat. Nothing fancy. I set up my presentation board and waited for someone else to take the glory. Yet Zain had walked straight over to me, without looking at anyone else's work, his bright blue eyes shining, an old-fashioned rosette in his hand. He stood so close I could count the strands of black hair that tumbled onto his forehead. But then he saw what I was submitting, and I could see the confusion on his face . . . followed by the disappointment. "I expected better, Sam," he said, and I was so surprised he knew my name I almost forgot to be annoyed at how condescending he sounded. He awarded the prize to the girl next to me. She'd created some formula that fizzed and exploded like a miniature volcano. Toddlers could have mixed that potion.

I went over every detail of that encounter with Anita. Arjun overheard us gossiping, rolled his eyes, and said, "I bet he was looking for a mix to steal back to the ZA lab."

Arjun was probably right, but something about the way Zain had looked at me made me feel ashamed for failing to live up to the Kemi reputation. Like he'd been expecting greatness and found me lacking.

Seeing Zain now, I'm taken straight back to that day. He still has his bluer-than-blue eyes and dark hair, almost jet-black, as his signature, his stand against the crowd. Normally the cool kids are defined by their golden blond hair—their attempt to emulate the princess in all things. But Zain is so cool he doesn't need to match. My hair is also so-dark-brown-it-might-almost-be-black, but no one thinks it's cool. It's an inherited Kemi trait: a clear marker of our eastern heritage that my mother's blonde Novaen genes haven't been able to impact at all. Sometimes I'd love to change it, but the cost of such a glamour is extortionate.

In addition to his apprenticeship to ZoroAster Corp., Zain studies Synths & Potions at University of Kingstown. It's not like I stalk him or anything. I only know that because that was the exact course that I would've wanted to take . . . if I wasn't going straight into full-time apprenticeship to my granddad after high school.

Despite the supposed ingrained hatred of synths that's swirling through my blood, I sometimes think it would be amazing to work in a swanky lab, with every ingredient at my fingertips, and never worry about money again. The Kemi gift is an incredible thing to have—or maybe was, a hundred years ago, when working with natural ingredients was the only option.

Granddad calls synths a travesty, an abomination. I'm not so sure. All I know is that there's no way any Kemi is going to work with synths, not while he is alive. I squash those dreams deep down into a locked box in my brain, disturbed that one look at Zain can make me want to change the course of my career and devastate my family.

The rage pouring out of the Queen Mother is palpable—

so thick I can feel it wrap itself around me, uncomfortable as a blanket on a hot summer night. I can't imagine what it must be like for Zol and Zain, at whom the heat is directed as sharp and focused as a laser.

"We've already ruled out Zain as a suspect," says the king. "He volunteered for a truth serum test."

"I still don't trust him in our palace," the Queen Mother says.

"Go back to your chambers, Mother. This is not your business."

I can hardly believe the king is talking to his mother that way. The Queen Mother rarely makes public appearances—and now I wonder if it's her choice or a decision made for her. The Queen Mother scrunches her face into an even deeper frown, but she doesn't protest except with a single "Pah!"

I turn back to look at the princess. She's been still for so long; she's like a waxwork statue and just as flawless. *What is wrong with you, Princess?*

A bony finger brushes my arm and I jump like I've been shocked with electricity. The Queen Mother is touching me. I fumble over my etiquette—I really never thought I would meet a member of the royal family, ever!—and end up in a half-curtsy, half-bow that I'm sure pays no one any respect. The Queen Mother doesn't seem to mind, though, or she's too polite to fuss. She says, "Ostanes, is this your granddaughter?"

My granddad bows his head. "Yes, my lady."

"She is beautiful. So tall! That doesn't come from your side of the family, then." Her mouth is buried so deep in wrinkles it takes a moment to see that she is smiling. She leans in to my granddad. "I'm glad you're here," she says. "The Kemis never fail us."

I stand stock-still, worried my granddad is going to explode. But instead he says simply, "Your Majesty," and bows stiffly. The Queen Mother tilts her head toward me to say good-bye, and walks through the wall out of the room.

My arm tingles from where she touched me.

Movement from the princess draws my attention back again. I can't seem to look away for too long—her presence is magnetic, compelling. Then, almost so subtly I miss it, her eyes flicker toward the mirror. She stares at herself for a moment before dropping her eyes again. She brings her hands up to her lips, then slides them gently to her throat, all the while staring demurely at her lap. Then she flicks her eyes up again.

She smiles.

She's flirting with the mirror, and in that instant, I know the truth.

"She's in love with herself," I say in a voice barely louder than a whisper, and then I clasp my hands over my mouth.

Chapter Seven

Samantha

"WHAT?" HISSES ZOL.

Suddenly everyone is craning for a better look. It's clear that my theory is correct, even as I get squashed out to the edge of the circle. The Princess has risen and is standing by the mirror now, smiling and chatting to her reflection. She doesn't look ill at all. In fact she looks . . . radiant.

Renel clears his throat, trying to take back some control of the crowd. "Yes, yes, well done, Kemi." He glares at me. "Princess Evelyn was poisoned by a love potion we believe she made by her own hand."

Unbelievable. Love potions are dangerous—not to mention illegal—and the original recipe was wiped from existence by royal decree well over a century ago. Anyone who even writes out a new recipe in their private journals draws the attention of the Novaen secret service. Arjun thinks the fact that the royal family has that power is scary and oppressive, but at least it keeps people safe—except for, I suppose, the princess. I'm impressed. I didn't think it was possible for royals to mix their own potions. Their Talent is so strong, who knows what effect it would have on the ingredients.

"Attention. Attention!" Renel claps his hands. When no one turns to look at him, he touches his staff to the wall, and the window to the princess goes dark.

"She doesn't look like she's in mortal danger," says someone I don't recognize.

"Then you don't understand anything about the royal family and aren't fit for this hunt," snaps the king. "We dedicate our lives to keeping the flow of magic in check. If Evelyn's mind is compromised in any way . . ."

"She could bring the entire city of Kingstown to its knees," says my granddad. "Once again endangering us all," he mutters under his breath, so that only I can hear.

The king doesn't say anything, but his silence speaks volumes.

Renel steps up again. "Now you understand the gravity of the situation. We have enough doctors here to keep the princess in a stable condition. But that could change. How quickly we can save her is down to you.

"Now, there hasn't been a Wilde Hunt in over sixty-five years, so I must make you aware there are several rules that must not be broken. Not only will the royal family enforce the rules, but the hunt demands it.

"One: Only Participants called by Auden's Horn are eligible to compete in the Wilde Hunt. The first Participant or his apprentice to submit a potion that turns the horn gold will be declared the winner. Submit the wrong formula, and the horn will remain black.

"Two: You are the chosen Participants, but you still have a choice. You have twenty-four hours following the call of the horn to enter your name. Once you do, you are bound to the hunt. In return, you will be issued with royal-approved Wilds passes, giving you access to anywhere you need to hunt for ingredients.

"Three: In addition to the Participant and his apprentice, one Finder may be chosen per team.

"And finally: Since a love potion antidote is a mirror cure, the winning potion must be as close to the princess's formula as possible. That means that all ingredients used in this Wilde Hunt potion must be natural."

"Your Highness, with all due respect, that is preposterous!" Zol exclaims. "We could have a synthetic potion prepared in days . . . Hunting for the ingredients could take weeks."

The king sighs. "Zol, this is my daughter's life at stake. We cannot take any chances."

"Auden's Horn called you because you are a master alchemist, in addition to your synth mixing, isn't that correct, Zol?" says Renel.

"Well, of course, but . . . ," Zol splutters.

"Then you will know how key it is that we follow these rules exactly."

"How are you so sure that no synths were used in the manufacture of the princess's potion?" Zol asks. "With the exception of a few of these old-timers"—he looks pointedly at my grandfather and me—"almost no one operates completely synth-free anymore. This is the twenty-first century, after all!"

Renel reaches into his suit pocket and pulls out a slim journal, its pages edged in gold. "This is the only remaining evidence of the princess's mix. She began a record of her formula, although she only got as far as to write down a single ingredient. But one thing she did specify is that her potion was made with one hundred percent natural ingredients. It appears she feared that using synthetics would be too easy to trace. So I will reiterate: The potion needs to be completely natural."

Zol scoffs, but doesn't protest again.

Renel continues. "Those who choose to participate will be given the name of the ingredient the princess wrote down as a head start. After that, you are on your own. The prize for the correct potion is one million crowns and access to a private stream of Novaen royal magic for twenty-four hours." His nose wrinkles as he mentions the prize, as if it should be of no consequence when it comes to saving the princess. It's of big consequence to everyone else, though. "Since love potions are illegal, you will also consent to having the ingredients and any record of the formula wiped from memory."

Despite the dangers, there is an excited buzz in the room. A Wilde Hunt. A chance to create an illegal potion for the royal family. A natural potion. This is freaking awesome.

"Zol Aster, do you still want to be first to join?" asks the king, one eyebrow raised.

Zol stands up straighter, adjusting his tie. "Of course, Your Highness. Synth or natural, ZoroAster Corp. are the best potion-makers in Nova." Now it's my granddad's turn to scoff, though Zol continues as if he doesn't hear. "We would be honored to pledge our service to saving the princess." Zol and Zain approach the horn, in its curious floating gold light. Once, they might have had to write their names on a piece of paper to enter the hunt, but not anymore. Now there's an electronic pad sitting in front of the horn. Zol places his forefinger on the pad and it scans his fingerprint, then Zain does the same. Something inside the horn fizzles and smokes.

They are entered in the hunt.

But before Zain has lifted his finger from the pad, the horn shakes, then blasts out the resounding trumpet sound I heard on the Royal Lane. Instinctively, we all turn toward the Summons. Then someone else steps through the screen—without needing to be pulled through. A woman, dressed in a long hooded robe the color of swirling mercury, of molten silver. The edges are ragged and torn—so old-fashioned in style she looks like she's walked out of the pages of a historical novel. With her comes a smell—sharp and metallic, like the copper taint of a bad penny.

Guards melt out of the shadows, and what feels like a hundred men in suits surround the woman, wands drawn.

When she lowers the hood and shows her face, I'm instantly grateful for all those guards.

"No . . ." The king stands up so fast, he almost topples his throne. "There must be some mistake! Renel, check the horn's call."

The woman grins, all perfect teeth and pale pink lips. "It's nice to see you too, brother." She would be beautiful if she wasn't so terrifying. Her hair is as gray as her cloak, and her veins, visible through her translucent skin, are black as night. I know what that means. It happens to alchemists who meddle with ingredients that stain the soul as well as a person's hair, eyes, and skin. I shiver with disgust. No one uses dark potions anymore in Nova. The rumors say there are still some on the continent, deep in the forests of Gergon, who do. This is proof of it.

"I'm sorry it took me so long to get here," she continues. "I suppose it was hard for the horn to track me down. It's quite rude of my own family to take away my passport and block me from transporting into my home country, isn't it? But Auden's Horn doesn't care about our arbitrary laws, borders, and exiles. It called me as a Participant, and there's nothing you can do about that."

The king shakes with rage, his face a bright shade of red. "But you're no alchemist!"

"How would you know what I am, Ander? Oh, don't you worry. I've always been fond of my niece, which is more than I can say for you. Now, what's wrong with her?" She snaps her fingers at the guards. "Move out of my way. I need to see the princess."

"Don't you dare," the king shouts.

"You can't stop me. I've been called."

"Of course I can, I'm the king!" he splutters.

"Always trying to bend the rules, when it suits you. I think you'll find the horn has made its choice. As a master alchemist, born of Nova, I am more than qualified to be in the hunt," she says, striding toward the window. "If I choose to." The guards fire blasts of magic at her, but the spells fizzle out before they reach her. She places her finger on the glass, her long curved nails scraping against the window. The glass turns clear.

The room is silent, holding its breath as the woman observes the princess. "A love potion. How quaint a thing to put her life—and the country itself—in mortal danger. Rather reckless that you would allow this to happen under your roof, King Ander. All the better for me, though." She walks over to the horn, placing her finger on the pad.

The Horn sparks once more.

She turns to the crowd, and my skin crawls as her ice-blue eyes glance over me. Thankfully, they don't linger long as she regards each one of us in turn. "I will be the one to save my niece. I suggest you all bow out gracefully now, while you can." With two bounding leaps, she jumps into the Summons, disappearing back to wherever she came from.

The king's voice breaks the shell-shocked silence. "What are you waiting for, get after her!" he bellows to his guards. They leap through the Summons, attempting to follow her trail. "As for the rest of you, I will double the hunt's prize. *Two* million crowns and forty-eight hours of power, to whoever finds the cure before that woman."

"Who was that?" I whisper to my granddad, when I've finally stopped shaking.

"Emilia Thoth," he says, his voice grave. "The king's exiled sister. Come on, Sam. Let's go home."

"We're not joining the hunt?" I ask.

But I already know the answer to that.

Chapter Eight

Princess Evelyn

SHE'S OVER THERE, BY THE MIRROR. I CAN just about spy her out of the corner of my eye. My god, she is so beautiful. I should go over to her. I should say hello.

The truth was, she felt paralyzed with doubt.

I wish I was as bold as her. She decided to risk another glance, and she turned her head slowly, ever so slowly, over her shoulder. *Oh! She's looking directly at me.* Her eyes met the other girl's, but she dropped them quickly. *Breathe, Evelyn.* Her breath came and went in deep waves, and she felt her cheeks fill with heat. She couldn't remember if blushing made her look more beautiful or just odd, so she didn't want to risk turning around again.

Frankly, Evelyn couldn't quite believe the girl had the nerve to follow her here, into her private chambers. She should go over there and confront her, but she was nervous. Evelyn scolded herself. A Novaen princess should not be such a coward.

She spun around, taming stray strands of her hair. Then she swallowed and looked up at the beautiful stranger. "What is your name?"

"What is your name?" the girl replied.

"Evelyn."

"Evelyn."

"Truly?"

"Truly."

That was it, then. It was fate. Somehow, they shared the same name. She could see the truth of it written on the girl's face—this was no joke. The two of them, the same, one half of the other. But it would not do for them both to be called Evelyn. "I will be Eve, and you Lyn."

"I will be Eve, and you Lyn."

Ah, the girl was simply being amusing. Eve could see the twinkle in Lyn's eye. It was fine; she could see they understood each other.

She had never felt so connected to someone before in her life. She could hardly believe that only a few hours ago, she had almost made a hideous mistake. There had been so much pressure for her to choose a partner—pressure from her parents, pressure from her magic—that she had plotted to potion Zain. He was all right, but he was so butch, so male compared to the exquisiteness that stood before her. Thank goodness Lyn had caught her eye at the last moment.

Eve had always known that it was her duty to make

sure she handled her power responsibly. She could hardly complain about her privilege, but the thought of being with someone that she didn't love for all of eternity had terrified her into desperate measures. Her parents didn't love each other, not at first and not now. Eve knew they were always off dallying with other members of the court—the intrigue kept the gossip columns in business. Her mother had readily agreed to the marriage, though, for the power and a lifetime of the very best of everything.

It was rare for any royal to be as lucky as Eve.

She had found her true love, and just in the nick of time. Lyn. They could marry soon. Preparations for a wedding had been in the royal family's press book since she was sixteen; they could pull it out in a month if they wanted to.

The media would love and loathe that. It would give them a month's worth of blanket coverage, but they'd have less time to speculate over her dress, the color scheme, the music . . . there was nothing like a royal wedding to spark a media storm. And one with two beautiful brides? It would be a frenzy! An enormous celebration. Street parties and teacups printed with their faces and photographs in all the magazines. It thrilled her to think about it.

She had to get planning! No high street dress would do this time, she needed a top designer. She wondered if House of Perrod would be free. Who was she kidding? They would drop everything for her . . . .

Voices interrupted her reverie. "What are we going to do, Ander?" It was her mother's shrill voice. Eve could sense her over on the far side of the room, pacing in a circle, her high heels tapping on the floor. It was strange to have her there, but then Eve remembered—they must have come to meet Lyn. Of course they would need to meet her before they announced an engagement! She couldn't remember her mother ever caring about her in a way that felt maternal—nannies and royal advisors had raised her. But she could imagine her parents caring about who she married. They would be so relieved.

Her father was in the room too, and he sat on the throne he brought with him from place to place.

"We can't do anything," came her father's reply. "The hunt has been called."

"But you're the king. Surely you can stop this? How can we trust those quacks to come up with the cure for our daughter when she is involved! Your vile sister Emi—"

"*Don't* say her name in this palace," the king fumed. "You can't be sure . . ." He paused, and then whispered, "That you won't be calling her presence right into this room." There was only one name that could fill her father's voice with such fear. Her aunt, the exiled Emilia Thoth. At eighteen, she left the palace, allegedly to go to university in Gergon. Instead, at twenty-one she staged a coup to steal the crown—an attempt that ended with her official exile from Nova.

Emilia didn't believe in the contract that bound the royal family's power to Nova's elected government. The agreement turned them into figureheads, held in the utmost regard but unable to exploit their full capacity for magic. The result was peace and democracy for the country. It worked perfectly.

Only Emilia and her power hungry followers didn't think so. The whispered rumors said she still lived in Gergon, where a royal family ruled with fists made iron by magic. Gergon never verified claims that they harboured Emilia—to do so would be tantamount to starting a war—but it wasn't hard to guess that they'd want her there, in their back pocket, in case anything went wrong in Nova.

Because the one thing the king and queen couldn't get away from was that Emilia was next in line if anything happened to Eve.

"We've sent a team of agents after her through the Summons," continued the king. "We'll find her and stop her before anything can happen to Evelyn."

"You don't know that! And what of the other Participants? They're all at risk now."

"Someone will just have to cure Evelyn before she causes too much damage, and then Emilia will be banished back to wherever she came from. The Participants know the dangers when they sign up."

"Ha! Do you think they're prepared for dangers like your sister? She will stop at nothing to eliminate the competition."

Her father squirmed in his throne. "There are ten Participants competing against her—and still others that haven't joined yet. Besides, Zol will win."

"He had better. Where is that man, anyway? I need to talk to him about his wretched son."

As if her mother's voice had Summoned him, a door appeared in the stone wall and Zol and Renel strode in. Eve rolled her eyes—seeing Zol made her think of Zain. How glad she was that the potion hadn't worked. Now he was free to find love too. The locket had been empty, so she must never have completed the mix in the first place. Or did she have a change of heart and dump the contents? It was so hard to remember. Her brain felt fuzzy, events rubbed from her memory like chalk from a blackboard. But then she lifted her eyes to meet Lyn's and instantly felt her worries melt away.

"We have a lead on the first ingredient for the hunt," said Zol.

"There's a hunt?" At this, Eve perked up. "That's exciting. But there is no one here in mortal danger . . . What are they looking for? I do hope it's a good luck potion for my marriage—that would just be wonderful."

Zol looked at her in such slack-jawed wonderment that Eve laughed. She didn't think she had ever seen Zain's dad look so uncomfortable in her presence. "Your marriage, Princess?" he asked.

"Oh, silly me. I haven't even told my parents yet! Mum . . . Dad . . . I want you to meet someone. This is Lyn." She gestured to her love, who stood frozen still. "You should curtsy," she whispered to Lyn. When she still didn't move, Eve laughed. "Of course, you don't know how! Please don't take offense, mother, she's new to all this royal nonsense. I'll show you, Lyn, it's easy." Eve curtsied in the mirror, and to her delight Lyn did the same. "Oh, that was perfect! Don't you just love her?" she said to her parents. "We want to marry as soon as possible!"

They all stared at her, not saying a word, but she shrugged and turned her attention back to Lyn. Her parents would come around in time.

"If you had controlled your son, this would never have happened in the first place!" the queen hissed.

"Oh, don't worry, I will be speaking with him," said Zol, his voice dark with anger. "And we will be the ones to find the cure, mark my words. As I said, I already have a team in place tracking down the first ingredient and researching the rest of the mix."

Eve sighed. It was clear that all this adult talk was boring Lyn. That just wouldn't do. "So, when am I going to the party?" Eve said, her bright voice cutting through all the tension.

All eyes turned to her. "I have my big announcement to make. Set up a television interview. I want nationwide coverage. Oh, and get a photographer for our official portrait. I want to introduce Lyn to the entire world!"

Chapter Nine

Samantha

GRANDDAD AND I SIT SIDE BY SIDE ON THE tram ride home. We left without joining the hunt and were escorted through the palace, ending up in the courtyard of the castle at the top of Kingstown, which was empty following the cancellation of Evelyn's concert. I guess there is a connection between the two buildings, after all.

Despite my granddad's stubborn refusal to join the hunt, my head spins with everything I know about love potions. There are endless myths surrounding them—it's going to be hard for the Participants to separate the truth from fact. But even though they were banned before his time, I'm positive that somewhere in our store there is a lead on the original recipe. Who knows, maybe the recipe itself is actually stashed away somewhere, amidst the hundreds of books and the significant archive of Kemi alchemist grimoires—or potion diaries, as we call them now. This could be what the Kemi family has been waiting for—the chance to bring back honor to the traditional alchemists, the first potion-makers. And if it brings a little glory too, what's the harm in that?

I bring up the hunt again, but Granddad waves his hands at me and tells me to shush. He mumbles something about the "audacity of royals."

"They think they can just drag me up to their palace, without even a word of apology for the interruption. Three mixes, ruined. I'll have to start all over. And I bet they won't reimburse us for that time either."

"Granddad, this is the princess. Of course they think she's more important than our mixes. Is it because of Emilia that you don't want us to compete?"

"I'm not scared of some royal pretender."

"Then what is it?"

He harrumphs and buries his nose in an old newspaper he finds on the seat. I give up until we reach the Kemi Street stop.

Our home is at the back of the store, so we walk past the front door and down a narrow alley, dodging the overflowing rubbish bins that are ready for pick-up. We enter straight into the kitchen, where Mum is dishing up a plate of fried rice and pork belly for Molly. Dad stands by the sink, his arms crossed in front him, eyes fixed on the back door.

"You're back!" shouts Molly. She jumps up from her seat and wraps her arms around my waist.

Granddad steps past me and continues in his slow, unhurried way, as if he hasn't just been called to participate in a Wilde Hunt. He ignores the rest of the family's curious faces and heads straight into his lab, shutting the door behind him. My parents don't look too concerned—they're used to his surly moods, and they know they'll get more information out of me anyway.

"Sarah's mum sent me straight home as soon as we found out the concert was canceled," Molly says. "I don't understand—why would the princess not want to have her party?"

I stroke her hair. "I'm sorry, Mols, I know you've been looking forward to the concert for ages. But I do know why the princess canceled her party. It's why Granddad and I were Summoned to the palace."

Now I have their full attention. I sit down on the chair next to Molly and relay the entire story to her and my parents. At some point, Mum puts food in front of me, and the next time I look down, I've demolished it.

When I finish, they're speechless. Molly is the first to break the silence. "But is Princess Evelyn okay?"

"Of course she is—we just have to do our best to save her." I smile at her, but I know my eyes tell a different story.

Mum interprets my look. "Molly, it's been a long night. Maybe you should get ready for bed?"

"But I want to hear what Sam has to do to save Princess Evelyn!"

"She'll tell you all about it in the morning."

Molly huffs and shuffles up the stairs to her room.

"So how is the princess really?" asks Mum.

I shrug. "Strangely, she looked fine. But imagine: She's in love with herself . . . things could go from fine to terrible very quickly, and the royals are worried. But that's not all. We were also joined by Emilia Thoth."

My dad turns to me sharply. "The king's exiled sister? How in dragon's name did she get through the palace security?"

I shrug. "Auden's Horn calls all eligible Novaen alchemists, even the ones the royal family has banished. I guess it didn't get the memo about her exile. The king didn't seem to have much choice in the matter." I shiver. "She looked . . . unnatural. What kind of person would do that to themselves?" Only the darkest experimental potions would have the ability to change a person to look like Emilia.

"Someone with a big grudge to bear," says my dad, his voice grave.

"How did Granddad respond?" Mum asks.

I almost don't want to tell them. But my face goes all red and blotchy when I try to lie, and I can already feel heat pricking the bottom of my neck as I think about it.

"Sam . . ." My mum puts her hand on mine.

I sigh. "He doesn't want to do it. He doesn't want anything to do with the Wilde Hunt and won't be joining."

She takes her hand away and shares a look with my dad. They might have a secret old married people language all their own, but I know enough about those looks to interpret their meaning. "But why? I don't understand. Why is Granddad so against the hunt when it could be a chance for us to prove ourselves to the whole world? At least it would be free publicity for the business! We could actually get the till ringing again!"

"If your grandfather says no, he has a good reason," says my dad.

"Plus, Emilia Thoth? She's what nightmares are made of. I don't want you anywhere near her warpath," Mum says.

"So I'm just supposed to let the princess go steadily insane even if I have the chance to cure her?"

"Someone else will help her, honey."

"But I could help her! You keep telling me I have this gift, but now that I actually have the chance to use it, you're not letting me!" My cheeks prickle with heat. All I can think about is the silent till in the store. The empty jars on the shelves that will never be filled. The years of pinching pennies, just so that Molly and I can have an education. Granddad taught me to be a proud Kemi, but how can I be proud? We've been offered a chance to prove ourselves, and we're just going to throw it away. It's typical. "I'm going to my room."

"Sam—" Mum tries to call me back to the table, but I'm already up the stairs, my eyes blurring with tears.

I throw myself onto the bed. I don't know why my family is being so difficult about this.

There's one other family I know who must be going through the same thing. I drag my laptop off my nightstand and onto the duvet. As soon as I log on, Anita pops up on the video chat, her face flushed with excitement. Her dark hair is tied back into a ponytail, and I can see the thick straps of a backpack over her shoulders.

"I've been waiting for you all evening, Sam, what took you so long? Dad said he saw you at the palace! We don't have much time to get to—"

She must register the look on my face, because she stops midsentence.

"Granddad said no," I say.

The image of Anita shakes as she reaches out and grabs her computer screen. "What? You're kidding? You haven't joined yet?"

I shake my head. "I know, I don't get it either."

"But a Wilde Hunt! It's practically a Kemi family tradition!"

"Maybe back in the day . . ." I take in more of Anita's

outfit, and it's clear she's dressed to go find an ingredient. I swallow down my jealousy and force a smile. "Now it's the Patels' turn."

Anita sees through my act, though. "Oh, Sam, you should be here. My dad was hesitant too. He won't actually participate in the hunt either; he's got commitments at the store he can't leave. But he made me his apprentice and Auden's Horn accepted my entry just a moment ago. Arjun is coming along as our Finder. We never thought we'd get an opportunity like this in our lifetimes. We might not have a hope of winning, but we're going to try."

There is a commotion on the screen, bringing into focus the familiar dark-eyed features of Anita's brother, Arjun, as he forces himself into the frame, his hair stiffened with just a bit too much gel.

"Hey, Sam, I overheard. That sucks."

I nod, but I have to bite my lip to stop myself crying.

Arjun looks at Anita. "Okay, sis, we gotta go."

"Good luck, guys," I choke out, waving as the computer screen goes black.

Our video chat over, I snap down the lid on my laptop. I change into my pj's and jump back on my bed, flicking on the TV that sits on the dresser in the corner of my room. There, in front of me, is Evelyn's shining face, her pearly white teeth bared in a perfect smile. EVELYN CANCELS BIRTHDAY PARTY, REASON CURRENTLY

UNKNOWN, the scrolling caption reads. So, the news of her poisoning hasn't broken to the media yet.

I feel a twinge of guilt. What could've driven Evelyn to mix a love potion when the consequences could've been—well, I guess not much worse than what actually happened to her? But then there is something else—a spark of admiration. She'd mixed it on her own—unearthed the formula for a potion so many try and fail to produce.

Someone will cure her.

It just won't be me.

They switch to a show reel highlighting the princess and Zain. IS A FALLING-OUT WITH A FRIEND THE CAUSE?

The newscaster's voice drones over the images. Speculation mounts as Zain Aster was seen entering the castle only hours before Princess Evelyn canceled her eighteenth birthday party. The images show Zain whispering in Evelyn's ear, his arm draped casually around her shoulders. They look so comfortable together, like co-conspirators or old friends gossiping. But then something catches Zain's attention and he pulls his arm away from Evelyn. I catch the barest of flinches from her, and the look in her eyes as she stares at him is full of longing. She really did love him. My finger hovers over the remote, but I can't bring myself to change the channel while Zain is on the screen.

The potion was meant for him. That must be what

the Queen Mother meant. He could've become instant royalty. I wonder why he didn't want that.

It's hard to believe that only a few hours ago Zain and I were in the same room together. Thinking about him, I almost blush, even though I'm alone. I roll my eyes at my own reaction, then finally switch over to a sitcom about a mixed group of Talented and ordinary friends who hang out together in a local bar. It was a pretty radical show in its time and I've seen all the episodes a thousand times. I don't take any of it in. All I can think about is the love potion. I wonder which ingredient the princess wrote down. I wonder where Anita and Arjun are off to. I scold myself. I need to forget today ever happened.

A few episodes later, and the house is silent. I tuck in under the duvet, but I've barely shut my eyes when I hear a tapping sound on my window, like stones are being thrown at it. I sit up in bed, pull the curtain aside, and find myself staring straight into the face of Kirsty Donovan, the Kemi family Finder.

Chapter Ten

Samantha

"KIRSTY!" I PUSH UP THE WINDOW AND HELP her crawl through into the room. She must have climbed up the outside of the house to my window using the drainpipe. Kirsty never does things the normal way. "What are you doing here?" I whisper.

I haven't seen her in months, but she looks just the same—glamour-free, tanned skin, dark-blond hair pulled to the side in a braid that looks practical but still beautiful, her toned arms on show as they always are except in the darkest months of winter. She's wearing her trademark uniform too—black vest top, gray-green trousers with innumerable pockets, tall boots. She's the epitome of a Finder. I suddenly feel incredibly awkward in my yellow polka-dot pajamas.

"I'm here to talk about the hunt, of course!" I can see her eyes are shining, catching the light from the street lamps outside.

"You heard? How?"

She winks. "Friends in low places, I guess. I'm a bit insulted that you haven't already asked me to be your Finder in the hunt, but I'll let you off. What's the first ingredient? We need to get ahead of the competition if the synths are involved."

I slump back down onto my bed. "We're not joining. Granddad doesn't want anything to do with it."

"Don't be ridiculous," says Kirsty. "Why do you think I came through the window? Of course Ostanes won't allow it; I've known dragons who bear less of a grudge than that man. But a Kemi has been called to the hunt. That could be you."

"They want my grandfather, not me."

"But you could do it."

"No way," I scoff.

"Why not? You might try to deny it, but you've got the Kemi gift. You know how to mix with the best of them."

"I'm nowhere near as good as Granddad, and I won't be able to compete with the synths. When they get those ingredients into their big labs . . ."

"Then think of it this way. You're the Kemi apprentice. I don't really get it since obviously you should be going to Kingstown Uni to study synths and potions because this is the twenty-first century, but fine. Your choice. But this is your chance to make that decision count. To make your name as an alchemist and put the

Kemis back on the map. You need my help, of course. And I'm offering it to you—free of charge."

Hearing Kirsty say this out loud makes the opportunity seem real, tangible—something I can reach out and grab with both hands. I'm surprised she's offering her services for free. Business is tough for her too. In the old days, every great alchemist would have their own Finder. If you were the Kemi master, you had a team of people you trusted to go out into the Wilds and collect ingredients. Simple, right? Sure, when you can only pick a certain leaf on the third new moon of the year, and if you miss that window, the next one's not going to be for another twelve months. Or when you have to track a sabre-tooth lion through the Aluptian mountains, risking death by mauling. It's a specialized skill too—to know what equipment to take, how to survive out there in the Wilds, and also to recognize the ingredients when you see them. The best Finders go out on assignment and come back with a million things you didn't ask for, but all of a sudden realize you need.

Synths don't need Finders, not when they can create the ingredients in a lab. Against her better judgment, Kirsty's been forced to become more of an entrepreneur, peddling pretty but useless trinkets like amethyst pendants and gullfish eyes to eager tourists. She even had a market stall for a while along Royal Lane, but Kirsty is no good at sitting still, and she knows it.

"I heard Emilia was at the palace," Kirsty says.

I nod slowly. The thought of Emilia's body, tainted by those dark potions, still turns my blood cold. "She says she's a master alchemist now."

"She hasn't wasted a moment of her exile. I've heard stories about her, too." Kirsty hesitates. "In addition to her alchemical training, she's spent all these years exploring the Wilds. I heard a ranger say there was no better Finder in the world. She could be a step ahead of the hunt already."

My eyes widen. "Alchemist and Finder in one?"

"She's going to be a formidable opponent. Even if she isn't trying to find the cure, she'll know exactly how to stop us."

I swallow hard. I hadn't considered the possibility that someone wouldn't want to cure the princess. But if the princess dies . . . then Emilia would be the next queen. And life in Nova would never be the same again.

I'm not sure if I'm cut out for this. Joining the hunt would mean going out there . . . into the Wilds. The untamed lands outside of the major cities and towns. The Wilds are carefully protected sanctuaries of nature, where streams of magic can flow unchecked. Access to the Wilds is strictly controlled. Granddad thinks the regulations around the Wilds are a joke—once the entire world was Wild, of course, but towns and cities have spread like fungus until only comparatively small acreages of wild land are left. There are reasons for this, of course. This is a modern world. Magic is unstable out in the Wilds, and cities are much safer places for Talenteds to live. Something about the more people pulling on the stream of magic, the stronger and more stable it gets. Like a rope made up of many twisting strings. Out in the Wilds, those threads get spread further and further apart, and become more likely to fray—or even break—with violent consequences. The magic in the Wilds is just too powerful for most Talenteds to control. In some places, it would be like turning on a tap and expecting a stream—but instead getting an ocean.

Of course, the Wilds are dangerous for the ordinary among us too: full of creatures waiting to bite your head off. And plants that might do that too.

The Wilds are for the adventurous people of the world, like Kirsty. They're not for people who would rather live their adventures through characters in books. I like staying home, thank-you-very-much, where I know I can always find a plug point for my laptop, I'm never ten steps from a kettle to boil for tea, and I can go to sleep wrapped up in the comfort of my own duvet.

"Alchemists belong in the lab," Granddad says, and he only leaves the building to play pétanque with the other old folk. Everything else he needs is here.

Sometimes we're more alike than I care to admit.

You've got the Kemi gift. Kirsty's words ring in my ears.

Maybe I do. And I can't keep holding on to these dreams without at least trying to make them come true.

I jump up from the bed, feeling more confident than anyone should in their pajamas. Adrenaline floods my system: it's impulsive, it's rash, but if I take any more time to think about it, I'll talk myself out of it. "Okay, I'll do it. First thing tomorrow morning," I tell Kirsty.

"Do it now," she says. "We need to plan for the first ingredient."

The clock on my bedside table reads 11:09 p.m. "It's late . . . ," I say, but then I know the royals won't be sleeping. "Okay, give me a second."

"I won't move a muscle," she says with a grin.

I tiptoe out into the hallway. The house is deathly quiet. When I was younger, Granddad used to make mixes deep into the night, but now he takes a sleeping draught at ten p.m. on the dot, so I know he won't waken.

When I reach the shop floor, I take a deep breath. The shop has an eerie appearance at night, the muted light from the street reflecting off the innumerable glass jars that line the back wall. The air is still. There's a dark screen in the corner, our Summons, and I place my palm on the glass. It's cool to my touch. I've never done this before, so I hope it works.

"Renel Landry," I say to the glass.

Renel's face appears beneath my hand, and I have to bite down on my tongue not to yell out in shock.

"Cutting it close, Samantha Kemi." He reaches his hand through the glass. I take it and brace myself. He pulls me hard, and within a blink of an eye I've arrived in the palace. It's not nearly as hard as last time.

The surprise must show on my face as he tuts at my ignorance. "Once you've visited a place, it's much easier to transport there again. You left an imprint of your-self along the magic streams." He walks briskly over to Auden's Horn, which appears to breathe in the flickering candlelight of the palace room.

"You know what to do," he says.

I step forward and place my finger on the screen. Just like it did with Zol and Zain, smoke pours from the mouth of the horn as if it is on fire. I feel heat on my face. "I'm in . . . but my grandfather isn't," I say.

Renel raises an eyebrow. "No Ostanes? I will have to talk to the family about this." For a moment I think they'll refuse to let me enter on my own.

But then he reaches into his pocket and pulls out a scroll. "Your Wilds pass, and the first ingredient," he says, then turns me round and I fall sideways into the wall behind me. The wall bends and breaks, then I'm back on the shop floor, skidding on the stone slabs, panting heavily. The Summons screen goes dark.

I take a few deep breaths, then run my finger along the edge of the scroll to break the seal. My heart stops.

I might have already missed my shot.

Chapter Eleven

Samantha

"AT LEAST WE DIDN'T WAIT UNTIL tomorrow." Kirsty looks down at the scroll. "I guess anyone who has to think too hard about whether to join the hunt is going to be out without a hope. This stuff is impossible to buy."

"Are we too late?"

Her watch is a complicated device with several different interlocking faces showing time zones and moon phases and tides. "We should just make it. If we leave now."

"What's going on here?" Mum stands in my bedroom doorway in her purple dressing gown. Dad is behind her, a beat-up paperback in his hand. I wasn't exactly discreet, running upstairs from the shop floor. I would have woken the Sphinx with my stomping.

As they stare at Kirsty and me, I know they've figured it out. But to my relief, they don't look mad. Only tired.

"Oh, honey," says Mum.

"I'm sorry. But I want to do this. I need to do this. This is my chance to . . ." I run out of words.

Dad reaches out to me. "It's your choice, Sam. But we can't pay to help you get any of these things. Kirsty's fees, your transport out into the Wilds, anything you might need along the way . . . Any of it."

"Kirsty will help me out. Help us out."

Thankfully, they seem to come to a mutual agreement. "You'll have to break it to Granddad tomorrow morning."

"I might not have time for that." I hand over the scroll.

Dad reads the name of the ingredient and draws in a sharp breath. "My goodness."

"What is it?" asks Mum.

"Full moon oyster merpearl. Crushed. Thirty grams," I recite, already having it memorized.

"Do we have it in the stockroom?" Dad asks.

I shake my head. "I just checked before coming upstairs." The jars had skipped straight from an empty jar of Merlin's beard to merrimack plant. No merpearl in stock—I'm not that lucky.

"But the next Rising is tonight!" Mum says. "I saw it on the news."

"I know." I knew it as soon as I read the ingredient.

"You don't have any time to lose, then," says Dad. He hands back the scroll. "Kirsty—you keep her safe."

"I will, John." She chucks me my backpack from the floor. "Meet me outside in five."

I nod, grinning and darting around my bedroom, throwing anything I can find into the bag, barely stopping to think about where I might be going. What do you pack to go fishing for merpearls? I change into my most Finder-like gear: cargo trousers, a black T-shirt, and warm hoodie. I throw in my waterproof jacket and a torch. Then I pack my most important item: my potions diary. It's a thick string-bound notebook with a sturdy brown leather cover. It's by far my most prized possession. In here are all my recipes, all my notes about ingredients, all my dreams of new and different mixes. It's my brain in paper form.

In our library we have potion diaries belonging to almost every Kemi going back nearly five hundred years. There are a few key ones missing: my great-grandmother Cleo's, for example, and the journal of Thomas Kemi, the founder of the store. But the remaining journals form the great archive of Kemi knowledge, and it is by far our biggest asset.

I slot mine in the front pocket of my backpack.

I kiss Mum and Dad good-bye and race downstairs and out the side door. I swing my backpack up onto the floor of Kirsty's 4×4 and climb into the front.

"Ready?" she says.

I bite my lip and nod. We have two hours to do a two-

and-a-half-hour drive, plus find a boat willing to take us out to the Rising at the last minute. I sense that our chances aren't good, but what else can we do?

Before another thought can enter my brain, Kirsty slams down her foot on the accelerator, her fingers reaching out and flicking a switch on the dashboard that sends a surge of heavy metal music into the night air. If anyone opened a window to complain, we wouldn't know it—already we're around the corner and bombing down the twisted side streets, aiming straight for the highway heading south: to the Wilds of Nova.

I chew at the edges of my fingers, the buzz of Kirsty's subwoofer not helping my nerves.

Some parts of the Wilds are more accessible than others, like where we're going—Syrene Beach. It's the closest Rising to Kingstown and the only one in Nova. No one will have time to get anywhere else. You have to have a pass to get in, but it's one of the easiest to acquire. Syrene Beach is always featured in any guidebook or tourism advert for Nova: "Come witness the only Rising visible from the shore!" "See the beauty of Aphroditas and her mermaid clan!" "Go wild in the Wilds: the hottest party beach in Nova!"

No one is quite sure why the mermaids rise in the middle of the night during the full moon. They might bear many physical similarities to humans, but researchers haven't been able to communicate with them in any meaningful way, at least not enough to give us any insight into their traditions. They're exhibitionists though, that's for sure. They rise up out of the sea and show off the beautiful pearls they've cultivated during the past month. They're competitive too, spending the month preparing for the occasion, which has all the pageantry of a beauty contest, and performing for all the people who crowd on the beach to watch them.

The most beautiful mermaid is called Aphroditas. If my guess is right and other teams from the hunt will be at the Rising, whoever gets the pearl from her will instantly have the most potent ingredient. That's the gamble the teams are going to have to take: compete for the attention of Aphroditas and potentially gain the most powerful pearl, or lose out and risk not getting a pearl at all.

Merpearls are the most popular engagement ring stone, even more so than diamonds or sapphires. In fact, Princess Evelyn has a merpearl tiara, the ultimate in extravagance. A vision of her picking her tiara apart to get one of the ingredients for the love potion plays out in my mind.

"Maybe we should have dragged my dad along."

"What do you mean?" asks Kirsty.

"Don't mermaids respond best to male voices?"

"How do you know that?"

"I read . . . a lot."

"Nerd."

I punch her on the arm and she laughs. "Don't worry, we'll figure it out. If necessary, I can teach you a few tricks to change the timbre of your voice."

"And that works?"

She nods. "Rule number one of being a Finder: you work with what you've got. Never count yourself out."

Kirsty barely takes her foot off the gas, and since the highway is deserted—and there are no signs of any police—we make good time. With a few minutes to spare, we pull up to the Wilds border, little pillbox sheds standing like sentries on guard in the middle of the road. I wonder how busy the beach will be. Packed for the Rising, most likely.

I stare down at the paper in my hand, the neat line of printed text. FULL MOON OYSTER MERPEARL. CRUSHED. 30 G.

The guard checks over our papers and flicks my shiny new pass with his fingers. Kirsty's pass is old and battered, even though she has to get it renewed every year she continues as a Finder. "You're late," he says with a smirk.

"Then stop stalling us," says Kirsty.

"Maybe I should take a closer look at these."

Kirsty leans out the window, grabs at the guard's shirt, and yanks him down toward the window. "Let us through."

I swallow down a dense ball of alarm at Kirsty's brazenness, but the guard laughs and tosses the passes back through the window and onto my lap.

His "see ya" disappears on the wind as Kirsty stomps on the accelerator again and we whip away into the night.

"That's Duke. We used to date," Kirsty explains. "But then I realized he was a loser and we split."

I've never seen Kirsty like this before. In her element. Her eyes are filled with determination, her jaw set. She catches me looking and grins wide. "Having fun yet?" She shifts gear and speeds up even faster. I grip the edge of the seat, my knuckles white.

A huge illuminated sign wings toward us: SYRENE BEACH, 5 KM. You wouldn't need a sign to know you were getting close, though. White lights reach and dance in the night sky. Occasionally one changes color, into brilliant magenta or electric blue, and tints the stars an unnatural shade.

A shiver runs through me. The Wilds always do this to me. I tilt my head to look out the window. Someone down by the beach turns a beam into the night sky, projecting out the massive snarling face of a bear. The University of Kingstown mascot: the Ursa Major.

Kirsty swings onto the exit ramp and slows as the paved road leading up to the beach becomes rutted and pot-holed. The car thrums with the deep reverberations of speakers blasting dance music to happy revelers. Far in the darkness, the horizon lifts and sways, and then the smell hits me—sharp and salty and fresh. The sea. We've arrived.

We grab one of the furthest parking spots from the sea—not by choice, of course. The lot is absolutely packed, mostly with party buses covered with graffiti like someone vomited color all over them. I start unpacking my backpack, but Kirsty shakes her head. "No time," she says. She grabs a torch from the inside of her car door.

We hurry past students drinking pale gold fizzy beers in meter-long flagons, the cheapest they can get their hands on. More impressive are their glamours, glow-in-the-dark inks tattooed over tanned skin, and the Talenteds with lights embedded in their hair and down the lengths of their arms so that when they dance on the sand it looks like the stars are dancing with them.

"Gawk later," says Kirsty, pulling me along. Her eyes turn toward the sea. Following her gaze, I can see we're already late. Out of the darkness, rising and falling with the waves, is a flotilla of lights, huddled together like seals in a storm. All of a sudden the sky around the boats lights up. There's a massive floodlight pointed down at the waves, and it's coming from one of the boats out in the middle of the ocean. "Boat" isn't really the right word for this particular object—"yacht" might be closer, perhaps "floating palace" even better. It's no surprise to see the huge letters that adorn the front of it: ZA. ZoroAster are already here.

The floodlight illuminates the other boats that are

crowded into the same area—other yachts, but also smaller fishing vessels and even, I think, a Jet Ski.

We're racing down the beach now, toward the jetty. The light from the crowd of boats doesn't quite reach the end of the dock, but I can see a commotion is building. A girl yelps in frustration and my heart leaps—I'd recognize that sound anywhere.

"Anita!" I shout at her. Kirsty and I have reached the dock, sand making way for rough planks of wood haphazardly nailed together.

"Arjun, look who's here!" Anita shouts over her shoulder, and her brother's head pops up from the end of the dock. His face is scrunched into a frown, but it softens when he sees me. Foam from the crashing waves fringes his dark brown hair with a white crown.

Arjun is sitting in a rickety-looking rowing boat that I'm convinced is taking on water from the way it dips at one end. Also in the boat is an old man dressed in a ragged white shirt, waterproof trousers, and a black jacket. A jagged scar runs across his face and I wonder what Wilds animal gave him that injury. He's a fisherman. Licences to fish the Wild waters are rare, so he's most likely a poacher. That means he's dangerous.

The boat rocks against the dock as a wave crashes beneath us, and seawater seeps through the eyelets of my laces.

Kirsty's boots pull up next to mine with a firm, confident step. I bet her shoes are waterproof—there's no telltale sound of squelching toes from her.

"Edgar," she says, addressing the old man with her hands on hips. "What's going on here?"

The old man fidgets with the collar of his salt-stained coat. "Well, Miss Donovan, I've been trying to negotiate me a fair deal with these young pups to get out to the Rising."

"Negotiate?!" Arjun explodes. "Cheat, steal, swindle, maybe."

A small smirk appears on the old man's face. "I heard the rumors too, ain't I? This ain't no normal voyager out to see the clamwhackers."

Anita, Arjun, and I reel back. I've never heard anything as offensive as the man's blatant insult to the mercreatures, but it just spurs Kirsty on. She reaches down into the boat and grabs Edgar under the armpit. She pulls him upward and—as if the sea is momentarily on our side—a wave rises up beneath them to push him up even higher. She drags him onto the dock, then drops him like a stone.

Anita and I dash into the boat before Edgar can regain his footing. "I know for a fact that you don't own this boat, Ed. You lost your license to sail when you tried to snare that narwhal. So find some other Finder to swindle." While Kirsty talks, she unravels the length of rope attaching the boat to the dock. With a firm shove from her boot she pushes the boat away and jumps in before it floats too far.

"Get the oars!" she yells. Anita and I scramble to grab them, and I shove one toward a slack-jawed Arjun. Kirsty takes the other one from Anita and roars out, "Stroke! Stroke!" until she and Arjun fall into a fast rhythm.

And still those lights look a long, long way out to sea.

"We're not going to make it," Anita mutters beside me.

"What do you mean?" I ask.

"Listen! Can't you hear it? The Rising is beginning."

Chapter Twelve

Samantha

AT FIRST I CAN'T HEAR ANYTHING BUT THE rise and fall of the oars in the water, but then the first few notes reach me. It's coming from where the other boats are huddled. There's a loud snap, and the floodlight from the massive yacht blinks out.

All the other boats turn their lights off too, and my eyes have trouble adjusting to the midlight. The full moon seems obscenely large without the halo of other lights diminishing its brightness.

It's then that the first shell rises. At first it looks like another wave cresting far out at sea, but then I realize it's the scalloped edge of a mermaid's clam shell, as wide as our rowing boat is long. All other sounds have quieted down and the sea is as still as glass. This makes it easier for Kirsty and Arjun to propel us through the water, but Anita and I are frozen at the bow of the rowboat, paralyzed by the thought that we might have made it this close but yet still be too far.

The moonlight glints off the pearlescent lip of the clam shell, disappearing into its numerous ridges and sparkling again on the swells. Another shell rises a few feet away, this one a more blushing pink than the first. They seem to multiply then, every shade of a dusky rainbow—from deep-bruise purple to silvery gray to almost bronze. The numerous remedies that can be made from the delicate inner lining of the shells rise in my mind:

Oyster Shell: for rosacea reduction—to soothe reddened skin. Also for bone strengthening—can help with early onset osteoporosis.

Anita stares through wide-angled binoculars, chewing at her bottom lip.

"Has Aphroditas risen yet?" Kirsty asks over her shoulder, her voice straining with the effort of rowing.

Anita shakes her head. "I don't think so . . . wait . . ."

I squint my eyes to try to get a better look, and then I squeal with excitement as I follow where Anita is looking. A shell is rising; white, a brilliant, pure white that is brighter than any of the others. And it's larger than the others too: the moon itself lifting up out of the sea. Although the water stays calm, the boats spread out and away from this shell, offering the respect that it deserves.

And then the shell starts to open.

Her hand is ghostly white and it shimmers too, as if her skin is radiating the light from the full moon. Her fingers are too long, more like twigs than flesh, and fine, translucent webs join each one to its neighbor. In one swift movement she flings open the lid of her shell and she is revealed in all her glory. Her hair would make even the most beautiful supermodel in Nova green with envy—it moves with a life of its own, as if it's still underwater, floating and undulating through unseen currents. The pink-white strands appear to glow in the moonlight, tumbling around her naked upper body and wrapping around her waist, where skin meets scale. Her beauty astounds me, takes my breath away. Yet it's the strangeness of her that is most stunning—she is so close to human, and yet not. Her eyes are milky pale, as if she is blind, but she stares out at the crowd of boats, examining us all. If anything can draw attention away from her, it's the jewel around her neck—a pearl of such perfect roundness and sheen that it puts other stones to shame.

"Aphroditas," Anita whispers, as gobsmacked as I am. Aphroditas is queen of the mermaids, and like tonight's full moon, however many times you see her, she's always captivating.

We're drifting now. Both Arjun and Kirsty have stopped rowing, although the momentum of the water is still carrying us toward the circle of boats. There is a gap, ready-made for us. We might make it after all.

And just as well, for the next few seconds are a scramble. Shells open everywhere, following Aphroditas's lead, and there are mermaids and pearls appearing faster than we can keep up with. They fill the circle with their laughter, splashing each other and giggling and generally ignoring us.

Immediately, the other teams attempt to grab the mermaids' attention. Right across from us, with the prime spot in front of Aphroditas, is the ZA ship, with someone standing on the prow, their arms outstretched. Recognition flicks through my mind, and I grab Anita's hand.

"What is it?" she asks.

"Quick, can you lend me your binoculars a sec?"

"Sure." She lifts them from around her neck and passes them over to me.

I point them toward the yacht and adjust the focus. A man in a sharp three-piece suit comes into view, his hair slicked back with gel in the latest style. He's holding a wand that is studded with sparkling diamonds, and he touches the tip of the wand to his throat. Then he opens his mouth and starts to sing.

It's Anita's turn to grab at the binoculars. "Oh my god," she says, unable to keep the awe from her voice. "Is that who I think it is? Have they really got Damian out here?"

"Trust Zol to pull out all the stops," mutters Kirsty in the back. "That's Aphroditas secured, then."

I can see what she means. Aphroditas drifts toward the

ship, intrigued by the mellow richness of Damian's voice. Damian is the hottest pop star in Nova at the moment, and this is about to be his most captivated audience. This is the biggest stage Damian could wish for.

"Okay, it's our turn. Arjun, are you ready?"

Arjun nods grimly. "I'm not quite in his league, guys. And if I hear so much as a giggle out of any of you, you're going overboard."

Anita and I shuffle out of the way to give him space at the front of our little rowing boat. He opens his mouth, but at first, nothing comes out. He turns and looks at Kirsty, a sheen of sweat on his brow. "What should I sing?"

"Start small," she replies. "A nursery rhyme or something."

He turns back to the water and at the small group of mermaids whose attentions haven't yet been secured. Finally he chokes out the first few notes of a children's song about the sea:

**From the beach, to the waves, on the sand.
Mermaid's tails, sandcastle pails, hand-in-hand.**

His voice is sweet, lilting even, but it doesn't compare to Damian—who has enchanted his own deep, honey-smooth voice to project across the water. The three of us wait with bated breath as Arjun sings.

Finally, after Arjun switches to an old folk song with a slightly more prominent beat, one of the mermaids tilts her ear in our direction.

"Yes, Arjun, keep going," whispers Kirsty encouragingly. Arjun clearly spots the mermaid too, and focuses his voice on her, trying to make it sound like he's singing to her alone. Her tail flicks, a graceful motion like a petal in a breeze. Her long, mauve-colored fingers caress the pearl around her neck as she listens. Kirsty nudges me. "Arjun's doing well. See that pearl? That will be perfect. And there should be enough essence there for both teams."

Teams. She's said it, now, and I didn't even think of it before. I am a team against Arjun and Anita. Although we will help each other out along the way, only one team can win the hunt.

Arjun's mermaid is moving toward us. We're riveted by the action, so engrossed that we don't notice the superyacht ZA creeping in front of us. Kirsty, the sharpest of the four of us, yells, and immediately pulls at the oars to get us out of the yacht's path. While Damian sings to Aphroditas, the yacht is going to block our path to the Rising.

"Hey!" Kirsty drops the oars, stands up in the boat and screams. The action rocks the boat severely, and water sloshes into our hull. "That's illegal! Get out of our way!"

The yacht keeps on coming. I almost laugh. Who are we going to complain to if they prevent us from accessing a pearl? No one will care. This is a Wilde Hunt. All rules except the hunt rules are out the window.

It's a lot darker out here, outside of the circle. We stare in dismay as the waves rock our boat further from the action, further from the gathering of mermaids.

Arjun's voice breaks.

"Don't stop singing," Kirsty says, her voice grim. Her gaze is focused away from the boats, at a seemingly dark patch of the ocean. I follow her eyeline and struggle to see anything but the gentle rise and fall of the waves until—wait!—there's the tiniest ripple on the surface.

"There's another," whispers Anita beside me. Another mermaid? I'm at once hopeful and afraid. A mermaid outside the ring of the Rising is almost unheard of. But there are other creatures in the ocean, ones that would be much less delightful to meet. A fin appears out of the water, and although I only glance at it for a second, my fear is eased: she's definitely a mermaid. But the fin has a deep gouge out of it, as if she's recently been attacked, and I hope she's strong enough to produce a pearl.

A few feet away from the boat, she reemerges. I have to stop myself from recoiling—her face is full of wrinkles, the thick bands of her hair in tatters—she must be ancient, but, if she's like any other mermaid, she's also vain. If she sees surprise or disgust on any of our faces, she will surely bolt.

She approaches the boat, her lips widening into a grin. But that grin is a horror . . . teeth sharpened to a point, more shark than human. Worse still is the stench—rot, decay and mouldering fish. Anita and I both have to hold our breath, but luckily her attention is fixed on Arjun. He's white as a sheet but holding his nerve well, and Kirsty's hand on his shoulder is lending him reassurance and encouragement.

He sings and his voice barely wavers. I never even knew Arjun had it in him, but as I look into his eyes I see he is locked in a kind of trance with the mermaid.

Kirsty's fingers dig a little deeper into his shoulder.

"Can you do anything to help him?" I ask Kirsty.

"He's doing everything right. He just needs to hold on a little longer . . ."

The other boats are leaving now, their engines rumbling, and if their wake interrupts the trance—or more likely, if they continue to play dirty and deliberately try to break it—we will lose the pearl forever. The fact that we haven't even seen the pearl yet is a bad enough sign.

Arjun's voice takes on a more urgent quality, but the mer . . . "mermaid" hardly seems like the right term, "mercrone" seems more accurate, will not be rushed. Slowly, ever so slowly, she reaches down into her shell and brings out the tiniest pearl I have ever seen, barely a seed.

Arjun extends his hand out and she reaches to meet his. But then the ZA yacht blasts its horn, attempting to scatter any remaining mermaids.

Including ours. But there's a glint of cunning in her eye as she spooks . . . and snatches at Arjun's arm in the process.

All at once the boat tips, the trance breaks, and the mercrone dives. Anita and I leap for Arjun, grabbing him by one leg each.

"Keep hold of him!" Kirsty cries as she fumbles through her bag. Between us, we are stronger than the sea creature and she surfaces again, hissing and spitting through her teeth.

Then with a powerful flick of her tail she bends forward and bites his upper arm. Arjun's screams fill my ears and I beat at her with my fist while still maintaining my fierce grip on Arjun.

"Sam, pull him back!"

I throw my other arm around Arjun as Kirsty tosses a handful of powder in the mercrone's face. Now it is her turn to scream and she releases Arjun, her hands clawing at her face. She dives. With a final tug we pull him into the middle of the rowing boat, collapsing on top of one another in a big pile.

"Alkali," Kirsty says. "It reacts with the salt in their skin and burns them."

"Serves her right," say Arjun, wincing as Anita wipes his bite wound with a natural anaesthetic. Aelgi, for wounds of the sea—to help the blood clot, to prevent scarring.

"As does this . . ." He opens his palm, and in the center of it is a little pearl.

Anita and I let out a whoop of joy. The first ingredient is ours!

I catch Kirsty's eye as she pulls the first stroke back toward shore. She shakes her head at me.

"Hey, Arjun, can I take a look?" I ask.

He places the pearl in my hand. I roll it between my fingers, and it disappears into the pads of my fingertips as I press down. I pass it back over to Anita.

It's too small for two teams to share. Less than twenty-four hours into the hunt, and the Kemi family is already out.

Chapter Thirteen

Samantha

KIRSTY DROPS ME OFF IN SILENCE. WE'VE been silent most of the way home. Anita and Arjun offered me a lift back in their car, but I couldn't face the excited talk. Plus, I didn't want them to have to feel sorry for me—they have more important things to worry about, like figuring out the next ingredient.

Oblivion, or permanent amnesia: mix four strands of jellyfish stingers with two cups of Lethe water. Heat until warm and then drink from favorite mug.

That's what I need right now. Anything to forget that I disappointed Kirsty, disgraced my parents, disobeyed my granddad, and failed at the first hurdle.

I stand in the alleyway for a moment, my back up against the wall. I close my eyes and breathe—anything not to cry. The first signs of light are creeping onto the horizon, the dawn of a new day. It was stupid to try. Who do I think I am, going out into the Wilds with Kirsty without a plan? My first taste of adventure, and it's bitter.

At least I can get out of my wet shoes.

I pluck up the courage to walk through the side door and into the kitchen. The whole family—except Granddad—is sitting at the table, waiting for me. They don't immediately look up, and for a split second I wonder if they don't know the news yet. Except that Mum gets up and takes a plate out of the oven, a plate piled high with a stack of pancakes—my favorite. There's real maple syrup out on the table, the expensive kind. And that's when I realize, they know. Of course they know.

Suddenly I can't help but let the tears well up in my eyes. Mum is over to me in a flash, and I fall into her open arms. "It's okay, sweetie," she says, brushing her hand over my hair, like I was Molly's age all over again. "You tried."

I nod into her shoulder, then finally extricate myself from her embrace. "I just thought . . ."

Dad and Molly are behind her. Dad looks at me with a mixture of concern and I-told-you-so, whereas Molly is distraught that her big sister is in tears. I really thought we had a chance to change things here. Now I have to put my hopes back on the shelf.

I wipe my cheeks and Mum walks me over to the table, sitting me firmly down with her hands on my shoulders. "Eat, young lady. You've had a long night . . ."

I pour the red-gold maple syrup over my pancakes

(maple—for comfort and lethargy, to warm the blood) and slice my knife through the entire stack.

But then I notice something unusual. Apart from the scrape of cutlery on plates, there's no background noise. The screen above the kitchen countertop is blank.

Mum and Dad always watch the casts in the morning, even if it's early. It's a daily ritual: Whoever's in the kitchen first turns on the casts and checks the weather, news, and traffic for the day. I try to keep my voice casual. "So can we turn on the TV already?"

My parents hesitate. I grab the remote, and my worst fear materializes on the screen.

It's our old family crest. The only reminder that the Kemis were once a great family now has a giant red X slashed over the top of it. A voiceover begins.

"After the shock announcement about Princess Evelyn's condition, a Wilde Hunt was called late last night. Of the twelve alchemists to participate, first out of the hunt is Samantha Kemi, representing the formerly eminent Kemi family, who was unable to procure the first ingredient. For the rest of the teams, the hunt is still on as the race for the princess's cure becomes ever more urgent . . ."

Mum places her finger over mine, pressing the power button on the remote. The screen goes blank. "Why don't you get some rest and then you can come with us to Molly's gifting ceremony this afternoon?"

And just like that, my day has gone from crazy to normal. "I will. I just have to do one thing first."

I stand up and reluctantly push the heavy wooden door that leads from the kitchen to the lab, ready to apologize and face my granddad's wrath.

The lab exists in semipermanent darkness, the old glass windows too streaked with the smoke of old experiments to ever truly be clean. The smell of kerosene lights, boiling plant matter, and preserving fluid invades my nostrils, a smell both comforting and revolting. It takes a few moments for me to spot him, but that's because he's hunched over the table and so still he might not even be breathing.

As I walk toward him, his image distorts through the glass of a great round beaker—his bulbous nose made more prominent by the bending light, one eye suddenly becoming huge and green in the convex.

"Sam, come. Tell me what I am brewing." His voice is kind, without a trace of anger.

I draw closer and am bowled over by the noxious fumes emanating from the bubbling mixture. The substance is a rich magenta. I swallow the nausea rising in my throat and place both hands on the ancient, knot-riddled, oak table. It's the small details that Granddad reminds me are the most important. Like mixing potions on an organic surface so that the natural ingredients remain potent. We try to stick to natural materials, though it isn't always possible or practical. From the other end of the table, Granddad pours two drops of a bright gold liquid from a small vial. The liquid is pumped through a maze of delicate glass tubing, looping around and around, each time having a little air added to it, before it finally drops into the potion in the beaker.

I hold my breath and bend closer for another look. "Um, it looks like . . . some kind of headache potion?"

Granddad tuts at me. "Why would I add goldenrod to a headache potion?"

Goldenrod—for sore throats and empty wallets. Granddad's right, of course. Not for headaches at all.

"Concentrate, Sam!"

But the remedy won't come. I've been up all night, and I'm almost asleep on my feet.

Granddad sighs. "The hunt is a fool's errand, Sam. You can't hope to revive the fortunes of alchemists just because of some quest. While synthetic ingredients still dominate, there's no place for us."

It's this kind of talk that makes an old frustration wring my stomach. "Why though, Granddad? If we update some of the store systems, replace some of the empty ingredients, maybe do a bit of advertising . . . there are people who remember the Kemi name. People who would shop here again if they knew we were back in action."

He shakes his head. "No. All we can do is keep on

studying our craft, so that our knowledge hasn't died out when the world finally comes to its senses."

"But the princess . . ."

"I won't help the royals. This is a mess of their own making. And how can you trust people who exile their own family?"

"You mean Emilia."

He nods. "They're terrified the princess's power will pass to her. I've been in a Wilde Hunt, Sam. You know that. And let me tell you, the 'rules' of the Wilde Hunts don't mean anything to the royals as long as they get their cure. I was apprentice to your great-grandmother, and by all rights she should have won that hunt. Zoro Aster stole the potion from her and submitted it as his own. Auden's Horn accepted it. Then Zoro Aster told everyone the potion was made from synths, establishing his company's legitimacy forever."

"But then someone should tell the royals!"

"You think we didn't try that? But your great-grandmother had lost her potion diary detailing her formula. Without that, it was our word against his. And the blasted royals had their cure, so what did they care? They had no problem stripping us of our commission and handing it over to Zoro Aster and his new synth company. Centuries of loyal service, forgotten just like that. Your great-grandmother was never the same again. That's why you can never trust the royals or the synths."

I have so many more questions, but I'm too tired to ask them. Besides, he's turned back to his potion.

"I'm going to get some rest," I say.

Rather than go straight upstairs, though, I stop by the door to the library—my favorite place in the entire world. Maybe a quick look in there will make me feel better.

Surrounded by the books, my mind drifts back to the love potion. Somewhere in this room, there could be an answer. Anita and Arjun still need the right recipe; they're not out of the hunt yet. Maybe I can help them.

I run my fingers over the crinkly gold writing on the spines, the titles barely decipherable after years of neglect. They are almost all recipe books—some clearly written by mad wizards with no idea how to put a potion together, but most full of useful knowledge.

I stare at the huge wall of spines in front of me. There isn't a book called *Best Recipe for Love Potions in Here* but one of them must contain a clue. I pick three of the most likely tomes off the shelf, bundle them into my arms, and take them over to the desk in the center of the room.

The title on the first one has all but peeled off, but on creaking open the front cover I blow a cloud of dust from the title page and read: *Foure Hundread Emploies for Pricolici Breathe.*

Great. Four hundred uses for the breath of an animal that has been extinct for three hundred years.

Who am I kidding? I live for this stuff. If not for the stale words and ancient advice within, then for the crackle of the parchment as I turn each page, delicately peeling the paper apart from its neighbor. The letters cling to each other like lovers, ink solidified by time into glue.

I carefully leaf through the rest of the book. Nothing. But this is the thrill of the hunt for me—the research, sifting through words like they're grains of sand, hunting for diamonds. The fourth stack of books is where I find the first sparkle of a gem. It's the word "philtre"—the old word for love potion. But the excitement dies as quickly as it comes when I see evidence of the purge that happened well over a century ago, when love potions were classified as illegal. The first two sentences are still there, the thin black cursive letters dark spots upon the page: *A philtre is one of the most dangerous potions known to mankind, for both the preparer and the taker. Proceed with the utmost caution.* After that, the letters huddle together in a thick black mess, as if they are trying to avoid the spell to make them disappear. In the mass of letters I can make out a few ancient words—indicum and eluvium—but I have no idea if those are relevant or just a jumble. I've heard that the older a recipe is, the harder it is to truly destroy it. And now the evidence is there on the page, right in front of my face.

Maybe I need even older books—and I know where to find them.

It used to be one of our weekly rituals, a special secret between Granddad and me. I don't know if he has ever taken Molly, and I've never asked—I like to pretend that he shared his love of books with me and me alone. I return to the front of the library and grab the key from its hook inside the doorway. It always puzzled me that Granddad kept the key out in the open, where anyone could grab it. Then his words ring in my ears. "It takes more than a key to open a door, little girl. You have to know where the lock is too."

And I do.

I haven't been in the room other than when Granddad has taken me, and as I touch the key, I feel a chill run down my spine. It's never been expressly forbidden to me to enter the room on my own, but I've never had a reason to go in either—most of the books are so old, they are written in an ancient language I can't read.

The chill from the key is enough to make me pause. I hold my breath until my lungs burn, my heart beating in my ears. I don't know what I'm listening out for—there's nothing but a subtle hum from the lightbulb, and the muted clattering of pans in the kitchen from Dad doing the dishes. I let out the breath in one big whoosh and shake out my limbs, then pad over to the far side of the library.

I have to crouch down to reach the right shelf, and it makes me suddenly smile to think that I am so much taller now than my granddad. He's always seemed like such a giant in my life, but now at five-eleven and still growing, I tower over him—and most of the girls (and some of the boys) in my class. Sometimes I despise my lanky frame, and the massively overgrown feet that come with it, the arms and legs slightly too long for my body. Once, at Anita's older sister's wedding, the Patels tried to dress me in their traditional clothing—a beautiful blue-and-gold stitched shalwar kameez that made me feel like a princess—except for the fact that the trousers stopped way too high above my ankles and made me feel like a giant playing dress-up in a princess's clothing.

The red book stands out to me on the shelf like a sore thumb, but I can see how others would pass it by without a second glance. I take it down from the shelf and, sitting behind it, obscured in the shadows of the library shelf, is the lock. I slip the key in, turn it a quarter of the way, and feel the entire bookshelf jump to life and swing out toward me.

Chapter Fourteen

Samantha

"SAM! TIME TO GO!" MUM SHOUTS UP THE stairs, not realizing I'm in the library. I glance down at my watch, and my jaw drops. I've been studying books for almost four hours nonstop.

I walk back through the lab and into the kitchen.

Mum frowns. "I thought you were in your room, resting?"

"I got a bit . . . distracted." Tiredness hits me like a freight train—a minute ago I was fine, now I'm exhausted. There's no mistaking what kind of potion I need.

Caffeine—for alertness and rejuvenation.

There's a small amount of coffee left in the bottom of the carafe from breakfast, and I grimace as the cold, bitter drink slides down my throat. Better than nothing. "I'll be fine, Mum."

She smiles wryly at me, giving me a quick look up and down. "We can wait ten minutes for you to shower and change, if you want?"

I look down and I can see what she means—I'm still in the same clothes I wore to the Rising. The bottoms of my trouser legs are caked in salt from the sea spray, and I wrinkle my nose as I realize I smell more mollusk than teenager. "Good plan," I say, before running upstairs.

A few hours later and we stand up in a jubilant ovation, as Molly's class of twenty step forward and take a bow. Molly is wearing a pair of beautiful silk gloves—her object—the iridescent material catching the stage lights and making her hands seem like they're glowing.

Maybe they are. The rest of her certainly is. Her smile reaches to both ears, and she radiates happiness. Against the other students, she's like a beacon. But then again, I am biased.

Of course her object is a pair of gloves. My gorgeous, sweet sister has no use for an aggressive object like a wand or a staff. She will be a healer, a teacher. Her magic will be gentle.

But she'll need her own pair of gloves eventually, and gloves are costly. They have to be made from material that will grow with her, mould to her hands like a second skin. The best material would be changeling leather—super malleable, but nigh on impossible to get hold of nowadays since changelings are at risk of extinction. Silk gloves, like the ones the school have lent her, would be more practical—there are worms in the southern caves whose silk shapes itself around any form. One of the big malls on the outskirts of Kingstown sells them.

Molly practically skips off the stage and rushes over to find us in the audience. I shift from one foot to the other as she chats to my parents. A few people stare sidelong at me and cover their mouths to whisper. Almost everyone is talking about the hunt, although not directly to our family. There's excitement, but there's fear for the princess too. No one knows what will happen if the hunt doesn't succeed.

Mum catches my eye. "Will you stay and watch Molly for a while, until she's ready to come home?"

Molly puts her hands on her hips. "I don't need looking after anymore, Mum. I can make it home on my own."

Mum smiles and puts her hand on Molly's head, but her eyes stay trained on me. "Be back in time for dinner, okay? I don't want either of you wearing yourselves out."

I shrug. "Sure thing."

Our parents leave, and Molly shoots off to hang out with her Talented friends. I slump down onto a plastic orange chair and watch as they compare notes on their new objects—Molly's best friend, Alex, was given a ring. Rings are pretty rare but powerful conductors of magic. She'll probably go into politics or business—something that requires a mix of power and subtlety. None of them will have to worry about their futures now; there's plenty of demand for strong Talenteds in all sectors. I pull out a book and try to read. My eyelids are so heavy, I could drift off at any moment.

"Sam?"

Molly's quiet voice snaps me out of my daydream.

"I'm ready to go," she says. She tugs at the edge of her glove.

"Already?"

"Yeah, I'm kinda tired."

"Everything all right?" I stand up to go, slipping my bag over one shoulder. "Gloves bothering you?"

"I'm just not used to them yet." We walk out of the stuffy auditorium and into the warm summer air. The breeze picks up as we stroll in the direction of home.

"That's understandable, but it's exciting, isn't it?"

"I guess."

I frown. This isn't the Molly from a few minutes ago— smiles and giddy laughter. "Okay, seriously, what's up?"

She shrugs. "I thought Granddad might come."

I pause. "I think he had some mixes to catch up on."

She shrugs again.

I decide to change the subject. "So are you allowed to show me what you can do with those gloves?"

Molly looks up at me, her blue eyes sparkling. "Really? You wanna see?"

"Of course!"

She looks up and down the street, but we're the only ones around. She reaches up to where a summer-blooming magnolia tree is leaning against a garden fence, its long branches dangling across our path. She finds one bud that hasn't yet bloomed and wraps her gloved hands around it. She closes her eyes and whispers a spell. Ever so slowly, the bud begins to grow, unraveling into a stunning white flower.

My jaw drops. "Oh my god, Molly—that's amazing!"

"Thanks." She beams. "I'm really hoping I'm good enough to get into medical school."

I laugh. "That's years away; you don't have to think about stuff like that yet."

A frown creases the smooth skin on Molly's forehead. "Of course I do. I mean, I'm not the one with the Kemi gift, like you have. I don't know what I'm good at."

"A gift which is useless," I mutter, gazing at the magnolia she's opened. "You're the one who's going to be rich beyond your wildest dreams and have the big fancy career."

"And if not . . . all the money Mum and Dad spent on me will have been wasted."

The flower bursts into flame.

We both start screaming. Molly releases the branch, backs away and starts running. I grab the branch further down, trying to snap it off before the flames hit the main tree. After a few tugs, it rips away, and I stomp on the burning embers of the flower.

I look up. "Molly!" I shout. But she's gone.

Chapter Fifteen

Samantha

BLUE AND RED FLASHING LIGHTS FLARE over Kemi Street, and my heart pounds in my chest. My thoughts instantly jump to Molly. I dash past police vans and fire engines mounted up on the curb and burst through the front door of the shop.

The scene inside is a disaster. There's paper strewn everywhere over the dark hardwood floors. A man in a navy-blue uniform barges past me, carrying a toolbox. Forensics. More men in suits stand behind the till; I still haven't seen my family.

"Oh, thank goodness you're here," says Mum, coming through the door to the library. She has to shove the door to get it open over the debris. I finally breathe again once I spy Molly standing open-mouthed behind her. And for good reason. If I thought the shop floor was a mess, the library is worse. Pages scattered to the wind, hardback covers ripped apart and strewn across the room. No shelf has been spared the torture—no matter how ancient the book, how delicate its contents, all of it is in complete and utter shambles. We pick our way through what was once Granddad's prized collection, over to where the forensics team are clustered around an open bookshelf. The door I unlocked before Molly's ceremony.

The door I'm not sure that I locked again.

The very ancient room, by contrast, isn't in shambles—at least they had that much sense. But there are gaps in the shelving like a mouth with teeth missing, and black scorch marks on the walls. Then the smell hits me. It's acrid, metallic. I reel backward from the ancient library and away from the stench.

"Who did this?" I whisper. This is Granddad's whole world and it's been violated. And it's my fault.

One of the detectives approaches me. "Are you Samantha?"

I nod, but my actions feel separate from my mind. Like I've disconnected.

"I know this is hard, but you have to help us out, here. Whoever broke in to steal your books also attempted to burn the store down. Luckily you have some kind of built-in security system that put out the fire."

A security system? I didn't think we had anything other than an old-fashioned deadbolt on the front door.

"Samantha?"

I've drifted away. I try to focus on the detective. "Um, this morning I was in the library as I thought I would do a bit of research on love potions . . ." I look sideways at my mother, chewing the corner of my lip.

"But you're out of the hunt," says the detective, scribbling in his notebook. "You do know that love potion recipes were banned over a hundred years ago. If your family was hiding one of them, that could mean serious consequences . . ."

Heat rises in my cheeks. "We weren't hiding anything! Sometimes those censoring spells disintegrate over time. It was a long shot but I wanted to see. Then I thought the book might be in the ancient library, and then I had to leave . . ." Tears well up in my eyes. "I'm so sorry, Mum!" I bury my face in my hands.

"It's not your fault, honey." Her voice turns hard as she speaks to the detective. "You've got the answers you need from my daughter, now you just focus on figuring out who did this."

"Yes, ma'am. We've had some petty vandals loose in this area. We think they saw this as an easy target."

"Vandals who steal only books?"

"We don't know yet what books are missing, which will make them harder to track down. Mr. Ostanes is being . . . less than cooperative." He scribbles down some notes. "Well, we think whoever it was saw you all leave the house."

"So you think this was premeditated?" my mother squeaks.

The detective hastens to soothe her. "Nothing is certain yet. We're working on a number of theories. For now we're going to have to close your store for a few hours, dust for prints, do a thorough investigation . . ."

"Absolutely not!" Granddad appears in the doorway. "Out, out, out. I don't need all you Talented busybodies in my house. We'll let you know if we want you."

The detective holds his hands up. "I think we're just about done here anyway. If you don't want us to do any more . . ."

"You've done quite enough, thank you."

The detective stares at him for a few seconds, and then nods. Not many people are brave enough to argue with my granddad when he's in one of these moods, and the detective is no exception. He snaps his fingers at the rest of his team, and they all shuffle out of our front door. The detective turns around to say something, and Granddad shuts the door in his face.

"Dad, are you going to tell us what's going on?" my dad asks.

"No. And we don't need any of those pesky policemen around because I know exactly who did this. John, Katie, I need you to take Molly and leave us," says my granddad to my parents.

"Why?" my mum asks, flabbergasted.

"Dad, be reasonable! This is our home that was attacked too."

"No. This is alchemist business and my apprentice is the only one who can stay. Now all of you, leave!" My granddad is at his most terrifying when he's like this. They obey his order. I want to reach out to them, to ask them to stay, but if this is important Kemi business then I know I have to listen.

"Can you smell that?" Granddad asks me once they're gone. His wide nostrils flare. "Whenever a Talented performs magic, they leave their own scent, a trace. It's normally undetectable, but not in here. Not in our store."

"A Talented did this?" I open my eyes wide in alarm.

"Don't you recognize the smell?"

I concentrate. It takes me a couple of beats, but my memory catches up with my senses. I do recognize it. It's the same sickening metallic scent that invaded my nose back in the palace.

"Is it . . . Emilia? What would she want with our library?"

Granddad nods. He reaches out and touches the black powder that streaks the wall. They're not scorch marks at all. "Most likely the same thing you hoped to find. When she couldn't get what she wanted, she attempted to set fire to all these ancient books. But this powder neutralizes spells."

"How is that possible?"

"Because the knowledge contained within these walls is worth more than either of our lives to protect. Every Kemi has known this. And when Thomas Kemi won the first Wilde Hunt, he spent his prize-winnings building this store and with it, many special protections against magic interference, reinforced with every win since. So that no Kemi would ever have to worry about the likes of Emilia Thoth."

"And so the missing books?"

"I took them so that the police would call it a robbery and be done with it. But nothing ever gets taken from the store while a Kemi master is in charge. Nothing."

Chapter Sixteen

Samantha

THE NEXT DAY MY ALARM BLARES, AND I curse myself for not turning it off. I feel like I could stay tucked up in bed for a hundred years. Instead, I delay the inevitable by staring at the glow-in-the-dark stickers on my ceiling. I stuck them up after I'd been to a party at my classmate Ella's house—one of the few Talented parties I've ever attended.

Her house was one of the massive mansions almost at the base of Kingstown Hill, and I had pulled up on my bike, cycling past limo after limo queuing to swing around the semicircular driveway and drop off their dressed-up inhabitants. When I had heard "house party," I'd automatically thrown on my favorite T-shirt, dark jeans, and scuffed-up ankle boots—turned out, this was the wrong look. As Wilhelmina stepped out in a sparkly strapless ballgown, I almost made a U-turn right then and there. But Anita had spotted me, and she was as dressed down as I was.

"You're not leaving me to face them all alone," she'd said, and I'd grudgingly gone with her through the vast double doors, feeling stronger with her by my side.

Strangely, I can barely remember the details from that party now—the beginning of it swallowed up by my nervousness, but the rest dominated by a single detail: Ella's bedroom. Her parents had opened up the whole house and Anita and I had gone exploring. A few times that made us the unwitting interrupters of closet hook-ups, but most of the time it led to rooms more magnificent and wondrous than the rooms that came before it. But Ella's bedroom—I will never forget it. I opened the door and gasped—the ceiling was completely enchanted to look like the night sky. But not just the night sky as you would see it on a normal night in Kingstown—a fuzzy gray-black background, stars drowned out by the light pollution or clouds—but the kind of sky you could only see from the top of a mountain, the pitch black cut by swaths of stars, milky-white galaxies shot through with purple, and dark, swirling nebulas.

That night I'd come home and plastered plastic stars all over my bedroom ceiling. It didn't quite have the same effect, but it was the closest I was going to get.

Now I shut my eyes tightly and try to convince myself that the past two days were just a dream, a blip easily wiped from my memory. Well, except for the fact that I know when I go down for breakfast I won't be able to watch the news—that part of the routine won't be added back in for a long time. But maybe going back to work in the store, helping to restore some order after the chaos of Emilia's attack, will make me feel normal.

The first few hours of the morning tick by in blissful solitude. I fix the bell above the door and get started on clearing up the mess. The terrifying thought crosses my mind that maybe the media will come by the store, bearing flashbulbs and voice recorders, to capture the Kemi family's misery on air. Yet obviously our early exit from the hunt isn't even news enough for that. We are forgotten as quickly as Princess Evelyn's early suitors.

Once I've piled up the scraps, I tie back my dusty hair and sit down cross-legged on the floor, trying to match them up like some enormous jigsaw puzzle. A line of text on a torn corner catches my eye—I swear it matches with another scrap of paper I've seen. I absentmindedly clamp the first bit of paper between my lips while I reach across the floor for the other.

As luck would have it, that's when the bell rings for the first time that day. I snatch the paper from my mouth and yell out, "Excuse the mess, but we're just clearing up from—"

The words die in my mouth as I take in who has walked in the door. Zain Aster.

Blood rushes up to my cheeks and I am immediately annoyed with myself in case he mistakes my flushed look for being attracted to him. So I throw him a good scowl just in case.

To his credit, he flinches. "Hi, Sam."

I move behind the counter, putting a big, solid object between us. He's wearing a black T-shirt and jeans, which is so different from the school uniform I was used to seeing him in before he graduated. Purposefully avoiding eye contact until the last possible moment, I catch a glimpse of glamoured tattoos shifting round his bicep. If he were anyone else, I'd say they were cool, but I keep my mouth firmly shut.

Finally I make eye contact. "Can I help you?"

"Nice store. I mean . . . I'm sorry about the vandals. I heard about that. Did they take anything important?"

"No," I say curtly. Zain jams his hands in his pockets and rocks slightly on his heels. It's such a self-conscious move that I realize he must be nervous. I almost laugh, but quickly stifle the smile in case he thinks it's for him, rather than about him.

"Look, I came by to say sorry 'bout what happened. At the Rising. That wasn't very . . . sporting of us."

"Yeah, generally cheating isn't considered to be 'sporting.'" What century did he think he was from, anyway? "But hey, you got what you wanted, I'm out—though I'm not quite sure why you've bothered to come all this way to remind me of that."

I'm expecting him to turn around and leave now his

apology is over, but instead he comes further into the store. He even dares to bend down and pick something up. If this counter wasn't between us, I'd snatch it right out of his hands.

"Don't touch anything," I snap.

"I'm just trying to help."

"I don't need your help. Besides, I have it mapped out where each book was torn up and I don't want to get the pieces mixed up." I don't even know why I'm telling him this; I want him to leave, but I can't seem to shut up.

"Look, I feel bad for what happened. Can I make it up to you in some way?"

"Aren't you supposed to be on the hunt?"

A flash of annoyance on his face. I finally feel like I might have got through to him.

"Yes, I am. But we have our researchers working on figuring out what the next ingredient is after the merpearl, and I wanted you to know that I tried to stop us blocking you at the Rising."

"And I'm supposed to thank you?"

"Okay, whoa." He holds his hands up. "You don't get it. My dad wants ZoroAster Corp. to cure the princess, no matter what. But I want to make sure she's cured, no matter who does it. We should all have a fair shot. That's why I came here, to tell you I'm sorry you're out. And to ask for your help."

"Well, the answer to that is no."

"Aren't you going to hear me out?"

"No. Why do you even want my help? Don't you have your researchers to do that?"

He leans forward on the counter and gives me a con-spiratorial grin. "They're all right, but I think you're better."

I raise an eyebrow and lean away from him. His blue eyes are full of mischief, and he's too close for comfort. "You do? Why?"

He laughs. "Come on, you're a legend!"

"No, my family is the legend. I'm just an apprentice."

"Don't deny it. I saw the concentration-boosting mix you were making for that competition. I came by your school a couple days before judging to look at how the entries were going. You're good. I don't know why you threw the competition, but I know you're the real deal. Look, I get if helping us is a step too far. But let me make it up to you for what happened at the Rising. I can show you around the main ZA lab, if you want?"

Despite myself, I'm interested. A tour around one of ZA's labs would be an incredible experience. Synth or not, I would give anything to see those mixers at work. It's also very hard to get an invite—the labs are normally closed off to the public, and the company likes to keep it that way.

But then I pull myself back to reality. "Thanks, but no thanks. I'm not going to work for the synths. Ever."

I suddenly feel self-conscious standing here in the run-down store, the ever-present reminder that this is what my life will amount to.

"Sometimes I wish I could work more with natural ingredients."

"Seriously?"

"Yeah, I mean, my dad trained as an alchemist, but he rejects all the traditional ways in favor of the synths. He hates that we have to go out into the Wilds too. If he could stay in his office and pay someone to go, he would. He doesn't trust me to go alone." A frown flickers on his face. "Plus, magic behaves differently out there."

I shiver, despite myself. "I guess when you're so used to relying on magic, you forget basic survival stuff."

"Something like that." His attention turns to a piece of crumpled paper on the counter. I'm aware of how close he's got since we started talking. I could reach out and touch the line of his strong jaw if I wanted to. Of course, I don't, but I feel almost as awkward as when I met the Queen Mother. Even at school, Zain always seemed more intangible than the royals. But he's not as perfect as I once thought. His hands are rough, and one finger is blemished by a nasty-looking chemical burn.

Witch hazel—to reduce scarring, blended with crushed anemone powder for skin reparation.

"Wow, wizard's beard? I didn't think anyone stocked that anymore."

I look up sharply from his hands and see he's studying the inventory list I'd been making before the Wilde Hunt started. This time he is close enough for me to snatch it away. "We don't have it either. I'm making a stocklist."

He's barely listening to me, though, because his eyes are cast upward and a look of awe descends on his face. He's taking in the shelves upon shelves of bottles, jars, and ingredients that disappear up into the high ceiling. I turn around myself and look at it all, trying to imagine what it must be like to see it for the first time.

"May I?" he asks, gesturing to come around the back of the counter for a closer look.

I actually nod, because seeing Zain in awe sends a surge of pride through me that I can't ignore—and I want him to be up close to really understand it.

"And none of this is categorized magically? Or digitally?"

I shake my head. "No, it's done by hand."

"Who maintains all this?" he says, releasing a whistle of amazement.

I shrug. "I do."

"Wait, seriously? I was joking! I thought it'd be impossible . . ."

I smile. "I've got a lot of time on my hands."

"Clearly."

I shoot another glare his way, but my face relaxes

when I see that he is smiling. "It is tough," I say reluctantly. "But I work in the store every weekend, so my goal had been to go through the shelves and take a proper inventory of everything. Hence the paper."

"Well, hey, you got as far as W. That's not bad."

I shake my head. "No . . . M, actually. It was labeled as 'Merlin's beard.'"

"Oh, I see. I'll help then. I'll start up from Z and you can work your way down again."

He seems totally genuine in his offer, but I'm still suspicious. "Won't your dad be wondering where you are? What with the hunt and all . . ."

"Yeah, but he knows how to get hold of me. And my dad thinks I'm visiting Evie."

It takes me a second, but the name clicks. "Wait, Evie as in Princess Evelyn?" I can't imagine being so close to a member of the royal family that I could casually drop their nickname into conversation.

He winces. "Yeah. I saw her first thing this morning, but she doesn't want to talk to me. At the moment she just sits there. Staring at herself. It's so strange."

"I'm sorry. I know you guys were good friends. Were you there when she . . . ?"

He nods.

My curiosity burns bright, but I don't pester him any more. I sweep my hair up into a bun and secure it with the pen that's in my hand. "Right, well, look at the labels, write down what's there, and if there's nothing in the jar itself, then put the ingredient on a separate list for the next Finding."

I search around the desk for another piece of paper for him to use, but he's already started jotting things down on a fancy tablet that I've seen advertised on the casts but have no hope of ever affording. "I'll flick the list across to your in-box when we've finished," he says, without turning around.

"Um, thanks," I say. I force myself to move, rather than stare at the back of his head. Anita would jump to all sorts of conclusions if she was here, watching him casually help me with the inventory. And Granddad would kill me—and probably Zain too—if he found him in the store. But I realize I don't care. He's already picked up his first jar. I would be suspicious of his interest in the Kemi family stock if I didn't also recognize the meticulous—scientific—scrutiny and care he has that I have myself.

We settle into a comfortable rhythm, Zain checking the stock while I settle back down to my shredded book puzzle on the shop floor. He occasionally mentions something interesting he finds or lets me know what's missing. He also talks about the stockrooms in the megapharmacies, and the braver I feel, the more I start to ask about ZoroAster. "I hope to work in Research and Development after I graduate," says Zain, after I quiz him about the different departments. "Researching new kinds of drugs, new formulas—there are so many places in the Wilds that not even Finders have dared to explore. With new, more advanced magic and technology, I bet we'd be able to find even better cures—stronger, faster, cheaper medicine for everyone. And who knows what new illnesses there will be in the future. Did you hear about that supervirus in Jung province?"

Words of agreement fill my throat, but I'm suddenly shy and don't want to agree with him. We keep working along the stacks, until his chuckle disturbs me. I look over and glare at him.

He catches my eye and laughs again. "I'm sorry," he says, stifling his laughter. "I didn't realize you had such a good singing voice. Big Damian fan, are you?"

I want to bury myself under the pieces of paper I'm holding. Then I can't help but laugh too. "Oh god, I never know when I'm singing to myself! I'll shut up."

"You don't have to stop for me. If you're embarrassed, I'll start and you can join in." He sings another pop song, and not only is he handsome and smart but he has a great voice too. I could really hate this guy.

I've spent so long on the floor; I yearn to stretch my legs. I grab my notebook and head over to the shelves. The ladders are still in place from the last time I'd climbed them—Emilia hadn't bothered with the stock, just the books. I nip up to the spot where I'd found the Merlin's beard and make a start. The song's refrain jumps into my head. But as I open my mouth to sing, I notice something strange. The remnants of a dust ring on the shelf. Two jars have been hastily pushed together to conceal it, but there's slightly too much space between those jars and their neighbors. I move the jars back to their rightful positions and ponder.

Merlin's beard.

Merrimack plant.

So what would be between them? Then it hits me. Merpearl. Merpearl, that wasn't on our shelves two days ago. Merpearl, that I failed to acquire at the Rising. Merpearl, the ingredient we'd had all along that someone had hidden so we wouldn't succeed in the hunt. And it isn't hard to guess who the culprit is.

I trip down the ladders, mind muddled with absolute fury, and land next to Zain. He's still singing, but he stops when he sees my face. He opens his mouth but I jump in before he can say anything. "Is that offer of a lab tour still on?"

"Sure."

"Could we do it now?"

"Um, I guess."

"Then let's go."

He carefully returns the jar he was holding to its exact position on the shelf. Then he follows me out the shop door. I stop to flip the sign on the front from OPEN to CLOSED, and slam the door shut behind me.

Chapter Seventeen

Princess Evelyn

SHE FELT HER HEART RACING WITHIN HER chest, but this time the feeling was pure agony. Why had Lyn not yet responded to her advances? Why did she still remain aloof? Did she not recognize the pain she was causing Eve; was she so cold-hearted and mean-spirited that she couldn't see how every moment they were apart was tearing her to pieces?

Eve had laid out a beautiful dinner for two with her best silverware and gilt-edged china, hand-decorated with the utmost care. She'd issued the invitation herself, written in her finest cursive on thick cream paper embossed with her seal.

Yet the seat opposite remained empty.

A small box sat on Lyn's place setting. Inside was Eve's favorite merpearl ring. But she wouldn't have the chance to propose, if Lyn never came. How could she refuse? This was cruelty, plain and simple.

An intense, real pain suddenly shot through the palms of her hands. She looked down and saw that she had been clenching her fists so hard her fingernails had pierced the skin and left little half-moon frowns, each of them stained red.

It should have been simple to find someone to marry her and to wear the crown. She'd known her whole life that one day the magic would become too much for her, and she needed to find someone to share the burden with. Her parents wouldn't let her forget it. And when she turned sixteen they had started an audition process. Over a thousand young men had signed up to try out for the part of her future husband. The media went into a frenzy over the process. Crown magazine even ran a weekly "Hot or Not" chart, ranking the latest suitors.

She entertained the idea because it felt like a silly game, right up until the magic overwhelmed her for the first time. She had a glimpse of what it would be like to lose control completely. Suddenly, the pressure felt real, intense, like she was trapped in an hourglass and the sand was quickly rising.

That was why it had to be Zain.

He was her best friend. She'd believed, foolishly, that he was her only option. She'd even asked him, once. They'd been seventeen and sitting between the turrets of the Western Tower, a wing her mother hated because no matter how many rugs they hung on the walls or magical heaters they fired up, draughts seemed to find their way through every crevice and set the china tinkling in their cabinets. Evelyn and Zain loved it, though—the wind seemed to chase them into hidden parts of the castle, blowing open secret doorways behind tapestries and whistling up cobweb-covered stairwells. They'd found a staircase that led up to the very top of the tower, and they could look down on the entire city of Kingstown. It was one of their favorite places in the world.

Sometimes she wished she could join the world below, like Zain could. He would tell her stories of his life at normal school, although she often wished he'd attend the elite academy that she did. She respected his decision not to let his high Talented status offer him too many privileges. She used to tease him for being obsessed with history. Zain had the inside track to synth superstardom, but still he insisted on studying the old alchemical ways—and mostly behind his father's back. That was another reason she and Zain explored the old wing of the castle. Zain wanted to see if there were any old books or grimoires hidden around, something that would give him an advantage that had nothing to do with his father.

She'd indulged him. She supposed that's why she'd thought she'd fallen in love with him—because he was her only friend, and she had been desperate not to lose him. Now that she'd met Lyn, of course, she knew that had been a false assumption. She hadn't loved Zain; she'd feared that getting married to someone else would mean spending a lifetime with someone she couldn't stand. At least she knew she liked Zain.

Up on those turrets, her head leaning against the stone wall—warm still, from the sun—she'd worked up the courage to ask him. "Would you do it if I asked you?"

"Do what?"

"Marry me."

He'd laughed, and at the time she'd found it cruel. "Some guy's gonna sweep you off your feet and you're going to forget all about me."

"What if that doesn't happen?"

He must've sensed something in her tone of voice, because he grabbed her hand. "Hey, chill. I just mean it'll never get to that point. You won't ever ask me because you'll have a million guys who want to say yes . . ." He stared at her, his brow furrowed. "And because you know I don't."

Her heart had stopped at that moment, even though she'd known the answer all along. He already bore the weight of a hundred obligations to his father; she couldn't force him into a marriage he didn't want on top of that. The whole point was that the suitors had a choice.

She didn't.

Marry or be married off. But this was the twenty-first

century, she'd thought angrily. That's why she created the love potion. She'd wanted to take destiny back into her own hands.

It seemed that destiny had other plans.

She stood up from the table and walked to the window. She could see Lyn just there, on the other side of the glass. She beckoned her over, but she simply beckoned back. Eve stomped her foot. She wished the other girl would stop being so stubborn and join her for dinner.

It was then that Renel entered. He was carrying a blanket, her favorite, made of the softest fleece and piped in silk. "Come, Evelyn. You've been in here for hours. You must be cold," he said.

She was cold. Her fingernails were tinged with blue, and goosebumps flecked her forearms. Maybe this was why Lyn was not responding to her. Maybe she was repulsed by her? "Yes, quick Renel, please bring the blanket. In fact, why have you let me get so cold, you foolish man? Should you not have seen my discomfort before?"

Renel allowed his normal, restrained pose to slip and replaced it with a relieved smile. For some reason, this made Eve even angrier. "Are you sure you gave the invitation to Lyn? Why is she waiting outside?"

"I . . . I don't know, Your Highness."

"And bring me a salve, man. Look what I have done

to myself." She held up her hands, which were now bleeding more freely. "I barely have the strength to heal myself. I feel like I've had no food or water for days. Maybe we can entice Lyn in with delicious food. Bring it out now."

"At once, my lady," said Renel, resuming his neutral expression. He clicked his fingers, and immediately a carafe of wine and a vast array of glistening fruit appeared on the table. Then he strode forward and made to place the blanket around her shoulders.

And as he did so, he stepped right in front of the window. Eve screamed and threw the blanket back in Renel's face. "How dare you block my view of Lyn! You rude, disgusting man. Have you learned nothing from your time here, you baseless, classless slave? MOVE, you fool!" Still he blocked her precious view, and so she willed a glass to her hand to prove to him she meant business. She directed the glass at his head with all the force she could muster. He ducked and the glass shattered onto the wall behind him. In that moment she caught a glimpse of Lyn again and saw the distress on her face. She rushed toward her, pushing Renel to the ground in her haste. She clutched the window separating her from her precious love, and was relieved that Lyn had finally decided to join her. Eve reached out to touch her through the glass, and Lyn copied her movements, echoing her.

Eve closed her eyes so as not to show Lyn the extent of her sadness. Still, she couldn't help the tears that welled up despite her efforts. "I am so sorry, Lyn, dear. I would never have expected Renel to do such a thing. I thought I could trust him. I will not be making that mistake again. I could never bear to be separated from you."

Chapter Eighteen

Samantha

ZAIN COULD HEAD TO ONE OF THE transport links to get to the ZA headquarters, but he opts to take the tram with me. It galls me that I, the poor ordinary one, have to pay for the rich Talented's tram fare because he hasn't the sense to carry any cash with him and he can't buy a single ticket with his fancy credit card.

We change three times to get across town to the heart of the science district. In contrast to the ancient stone buildings on Kingstown Hill, glass and metal skyscrapers dominate the landscape here, their sharp, shardlike silhouettes glittering in the sunlight. Most of the major synth companies have their laboratories in this district, each competing for the tallest tower or the most impressive architecture, but none of them manage to compare to ZA. If the other buildings are huge, ZA's headquarters are immense, dominated by a massive Z balanced precariously on the roof by magic. The Z is said to house Zol's office, and I wonder briefly what it must be like to have an office bigger than most ordinary people's houses.

Zantium—to reduce ego, maintain normal worldview, for empathy.

Thinking of the cure makes me giggle—the letter Z and lack of ego aren't two things that normally go together—and Zain looks over, one eyebrow raised. I shrug and turn back to the view.

The tram takes us straight into the building, and there are a few people in lab coats milling around, maybe on their lunch break. The workers on the tram must be ordinary, or else why would they be taking public transport? I want to ask Zain how many ordinary folk the company hires, but I also don't want to appear too keen.

We step off the tram and onto a platform that is so squeaky clean I almost have to shield my eyes from the brightness. My eyes dart to a man in a dark green jumpsuit, pushing along a machine that is buffing the surface. So there's one source of employment for an ordinary, then.

Zain uses his wand to open the door to the entrance. I wonder if it bothers him that his object is a wand. Wands are the most common object, and known for being unsubtle. Aggressive. A basic object for someone with such high Talented blood. His father's object is a stone ring. In the casts he's always wearing it around his neck rather than on his finger.

I once read about this experiment ZA had done to swap natural wands for synthetic ones, made of some kind of plastic. It hadn't worked—something about the magic only being conducted through organic substances, like wood. The fact still fills me with glee, and a hint of sadness—if only it was the same for potions, then the Kemi family might be as successful as ZA.

"So, is this, like, the son-of-the-CEO's entrance?"

Zain grimaces at me. "It's, like, the unpaid intern entrance."

My mouth forms an O of surprise, but then the door opens and saves me from having to say anything else.

Even for an intern entrance, it's impressive. The ZA logo shines out everywhere in a mix of glass and polished stainless steel. Zain heads straight toward a lift, so I follow him. In the warped reflection I catch a glimpse of myself, hair still up in a ragged bun, scruffy work clothes covered in a layer of grime. My breath catches as it dawns on me that some people would pay a fortune for the privilege of seeing what I'm about to—and I'm waltzing in with the owner's son like it's no big deal.

The lift travels down, not up, and I sense that the lab is bigger—much bigger—than I'd imagined. It beeps at us, thanking Zain by name for traveling, which weirds me out. "This is the R&D level," he says. "Thought you'd be most interested in this area."

I am, but I tell myself that's not that hard to guess. If Kemi's Potion Shop had any new customers, I would spend as much time researching new cures as I do mixing prescriptions for existing customers. My diary is as close as I get—my personal grimoire of formulas and mixes—annotated based on my experience with each ingredient.

I glance back at Zain, and he's typing away on the little tablet I saw him using at the store earlier. That's the rich person's version of my tatty journal. I'm not envious at all.

We're on some kind of walkway above the labs, but with full, almost 360-degree views of the workstations. I'm glad I'm wearing jeans. I think if I were one of the scientists down there I'd be a little unnerved to see a bunch of interns looking down on my work, but then the glass is probably glamoured to hide any spectators.

One of the scientists has a series of glass jars lined up in front of him, each one carefully labeled. He places them one at a time into a machine, which I assume is some kind of centrifuge. I squint through the glass, trying to read the tiny writing on the labels and figure out what he is making . . .

Zain's hand on my back makes my muscles freeze.

"Have you thought about applying?"

I scuttle sideways along the walkway, separating his hand from my back. "Applying for what?"

He frowns at me. "For an internship. Here."

"No," I scoff. "As if my parents would allow me . . ."

"Have you asked them?"

"What's the point?"

"But you're the real deal." He pauses for a second. "In fact, you're the best I've ever known at mixing."

Now it's my turn to frown. "And how would you know? The only time we've ever really talked was during that potions fair in high school. And I intentionally failed that."

Zain looks up and down the corridor. "I told you, I came by your classroom before the potions fair and saw your study aid cure. But there's something else. I took some of it. To be honest, I don't think I would've got through finals without it."

The walkway seems to shift beneath my feet. "You took my cure?"

"Shh—keep your voice down." He comes closer. "Yes, I did. And I would have kept on taking it if you had continued making it. I need it now more than ever and nothing I try to make for myself works half as well—and I'm the one who's doing my potions degree." His face goes bright red, but I sense it's not because of me that he's embarrassed. "Come on, Sam, I'm the son of the great Zol! You think he'd expect anything less than perfection? And with that mix I could just about maintain the right levels of focus without looking like I was trying too hard."

I let out a long breath. "Zain Aster took my cure."

His forehead wrinkles. "I guess I was desperate. I would have given you the prize, by the way. But you switched your potion."

"Yeah, because I was worried about people like you." I want to be disdainful of him—he's basically saying he cheated his way through his exams!—but instead I know exactly how he feels. I've felt that same desperation, that same pressure to perform. Maybe Zain is right. We do have more in common than I think.

"And there I was thinking your life was so easy."

Zain sighs. "It is easy, compared to most. I just don't want to end up like my dad."

"What do you mean?"

He shrugs. "Forget it."

We continue walking, and the labs below us start to fill up with more scientists returning to their workstations. We reach the end of the corridor, where a few white coats and goggles are hanging up on the wall.

"Put these on," he says, handing me a set. I shrug the white coat on over my jumper and put on the goggles.

"Wow, these are attractive," I say, catching a glimpse of my massive fly-eyes in the reflection of Zain's goggles.

"It's a good look for you." He smiles, and he doesn't sound as sarcastic as I did. It makes my heart skip a beat. Instead, I pull a face and he laughs.

We head down a spiral staircase, little metal teeth

digging into the soles of my ballet flats. I should probably be wearing boots in a lab like this, in case anyone spills any chemicals. The lab technicians ignore us as we walk through their workstations, one of them holding a vial up to the light and tilting it this way and that.

"Wanna see something cool?" Zain asks.

I nod. He walks over to what looks like a little tube and draws his wand. "Name me an ingredient."

The first thing that pops into my head is relatively obscure. "Eluvian ivy."

Eluvian ivy—for truth serums and binding potions.

He stares at me for a moment, his eyes searching my face. He opens his mouth as if he's about to ask a question, then decides against it. He points at the bottom of the tube, says a few words, and a second later is holding a clear glass vial filled with fine green powder. Eluvian ivy is written in neat type on the side. He hands it to me, and I take it.

"Awesome, right?"

Now that's service. But this powder bears no resemblance to the glossy dark green leaf with thin curling tendrils that I know as eluvian ivy. Looking at it makes my throat close up.

"Hey, are you okay?"

I shake my head, backing away from him slowly. "No, this is wrong. I'm a Kemi. I don't belong in a place like this."

"You're not just a Kemi, you're a great alchemist. You've got a mixer's brain. You could work here, with us, with all these resources at your fingertips. It doesn't have to be one or the other. You could be a mixer and not betray your Kemi heritage."

"If you think that's true, you know nothing about what it's like to be me." Heat flares up in my palms, threatening to dance all the way through my body. I need to get out of here.

My eyes dart around the lab until I spot a red sign marked EXIT. I make a beeline toward it. I bump into one of the mixers, who yells at me, but I barge past him. My palm slips on the bar of the door, but I push it open and escape into the fresh air.

Alarm bells scream through the building but I ignore them and keep walking, shedding the lab coat and goggles as I go.

"Sam! Wait!" Zain shouts. He runs up behind me and grabs my arm.

I yank my body out of his reach but force myself to turn around; now that I'm out of the coat and out of the lab, my heart rate slows. "I need to go home, I need to . . ." I look down. I hadn't realized I was still holding the vial.

"Hey, it's okay. Don't worry about it. You only set off the emergency alarm . . . and stole one of our ingredients . . . and probably the police are on their way here now. But it's cool." He's grinning at me, trying to break the tension.

"I know, I'm sorry . . . I shouldn't have come. Um, thanks for the invite." Like a reflex I extend my hand, and instantly feel like an idiot. His grin shifts from amused to bemused, but he takes my hand and shakes it. That humiliation over with, I spin on my heels and head toward the tram station. The sooner I can get away from here, the better.

Zain jogs to catch up with me and I almost scream with frustration. "Sam, listen—can we hang out again?"

"Maybe," I say, but it's a lie. I don't want to see Zain again. I just want to go home, be with my family, and pretend this whole day never happened. He's just a reminder of a life I can never have.

This time when I walk away, he doesn't stop me.

Chapter Nineteen

Samantha

BACK AT THE SHOP, IT LOOKS JUST AS I left it—obviously the rest of the family aren't back yet. That suits me fine. I leave the CLOSED sign turned around—it's only ten minutes until real closing time anyhow—and do a quick round-up of the sheets of paper on the floor, not bothering with my organization system any more.

Once the store looks reasonably respectable (as if I had spent all day clearing things up, rather than bunking off with Zain—did that actually happen?) I take the vial of synth eluvian ivy out of my bag and put it on the counter, staring at it as if it's radioactive. Bringing it into the store, I'm a rebel. I feel like I'm being watched; that the store itself is judging me for tainting it with the presence of a synth.

That wasn't just any panic attack. That's what being a traitor feels like.

But I have also been betrayed. If my life is so tied to the store that I can't even think of doing anything different without breaking into a panicky sweat, then I need to make this work for me. The hunt is my opportunity. One day I'm going to be the master of Kemi's Potion Shop, and I'm not going to go down without a fight.

I think of the missing merpearl and I know what I have to do. I have to make a potion. It's one that can be dangerous in the wrong dose, so I have to be ultra careful. I pull my journal out of my bag and turn to the page I need, reading the ingredients list several times over before beginning.

I walk over to the shelves and examine them, hands on hips, chewing my bottom lip as I go. I have several variables to take into account:

1. My subject is strong, and their mind will resist the effects of the potion.

2. They are familiar with potions, and if there is anything wrong with mine, they will notice it right away.

3. I definitely cannot get the formula wrong.

No. The consequences of that don't make me shudder; they make me want to vomit. But if I get this right, it could change everything.

The gathering of the ingredients goes quickly—I already know that I have everything I need in stock, which is quite a relief—and I walk into the back room with armfuls of jars. Once there I begin isolating the exact quantities of each ingredient, carefully measuring them out into wooden bowls. I then head back to the store and replace the jars on the shelves, so no one will be able to notice at first glance that they have been disturbed.

I return to the lab and begin the mix.

Each potion has a base formula that works for everyone unless they have a natural immunity to it. I have a natural immunity to sleep serum. The normal mix of lavender, chamomile, and sloth hair does little for me. But add a touch of melling bee honey, and you've got me. The sweetness triggers the cells in my brain that react to the potion and *poof!* I'm asleep.

I don't think my subject has natural immunity to the potion I'm making, but there is a good chance they have built up a resistance to it.

I've finished the base potion now, and it bubbles away over a tiny blue-flamed burner. The liquid is absolutely clear, so much so that if there weren't any bubbles, I might have trouble seeing if liquid was there at all. That's good. That's exactly how it should look.

But there is something missing, and like a lightning bolt it hits me. I almost sprint back to the store shelves, crouch down to the very bottom, and measure out half a teaspoon of a fine white powder.

The new bell above the shop door jingles, seeming louder than it ever has before, like an alarm going off in my brain. I hear my mum's voice before anything else, her delight at seeing the store returned to normal, followed by my dad's low tones, my granddad's shuffle, and Molly's light giggle. I stand up slowly, careful not to spill any of the powder.

"Oh, hi, Sam!"

"Hi, Mum. Good day at the shops?"

She nods while unwinding the scarf from her neck and throwing it over the hook by the door. "Yes, I think we have everything we need now. Who's hungry? I'm going to put dinner on."

"Me! Me! Me!" Molly skips along to every word, following Mum through the door into the kitchen.

"What's that you have there?" asks Granddad, nodding toward the spoon of powder in my hand.

"Oh—it's essence of wisteria . . . I'm making a potion for someone young, so I thought it would make it easier to digest."

"Well, don't forget to add a drop of rose oil to help the essence mix properly—or else you risk messing with your formula."

"Of course, Granddad." I say it with a smile, but inwardly I curse myself for almost forgetting that crucial step. I probably would have noticed once I mixed the essence in, or so I tell myself. "I'll just finish this up and then I'll come in for tea."

"Okay—don't be too long, sweetheart," says Dad.

The essence of wisteria goes in, as does the drop of rose oil. I take the potion off the boil and transfer small portions of the liquid into different vials until it's gone. I'm only going to need one vial for my experiment, but there's no point wasting a good mix.

I take a deep breath and walk into the kitchen. I wonder if anyone is going to take notice of how much I'm shaking.

"Molly, can you pour Granddad's juice for me and bring it to the table?" Mum asks.

"Do I have to?" she whines.

"Don't worry, I'll do it," I say. Molly's timing couldn't be better.

"Thanks, Sammy!"

I head over to the blender, where my granddad's daily dose of vitamins—spinach, lettuce, lemon juice, and a snip of the fresh wheatgrass from the plant on the windowsill—sits freshly pulsed. He never starts a meal without it—says it keeps his brain sharp.

I pour the gloopy green mixture from the jug into a thick-bottomed glass, adding my serum at the last minute. I almost drop the vial but I manage to keep my cool, slotting the empty back into my jeans pocket in one swift movement. I bring the glass over to the table and place it down in front of Granddad, which he acknowledges with a grunt, and then take my customary seat at the far end of the table. Mum places a plate of lasagna in front of me, and although the smell of melted cheese would normally drive me wild, my mouth is dry. Until Granddad takes a sip. And . . . nothing. He notices nothing amiss with his drink.

"Everything okay, Sam?" Mum asks. Everyone is already tucking into their dinners, but my cutlery is undisturbed.

"Oh, sorry," I say, picking up my fork and digging in. "Daydreaming."

"Well, eat up or it will get cold."

I take a few bites, and it's delicious.

"Anything happen in the store today?" asks Dad.

"Actually, Zain came by."

"Zain?" My dad seems puzzled.

I take another bite of food and keep chewing.

"Zain . . . as in Zain Aster?" says Mum.

I nod, and have to stifle a giggle at my dad's stupefied look.

"Bloody useless synth," mumbles the head of the table.

"Granddad!" scolds Mum. "Not while we're eating!"

"What did he want?" There is a reserved edge to my dad's voice too, although I am more intrigued by Granddad's outburst.

"I guess to see how I was doing after dropping out of the hunt," I say with a shrug. "We knew each other at school a bit."

"Oh, I have got to tell Sarah about this," says Molly, already taking her phone out and opening up TalentChat.

"She was really hoping to see him at the concert."

"No phones at the table," says Mum to Molly, who puts it away with a slight pout. Then Mum raises her eyebrow at me. "That's . . . nice that he came by. You never mentioned him before. I suppose ZoroAster are the main frontrunners in the hunt now."

"Zol and his band of minions couldn't mix a real love potion if the recipe came and danced in front of their faces," says Granddad.

"We could, though, couldn't we, Granddad?" I ask, not yet ready to make eye contact.

"Well, of course we could."

Mum tuts and says, "Enough with the hunt now, okay?" If she could reach to kick Granddad under the table, she would. And if I didn't have a feeling about what was coming, this conversation would have sent me over the edge. But I do, and so I'm able to be strong. She puts her hand over mine and squeezes it. "You tried with the first ingredient, Sam, but now you have to concentrate on the store again. You were getting so far with your inventory, weren't you?"

I smile at her, endlessly grateful that she's so protective of my sanity. But then I move my hand away and keep my gaze focused across the table. "We thought we didn't have the first ingredient, but we had it all along, didn't we, Granddad?"

Mum says my name in that loud *What on earth are you*

doing, Sam? tone and Dad slams his hands on the table so loudly the cutlery jumps. "Your mother said, enough!"

Amidst the commotion, I almost miss Granddad's answer. "Yes, of course, it's under the sink in the lab."

I can't look at Mum or Dad—even though both of them are quiet now, Granddad's words registering—as I'm paralyzed to my chair by my granddad's stare. His brow is furrowed, his lips pursed tightly together as if he's attempting to reassert control over his own mouth. He's looking at me with an intensity I can't bear, but I also cannot turn away or avert my gaze. He looks so angry. But there's something else. Something that gives me hope he's not going to murder me. Or maybe that's just wishful thinking.

"Molly," he says, not even breaking his stare for a moment. "Fetch me a glass of water." Molly jumps up from the table so quickly her chair almost falls backward onto the linoleum floor behind her, and rushes to the sink. "No, not from the tap, from the jug in my study." She goes immediately.

We wait until she returns. My parents are dumbfounded by my granddad's revelation and also not yet sure about my involvement.

"Dad," says my dad. "You knew the whole time—"

Granddad holds up a hand to stop him, and waits for the glass of water from Molly. He drains it, wipes his mouth, and takes a deep breath.

"I thought I was immune to truth serums, Samantha."

Mum gasps and the blood drains from my face.

"But somehow, you have created a mix that I am not immune to." To my surprise, he takes another sip of his juice and washes it around in his mouth. "Hmm . . . what is it? You adjusted the base formula—fortified it."

I can only nod, still cautious.

"And, of course, the essence of wisteria wasn't meant for a young child at all, but an old man. It's . . . inspired. I knew you were good at mixing, but I didn't realize you were this good. You will be a great master of alchemy one day."

I blush a deep red, but I can't allow myself to forget what this trouble has been for. "Then will you help me with the hunt? We can't let the synths win."

"I let the synths win a long time ago, Sam." He looks sad, tired. "But you are the alchemist who is bound to complete the Wilde Hunt. I won't stand in your way."

That's about as much as I can hope for. I jump up, run around the table, and kiss him on the top of his head, his fine white hair tickling my nose.

"But we're out, Sam," says Dad, scratching his chin. "It's already been announced."

"Plus, it's so dangerous," adds Mum. "We've already been robbed, for Talent's sake. ZA sabotaged you at the Rising . . . Who knows what they'll do if you ever get close?"

"If everyone thinks we're out, that could be our advantage," I muse. "I can do this, Mum. I'll be careful."

"Sam?"

I turn around and Molly is behind me. In her hand is a ceramic piggy bank, which she holds out for me. "It's not a lot, but it might help a bit."

"Mols, you don't have to do that!"

"But I want to. I know you can beat anyone else in the hunt." She puts the piggy bank on the table and gives me a hug.

"Molly's right," says Dad. "We'll help in whatever way we can. This is your dream, and we'll support it."

My eyes well up with tears. My mum pats my hand. "Eat, first. Finish your dinner. Then you can start making the world's most sought after potion, okay, honey?"

I grin; my parents' excitement is almost matching my own.

"But, Sam—if you ever potion your grandfather again, you will be grounded for life, got it?"

I'm not going to argue with that.

I devour the rest of my dinner and then head for my granddad's lab. Right under the sink, as Granddad had revealed, is the jar of powdered merpearl. It still possesses a slight glow of luminescence, a pink-white sheen. I tilt the jar round in a circle, and instead of behaving as normal powder does, it shifts more like a liquid. In fact, instead of tumbling in individual grains, it reminds me more of tiny waves crashing against the glass.

"It's beautiful." My dad's voice catches me by surprise.

I give the jar another whirl and watch it again. "This isn't powder from an ordinary mermaid pearl, is it? It belonged to Aphroditas. When we were on the boat, I was watching her. These were her colors." I peer closely at the label. COLLECTED ON FULL MOON NIGHT, 1942. "And it's as powerful as it can be; even though it isn't fresh, it will be strong."

"There was a time when Kemi's Potion Shop only had the finest ingredients," he says.

"I wish I lived in that time," I say, unable to tear my eyes from the merpearl.

"Maybe you will again. You know your grandfather means well. He saw the rise of the synths first hand, watched Zoro cheat your great-grandmother out of her win. Back then Zoro was trying to establish synth legitimacy. Now Zol is trying to protect it. And with Emilia coming out of the woodwork . . . it's so dangerous, Sam. I wish I could come with you. To protect you." He smiles sadly. "But you're the Participant, so I can't come even if I wanted to."

The same fears plague my brain. But if I let my fears act as my roots, I'll wither on the vine. "I'll have Kirsty with me. And I'll call Anita and Arjun—let them know I'm back in. Maybe if we can work together, we can make sure one of us comes up with the potion first."

He nods. "So what now? Have you thought about what ingredient might come next?"

I chew my bottom lip. "I've thought of something. But it's just a hunch. And if I'm right . . . I think I'm going to need a plane ticket."

Chapter Twenty

Samantha

"YOU'RE BACK IN!" SCREECHES ANITA DOWN the line.

"Yes! Granddad had some pearl powder stashed in his lab. Can you believe it?" The line is crackled and full of static, so I miss her next sentence. "'Nita, I can barely hear you . . . did you get my email?"

"Sorry, hun . . . distance call is expensive . . . got your mail . . . keep your pearl powder safe! Rumors are that someone had theirs stolen last night. Better to work together than let the Zs win! See you here soon."

"Wait! Where should I meet you?" I ask, but she's already off the line.

The phone buzzes again. "Anita?"

But it's not. "Sam, it's Kirsty. I'm coming to pick you up now. Your dad wired me the money to book the flights; I've got you some clothes, just grab your toothbrush and let's go."

"Okay but—" She hangs up before I can get the sentence out. What is it with people cutting me off?

I sit down on my bed, gripping the corner of my duvet. I'm about to travel halfway across the world from Nova to Bharat, a country with one of the biggest untouched areas of Wilds. The terrain in Bharat ranges from desert to rainforest to mountains to some of the world's most densely populated cities. The capital city, Loga, has over ten times as many people in it as Kingstown.

Not only have I never even used my passport before, but the first time is going to be to the country that's going to give me the biggest culture shock I could possibly experience. This is jumping into the deep end of adventure, with both feet and no lifejacket.

It's all to find real eluvian ivy. Ever since I saw it mentioned in that old book, and then Zain's reaction when I asked for eluvian powder in the lab, it's been my hunch that it's one of the ingredients. Typical that this time I know it's something we don't have—it's rare, and combined with the fact it's extremely volatile and needs to be kept in special wooden canisters, we don't bother stocking it. And it's dangerous for the Finders too. Its habitat is the deepest, darkest rainforests of the Bharatan peninsula.

I judge I have at least ten minutes before Kirsty rocks up, even if she jumps every red light and hops every curb. I dash around the house like a mad woman, but before shutting down my laptop, I log on to Connect—the most popular social network in Nova. I find a surprising number of people that I've barely even spoken to trying to add me as a friend—and twice as many again who are complete strangers. I've never been a huge fan of Connect, if only because it seems like just another place for Talenteds to congregate and exclude me online. So my profile is set firmly to "private" and contains as little information about me as I can get away with.

I scroll quickly through the new requests, deleting and denying as I go, but one name causes my finger to catch on the delete button. Zain Aster. Again.

I hesitate for a moment, then before I can talk myself out of it I hit connect. Immediately his profile unfolds on the screen before me. Strings of photos, the most recent ones catching my eye, as they were obviously taken at the Rising. Zain is standing next to his father on the yacht, Zol holding out the pearl in front of him in his palm.

Dad calls from the hall, "Kirsty will be here any second. Ready?"

Then I catch the status update. Zain's latest one.

Zain Aster is about to jump to Bharat. Madness. @ TheKTTransportLounge

My stomach flips at the thought, even though that's as good as confirmation that my hunch is right. It's a big country, I tell myself. The odds of running into Zain in the rainforest have got to be slim.

An hour later, and I'm sitting inside the terminal at Kingstown International Airport, waiting for Kirsty to buy magazines and snacks for the journey. Unlike Zain and his dad, there's no way we'd go to the KT Transport Terminal—it's just too expensive.

I open my diary, smoothing the pages on my lap. I thumb through the recipes, my neat scrawl covering the pages. I turn to a fresh page. Then I write at the very top:

Love Potion

*Full moon oyster merpearl. Crushed. 30 g.
*Eluvian ivy

I hear the telltale snap of a camera going off behind me and I slam the journal shut. I spin around and a young girl, not much older than Molly, is pointing her phone at me.

"Hey, what are you doing?" I ask.

"You're that girl off the TV, right?" she says. "My friends aren't going to believe this. You were in the hunt. Can I get your autograph?"

I hesitate for a moment. "Sure, if you show me the picture first?"

She shrugs and hands me her phone. I zoom in but breathe out a sigh of relief when I see you can't read the ingredients.

"Wait, can we take a selfie instead?" she asks.

"Um, I'm not—"

Before I've even finished speaking, she takes the picture. If this is going to be standard practice, I really need to work on my posing. The girl says a quick thank you and rushes off to join her parents.

"What was that all about?" Kirsty comes over and dumps her heavy carry-on bag on the seat between us.

"She thinks I'm famous, maybe?"

Kirsty purses her lips. "We're going to have to be more careful. It's not just the media we have to look out for; it's everybody with a phone. I somehow don't think your involvement is going to be a secret for very long."

"What should we do?"

"I have an idea; I'll send a message to my contacts in Bharat. Until we get there, be extra vigilant. We still don't know what we're looking for beyond . . ."—she drops her voice—"the ivy, and we need to change that." She gestures to her bag. "So pull out a book and dig in. We have a lot of research to do."

"What am I looking for?"

"Let's see . . . You think the ivy is an ingredient, but you're not sure. I'm going to trust your hunch, but one hunch isn't going to be good enough. Not if we want to beat ZA and the rest. They can afford to transport, which already puts them hours ahead of us. And the setback with the pearls puts us behind even the ordinary teams, like your friends the Patels. Down . . . but not out." She leans forward conspiratorially. "But we have an advantage."

"What's that?" I say.

She puts her finger on my forehead. "That." Then she moves it to hers. "And this. Your skill for mixing potions. My nose for finding ingredients. We're heading out into the deep Wilds now, Sam. If we can figure out what elements might go into a love potion, get a jump on what the next ingredient is, we might actually have a shot at this thing." A sequence of beeps sounds out from the overhead intercom, and we're ready to depart. "Come on. We've got a nine-hour flight ahead of us. Might as well make it productive."

Chapter Twenty-One

Samantha

THE HEAT OF BHARAT HITS ME AS SOON as we disembark from the plane, and I peel off the sweater I've been wearing. My pale blue T-shirt sticks to my skin. The humidity and warmth are so far removed from Kingstown weather it almost feels like we've flown to another planet.

"Wait here," Kirsty tells me, right before we leave security to pick up our luggage. When she's back, she has two silvery scarves in her hands. "Put one over your head."

"Why, is this the custom in Bharat?" I ask, winding the scarf over my hair.

"It will help you blend in with the crowd, but even better than that, it's perfect for thwarting any paparazzi that are around. Try it on me."

I take out my phone and snap a picture of her with the flash. The picture shows a bright white light obscuring her entire face. "This is genius!" I say.

She grins. "Right, now let's go." Kirsty shoots through the crowd in the arrivals area like an arrow from a tightly strung bow, and I struggle to keep up with her. I keep my eye out for cameras, but it's so busy it's impossible to tell who's coming and going through the sea of people.

All through the flight, we pored over the books Kirsty brought with her, but I'm having a mental block. I hope my brain is still ticking over the information, even as now I have to use all my senses to take in the sights, sounds, smells of Bharat.

"Over here!" Anita shouts at us, ducking under the barrier and throwing her arm around my neck. "Finally! Arjun's waiting in the truck. Come on, we're going to leave straightaway." Anita's eyes sparkle with mischief. "We're going somewhere no other Participants will know about. It's the kind of place you can only find if you have local knowledge."

Kirsty nods. "Lead on! Arjun is one of the best apprentice Finders I've seen in years, so I trust his instinct."

Anita blushes with pride for her brother.

Once we're outside, I have to take a moment to catch my breath. Everywhere is riotous with color and smell. Horns blare, voices are shouting, and tinny Bharatan music is blaring from an old-fashioned style boombox tied to the back of a scooter. I step back when I'm almost run over by a rickshaw, pulled by an incredibly thin but strong man, and carrying a girl in a beautiful, flowery dress with an ostentatious parasol.

"Careful!" says Anita, who takes my hand and navigates us across the road. I don't think I've experienced a more perilous crossing in my life. Not only am I dodging rickshaws but dark-windowed SUVs, motorbikes, and porters rolling massive luggage trunks stamped with the name of some luxury designer.

The truck that Anita leads us to has a smashed backlight and a bumper that looks like it's held on by duct tape and a prayer. Kirsty and I bundle into the back, while Anita squeezes in next to her brother on a bench-like front seat. Arjun isn't driving, though. "Sam, Kirsty, let me introduce our cousin, Vijay," says Arjun.

Vijay grins, then reaches out to the rearview mirror and grips a small statue of a god that's dangling there like the air freshener in Kirsty's car. He mumbles a quick prayer and pulls out into the mayhem.

No wonder he needs to pray. My knuckles have turned white gripping the seat (did I mention that there are no seat belts?), but Vijay seems to have some kind of magic sense that guides him through the traffic.

Even Kirsty looks grim, so I grip tighter and focus on holding on to the contents of my stomach. We don't head into Loga, the capital city, which disappoints me a little. All the way to Bharat and I'm not even going to be able to see the main attractions that adorn the postcards:

the red-bricked palace that once housed the Bharatan royal family, or the enormous gold-plated statue of the multi-headed elephant god. Still, once we're out of the city, the roads clear of the mayhem. Kirsty relaxes, and I follow suit. That's when it strikes me how tired I am. I feel like I haven't slept in days.

"So what do you guys know so far?" Kirsty asks.

Arjun and Anita shift in their seats so they are facing us. "We've got it on good authority that there are other teams out there looking for golden jasmine as the next ingredient," says Arjun. "Someone got in touch with our relatives who live in the Wilds to try to get a guide."

Jasmine. Bloom found across the Bharatan peninsula, into the Kang mountains and beyond, far into Shan province. I almost smack my forehead, it's so blindingly obvious. "Of course! That makes sense. It's the perfect ingredient for a love potion."

White jasmine flower is common enough, and readily available in most potion stockrooms, even in Kingstown. I've used it in plenty of potions, often reluctantly—as it is most often used to . . . ahem . . . increase virility. Yeah, when old Mr. Waters from the grocery store around the corner came in to ask for a virility potion, the unwanted mental images made me shudder. I even debated not putting the right amount of jasmine in, so it wouldn't work. Of course, that wouldn't do much for our already downtrodden reputation, so I just did my duty. But, when the new Mrs. Waters came in asking me personally to start fudging the recipe, I was happy to oblige. Anyway, that's by no means its only use: it's a versatile plant that can boost everything from self-confidence to simple happiness. The golden version is rarer but, when mixed with boiling water, unleashes heightened potency.

"So you agree? That's good. When you wrote about your eluvian ivy hunch in your email it was karma. We can get both of those ingredients where we're going."

"And where is that?" asks Kirsty.

Vijay decides to join in the conversation, and he turns around too. "To my village! We refused those other Participants. Why would we help them? The Wilde Hunt is a Novaen tradition; since we are no longer a Novaen colony, we have no desire to help your alchemists and Finders pillage our Wilds. But you, you are family."

"Uh, Vijay, maybe you better keep your eyes on the road?" says Arjun, who is now gripping the steering wheel and driving from the passenger seat.

To my relief Vijay puts his hands back on the wheel and focuses on the road again. I peer over his shoulder and see the speedometer pointing at 10 mph. Yeah, that's definitely broken. "Our village is important because it's said to be the resting place of the goddess Daharama," he says. "Goddess of love."

My eyes open wide at that. "Wow."

"The legend of Daharama is that every living thing

that set eyes on her fell deeply in love. Eventually she decided that in order to keep the number of people who loved her down to a minimum, she would live in a secluded village, far from the rest of mankind. Our village is that village."

"Really? I'm pretty familiar with Bharatan legends and I seem to recall that hundreds of villages claim to be the home of Daharama," says Kirsty.

Vijay spits out of his window. "Those other claims are heretical. Ours is the true one."

The fire has gone out of him a bit, and I'm annoyed at Kirsty for ruining the story. "Well, I'm not that familiar with Bharatan legend. Carry on? There might be a clue in the story that will help us build a love potion."

Kirsty shrugs her indifference and Vijay continues. "People still came to visit her, of course, including young couples who wanted her blessing to grant them a lifetime of love and happiness. She met anyone who made the long journey, but she always made sure to do so behind a curtain of heavy silk, so that no one could lay eyes on her. As a sign of respect and gratitude, her pilgrims would lay wreaths of jasmine flowers at her feet.

"Daharama lived in peace like that for a long time, but you cannot be the goddess of love without invoking some jealousies. Even hatreds. The legend continues that Daharama had one day without any visitors. She was very tired as she had not had a day free in many years. She decided to relax her mind by going on a walk through the nearby jungle, where she could gather up food and firewood and spare her willing servants from their duties for one day.

"But the reason she had no visitors was because of the jealous goddess Lakishi—her sister and opposite in every way. Lakishi had diverted the pilgrims in order to get Daharama alone. Then, as Daharama was walking in the jungle, Lakishi accosted her with her familiar, a huge white tiger known as Gar. But Daharama had at that moment chosen to lower her veil, to take a closer look at a beautiful jasmine flower growing on a tall tree. Lakishi caught sight of Daharama, and all of a sudden her hatred melted away, to be replaced with unconditional love.

"The problem was, the tiger also fell in love with Daharama. He saw Lakishi as a rival for Daharama's affection. He bared his teeth and growled most fiercely at Lakishi, who was too enchanted by Daharama to notice. She moved to give her sister a warm and loving embrace, but at that moment Gar decided to pounce. His great bulk threw both sisters to the ground, and Daharama's head was dashed upon the very tree she had been admiring.

"Realizing what they had done, Lakishi begged Gar to kill her too, which he did. Gar himself walked far into the jungle and died of a broken heart.

"Daharama's blood seeped into the ground where she

had been slain. The roots of that jasmine vine drank up her blood and now its petals are tinged with pink. We consider the pink flower that blooms there to be a gift from the goddess, that we are duty-bound to protect."

"It is the rarest and most potent jasmine bloom there is—way more than golden," Arjun says.

"Pink jasmine. I'm impressed. And it's worth a fortune on the black market," says Kirsty. "You'll give it to us just like that?"

"We have protected the flower for many generations, but for family, and for your princess, yes. We will permit you to take two blooms. Anita and Arjun have said you are as family to them, and so, to us."

"Then we are deeply honored." Kirsty reaches over the seat and places her hand on Vijay's shoulder.

"Thank you so much," I say, almost breathless at their generosity. "So we can go get the pink jasmine, then on to the eluvian ivy?" I ask, but it's not really a question. Already I can feel the potion building in my head, puzzle pieces turning, turning, and then finally slotting together. I pull out the diary and add pink jasmine to my list of ingredients.

Kirsty continues to interrogate Vijay on other ingredients native to Bharat, but my eyelids droop as we bump along the rutted road. I barely even wake as Kirsty hands over our Wilds passes at the border.

Waking up stiff from being tumbled about, I blink the

sleep out of my eyes and take in my surroundings. It's a complete swirl of green outside my window, lush jungle that occasionally sidles right up to the glass and brushes it with a long green finger. The road is nothing but mud—a far cry from the highway we were on before. I find it hard to believe that this is the main thoroughfare to the Patels' family village. But then, what do I know?

A little further down the lane, the jungle cuts away abruptly and the first signs of civilization appear: a string of flags strung from a tree, an abandoned wooden bucket overturned and sprouting a coat of moss as if the jungle is claiming it as its own. And a face suddenly appearing in the green makes me jump, but it's just the inquisitive look of a little girl.

Vijay slams on the brakes and I fly straight into his headrest.

"We're here."

Chapter Twenty-Two

Samantha

THE MOMENT WE STEP OUT OF THE TRUCK, children, barefoot and beaming, surround us. One of the girls takes my wrist and wraps a friendship bracelet around it. Kirsty digs into her pocket and finds a small hard-boiled candy in a sparkling gold wrapper. The girl squeals with joy and skips away, the treasured sweet already unwrapped and consumed.

"You might need a few more of those while we're here," says Kirsty, slipping a bag of them from her backpack to mine. I smile gratefully, wishing I'd had more time to prepare for my first trip outside of Nova.

Two children grip each of my hands, and together with Arjun we quickly step into the one-two-three-whee! game. Kirsty laughs and tells us that the love of being swung up high in the air is pretty much universal amongst kids.

We follow a dirt path through the jungle, barely wide

enough for three people to walk side-by-side, let alone play games, but somehow we manage. It's dark on the path, and I tilt my head back to stare at the canopy reaching over us, thick branches like the spindly roof of a cathedral, unwilling to let even the strong Bharatan sunshine penetrate down to the jungle floor. There's plenty of rustling in the trees from unseen creatures, but the atmosphere is incredibly peaceful.

The village itself melds into the jungle so neatly I don't realize we've arrived until the children detach from my hands and disperse around corners and under tent flaps.

"Follow me," says Vijay, waving an arm in our direction. He takes us to a building perched on stilts, the first floor high up above the ground. Although I see no cars here—just a rusty-looking motorcycle outside another of the huts—there is one major sign of civilization: an enormous satellite dish protruding from the second floor of the building like a kind of fungus. Obviously someone here is keen not to miss out on any of the latest casts.

The door of the building opens as we climb the first stair. A big man with a sharp pointed beard, wearing a turban and a bright orange tunic, steps out and spreads his arms wide. "Welcome, young Kemi!" he says. "I am Nalesh Patel, Vijay's father."

I smile and mumble, "It's Sam," but he continues on without waiting for me. "We thought you'd gone out of the competition permanently—I can't believe you let ZoroAster play that dirty trick on you with the boat."

I'm embarrassed to think the whole world must have seen that moment. "How much of the hunt are they showing on TV?"

"As much as they can. Everyone is now here in Bharat. Although I don't think the news has broken that you're back in the hunt."

"Good, and we'd like to keep it that way," Kirsty says. "The Wilde Hunt is the top news story at the moment and the world's eyes are upon it. That's why it's so important that we get one step ahead of the competition."

"And we've got a lot of it if everyone is here," I mutter.

"Not everyone. Didn't Anita say someone had their ingredient stolen? That's one team out of the hunt at least." Kirsty raises her voice. "So where's this pink jasmine you've been on about, Vijay?"

"Tomorrow, first thing in the morning, I will take you."

Kirsty and I exchange looks. "We're not going now?" I ask.

"It's going to be dark soon," says Vijay. "Too many big cats and even bigger snakes to be deep in the jungle at night. The trail to the jasmine will still be there in the morning."

I want nothing more than to rest up after the long flight, so I shoot a pleading glance at Kirsty. She looks

167

out into the forest, which is getting darker and more foreboding by the second, and the sun's not even set yet. I dread going in there, even though I can see Kirsty's itching to make a move. Maybe Finders are always on their feet, ready for the next adventure, but I'm an alchemist. I need my sleep.

Kirsty concedes. As we enter the house, the casts are projected onto a white sheet pinned up against the far wall. The screen is divided into four squares, each one depicting a different team. Zain is in one corner, arriving at the transport terminal. In a pair of gold-rimmed aviator sunglasses and a black leather jacket, he looks effortlessly cool.

I say "ugh" at the same time as Anita, which sends us into fits of giggles. She comes over and takes my hand, leading me away from the cast. "I bet the Zs walk around with their own stylists on the hunt. They care more about the cameras than the mix."

Suddenly the smell of cinnamon and caraway wafts into the room.

Cinnamon—for vitality of the mind, clearing blood clots, relief from colds and flu.

Caraway—for easing digestion, for clearer skin.

My stomach rumbles in anticipation, and Vijay thrusts a bowl of rice into my hands. I take the bowl to Mrs. Patel, Arjun and Anita's aunt who is dressed in a stunning dark green sari, and she fills it with a warm curry.

The first bite practically blows my head off—my Novaen tongue is far from used to the spicy heat. The Bharatan Patels laugh at my discomfort until Mrs. Patel takes pity and passes me a soothing yogurt drink. It comforts me that Arjun and Anita aren't looking too comfortable either, although Kirsty is wolfing the food down.

Next out is a bowl full of exotic-looking fruit. It's accompanied by one of the little girls who had been holding my hand earlier in the day. In her hand now is a crudely carved stick, stripped of its bark. Vijay gives her an encouraging pat on the back. "Go on, Pari," he says. "Show them what you've been practicing."

She hesitates for a moment, then takes one of the more complicated-looking fruits from the bowl, a pink egg-shaped object with green-edged leaves forming star-like patterns around the outside. She places it gently on the table in front of us, holding it with both hands until she's sure it will stand upright on its own. Then she lifts the stick, points it at the fruit, shuts her eyes and tilts her head back.

And then she does something I don't expect: She performs magic.

"It's a wand," I whisper, stating the obvious. The leaves uncurl from the fruit, creating a star pattern on the table and leaving the bright pink center looking naked and vulnerable. Then slowly the pink separates from the soft white flesh of the fruit. When it is completely peeled, she opens her eyes, and with a quick flick of her wrist, separates the fruit into quarters—one for each of us.

I look from the young girl to Vijay as we launch into enthusiastic applause. "Vijay—she's a Talented. And a powerful one if she can get so much from that wand out here in the Wilds. Is she going to school?"

Kirsty puts her hand on my arm to silence me, but Vijay shrugs his shoulders. "She will help out in the fields, like the other magicians. They can make the work a lot easier for us, which is why they are so valued." He enfolds her in a hug.

"Out here, the Talented are important, but their families can't afford to send them to proper schools like they would in Nova," says Kirsty.

It pains me to know that although I am ordinary, because I live in Nova, I still lead a better life than a Talented elsewhere. Maybe if I tell Renel about this girl, or even Zain, they might be able to help . . .

Kirsty registers the look on my face. "You can't 'save' every Talented kid you come across. And they need her here, too."

I bite my lip.

Now that dinner is finished, Kirsty, Arjun, Anita, and I move to the living room—a wide porch open to the air. There are colorful but well-worn cushions spread around the space, and a canopy of fairy lights overhead. It's magical. I happily sink into a cushion as Arjun lights one of the lanterns and the warm, spicy smell of incense fills the air.

Anita takes a seat opposite me and furrows her eyebrows. "Now, Sam, spill. How come you suddenly have Zain Aster on your Connect list? Since when are you guys best buds?"

In all the excitement, I haven't filled Anita in yet, and I can't help blushing. I try to assume an air of nonchalance. "He came by the store a couple of days ago. Said he felt bad about the trick played on me by their team."

"Wow . . . how nice of him." Anita raises an eyebrow in surprise.

"Yeah, real nice," says Arjun. He rolls his eyes. "I bet he just wanted the chance to poke around the Kemi supplies a bit to see if they missed anything in the robbery."

His words hurt, and the pain is unexpected. I frown at him. "ZA didn't rob us. Granddad thinks it was Emilia Thoth trying to stop us finding the recipe."

Anita shivers. "Dad told us about her showing up to the palace. Sounds terrifying—although surely she can't be strong enough to be a real threat. Hasn't she been living in exile her whole life?"

"Yeah, looking like she's been bathing in forbidden potions, not just dabbling in them." I remember the long strands of her slate gray hair, the pallid tint to her skin, the hideous curve of her nails. It makes me shudder that anyone could give themselves over to such horror. "I don't think anyone should underestimate her. This is the opportunity she's been waiting for. If anything happens to the princess, she's the next heir. She most likely robbed us. What if she stole that merpearl too?"

"Why does she want to participate in the hunt?" asks Anita, wrapping her arms around herself.

"Probably so she can make sure no one else gets the cure," says Arjun.

"That must be why she trained to be an alchemist," I say. "A Wilde Hunt gives her automatic entrance to the palace in Nova, overriding her exiled status. It's a long game she had to play, but it looks like her gamble paid off."

"Enough of Emilia," says Arjun. "If we stay under the radar, hopefully she'll focus on other teams that seem like more of a threat."

"But she's already attacked the Kemis once," Kirsty says. "We've got to be careful. Keep our eyes open and wits sharp."

"Let's check Zain's profile to see if there are any clues!" Anita winks at me and opens up her laptop.

"You can get a connection out here?"

Anita laughs. "Yep. No guarantee of hot water, but TV signal and internet connection? Always."

I reach over her and log in under my name, but when

we search for Zain, his profile is private again and the connect button is relit. He's unconnected me. It stings.

"Oh well," I say. "I didn't really want to hear about his hashtag TalentedProblems anyway." I shut the laptop and take a deep breath. "Anyway guys, I think I have a theory." The three of them turn their eyes to me, waiting expectantly. "It might be completely wrong of course, but . . . I've been thinking about the merpearls and eluvian ivy. They both have qualities you might need to 'build' love, like bricks. Merpearls, for beauty. Eluvian ivy, for loyalty. And now, pink jasmine, for passion. We're making the highest end, no-holds-barred potion possible, right? So I think after that it's going to be abominable hair."

"For loneliness?" Arjun blinks. "How does that fit in?"

I feel my cheeks grow hot. "Well, I don't know for sure as I've never been in love, but . . ."

"No, you're right," says Kirsty, and then she lets out a long breath. "Abominables are like penguins—they mate for life. Not only that, but they are single-minded in their pursuit of love. They roam the mountains in search of their one true love, resisting all other contact until they find it. Loneliness is the price they pay for that search. It's the perfect building block. No one but you could have put those ingredients together so quickly, Sam. It's inspired."

Anita leans forward. "So after we get the jasmine, we

find the eluvian ivy and then head up to the mountains."

Kirsty nods. "Yes, and the ivy won't be easy. It's vicious, to say the least." She throws me a long look, which makes me squirm. "We might be best splitting up and hunting down different ingredients, to move even faster. I don't suppose your granddad has any of those items stashed away somewhere, does he?"

I grimace. "I'll email my ideas back to my parents to check."

When I open my email, though, it's flooded with messages from other Finders, suppliers, and chancers attempting to sell me ingredients at ridiculously high prices. I can see that several are offering Aphroditas powder at an extortionate rate, and who knows if it's real or not?

"Anyone want to buy golden jasmine for two hundred thousand crowns?"

"You're kidding me!" says Arjun.

"Nope, look right here . . ."

"Obviously the sellers have caught wind of the next ingredient everyone is searching for. Anyone selling vastly overpriced eluvian ivy yet?" Kirsty asks.

I do a quick search, but there's nothing.

"Good, then at least we know we still have an edge."

"Or it might be wrong," I say. I lift my head from the screen as the smell of incense that had hung in the air so sweetly turns acrid in my nostrils. "Is someone sitting too close to a candle? It smells like something is burning."

Instinctively everyone pulls away from the nearest lantern, but there's nothing amiss. I look up, and against the darkening sky see a tall column of smoke. "Fire," I whisper.

All heads whip up, and then it's a mad scramble to see who can get off the balcony quickest. Arjun is through the door first, and a worried Vijay and Mr. Patel chase after him. We follow behind, Kirsty grabbing her bag and instructing me to pull on my boots. I do them up as fast as I can, almost sliding down the stairs in my haste.

"It's coming from the jungle," says Vijay.

"Come on, Sam, hurry." Kirsty snaps on a torch from her bag, and the beam illuminates the thick tangle of green in front of us, so dense it could almost be a wall. She tosses me another one, which I fumble and drop on the ground.

"We're going in there when it's burning?" I'd rather be heading in the opposite direction.

"This is the rainforest, Sam. And it's the rainy season. The trees don't burn like that on their own." Kirsty is already running. "That's where the pink jasmine is."

Chapter Twenty-Three

Samantha

I KEEP MY TORCH TRAINED ON KIRSTY'S BACK as we run. The last thing I want to do is flash it at the jungle darkness and see some huge spider staring back at me—or the glowing eyes of a carnivorous jungle cat.

More worrying, though, is that it's getting lighter, even as the smoke is getting thicker and heavier. The light seems to be coming in bursts from between the trees.

Suddenly one of those bursts is right in front of us, a python of orange and yellow flame writhing through the foliage. I can't help myself: I scream. Loudly.

The flames stop, cut off abruptly, just as Kirsty and I freeze. Then a woman's voice whispers a word, and a spray of blue light bursts all around us. The lights drift to the ground, illuminating the surrounding trees.

The spots take a minute to clear from my vision as my eyes adjust to the new light.

Kirsty adjusts faster than I do.

"Emilia."

"Miss Donovan, good to see you."

My vision clears. I see Emilia, her long gray dress and cape replaced by a sleek gray jumpsuit. She no longer looks like a burned-out alchemist, but more like a fierce Finder. I turn to Kirsty. "You know her?"

It's Emilia who answers. "Finding is such a small world, isn't it? Of course I know the famous Kirsty Donovan, independent Finder to Nova's once most prominent alchemists. She's a dying breed. When I wanted to learn how to find, I knew I had to learn from the best. The man who trained Kirsty trained me as well."

"Before you murdered him." Kirsty spits on the ground, which sizzles. "How did you find us here?"

"You might know how to cover your tracks, but that other team isn't so clever. I've been tracking them since they left Kingstown—although it was only when they picked up you two that they really became interesting. Now I can finish two teams in one—I do love being efficient. I mean, who knew those mild-mannered Patels were hiding a patch of pink jasmine up their sleeves. It seems like such a shame to have had to destroy it all."

Her formerly straggly hair is tied up into a sleek pony-tail, and on her back is a terrifying-looking flamethrower. All around her, soot is falling like some kind of perverse snow.

"It's not fair!" I cry, unable to help myself. All I can think of is the jasmine and our chances both going up in smoke.

"Nothing is fair in life or a Wilde Hunt, honey." Emilia steps toward me, but Kirsty is one step ahead.

"Don't come any closer! I have salamander dust and I'm not afraid to use it."

I shudder. Salamander dust—a nasty compound that burns eyes and skin, causing insatiable itching.

Emilia stops in her tracks. "This is your warning, Kemi. Today I destroy the ingredient. Stay on this hunt and I might not be so lenient with you next time." She pulls out a glass vial from her belt and throws it down in front of us.

Kirsty pushes me as thick smoke fills the air.

I fall to the ground, the heat of it burning my knees. There's a rush of sound through the forest and I almost expect it to be Emilia, back to gloat some more. But then the smoke clears and there's a sharp inhale of breath from someone surprised, shocked, at the scene in front of us: Anita. And an anguished howl from the next person to arrive: Vijay.

Emilia is gone.

A stream of Bharatan words spill from Vijay's mouth. It doesn't take a linguist to figure out what he's saying.

Anita sinks to her knees next to me. She buries her hands into the ash, swirling it around, as if she's searching for something.

"Well, she's really set us back now," says Kirsty.

"Wait, you're still planning to continue after that?" Anita asks. "She's not going to give up."

"And neither are we." Kirsty pulls anxiously at the end of her braid. She notices me noticing, then whips it around her shoulders. "Come on, Sam." She storms past us and heads back toward the village. I scramble after her.

"Can we track down more pink jasmine?"

"No. We're running out of time. We'll have to settle for golden. Source it somewhere else. It's the easiest ingredient on your list. We haven't been careful enough. This is a Wilde Hunt we're talking about here and we've committed the worst crime: underestimating our opponents."

Back in the village, Kirsty heads right up to a shack with a motorbike outside. She knocks, and talks to the man who opens the door, gesturing at the bike. They exchange heated words and there's a lot of gesticulating, but they come to some kind of agreement. Kirsty stands the bike up. "Grab your stuff," she says to me. "We have to go now."

"But what about Anita? And Arjun?"

"Look, only one team can win the hunt."

I'm momentarily stunned. "But they told us about the pink jasmine."

"And you told them about the ivy. You're even."

"What if we split up, like you suggested . . ."

"That was a possibility before, but the stakes have just been upped. Who knows how many of the other Participants Emilia has stopped already."

I'm about to protest again, but Kirsty continues. "Sam, they're slowing us down. We should have gone straight for the pink jasmine tonight. Emilia told us she traced us here because of them. Now I do know where to find eluvian ivy, so let's go."

"But eluvian ivy might not be an ingredient. It's just a theory!"

Kirsty holds me square by the shoulders. She stares me straight in the eye. "It's your theory, and that's good enough for me. If your instincts aren't right about this, then we're out of the hunt anyway. I trust you."

Her blind faith in me makes me proud and nervous all at once. But the more I think about it, the more the ingredients make sense—merpearl, jasmine, eluvian ivy, abominable hair. There's something else that I can't quite put my finger on, but those ingredients seem to fit in my brain, the jigsaw coming together. I can sense how they would mesh together to form the love potion, how each ingredient brings out a different quality in another. And more than that, I can visualize the mix, and my fingers itch to get started. I feel like I'm right, and Kirsty thinks so too. She nods, a slight smile on her face, and walks past me, back to Vijay's house, where she ignores the questioning faces of the family and grabs my backpack.

I want this. I want to win this hunt. We knew an alliance couldn't go on forever, that at one point we would have to separate—whether it was now or further down the line. So does it really make a difference when? And together we seem to have no luck whatsoever . . .

Arjun and Anita break out of the jungle as we're loading up the bike, the biggest backpack in between Kirsty's legs, the other on my back.

"Sam?" Arjun loads my name with accusation; he's already guessed what's happening.

"Where are you going?" Anita says. "I—"

Arjun stretches out an arm to stop her, to cut off whatever she's about to say. "They're leaving," he says, matter-of-factly. "Let her go."

"I . . . I'm sorry, guys. Kirsty—"

Now it's me he cuts off. "You're the Kemi, you don't have to do what she says. We're stronger together. I thought we said that if one of us wins it, that's better than some synth. And now we have an even bigger reason. We know that Emilia is trying to sabotage us. If we work together . . ."

I make a decision, throwing my legs over the back of the motorcycle. "There's no time. And we'll be safer apart. Emilia can't catch both teams at once."

It hurts seeing the angry look on Arjun's face, and

even more the wounded one on Anita's. "Wait," she says, dropping whatever it is she's been holding in her hands and running toward me. At that moment Kirsty fires the engine and pulls away. Anita yells out again, over the roar of the bike, and she reaches us in time to throw herself at my back, but then we start to gain speed and pull away from her. I look back over my shoulder to see her on her knees, with Arjun rushing over to help her, and a deep pit of guilt fills and overflows in my stomach.

When we stop to fill up with petrol, I pull the backpack off my back. There, imprinted on it like a slap, are Anita's handprints, blackened by soot and soil, staring at me in accusation.

Chapter Twenty-Four

Princess Evelyn

AH, NOW THIS WAS BETTER.

She had finally, finally been allowed in a room alone with the beautiful Lyn. In fact, everywhere she looked, she could see her, reflected again and again in beautiful mirrored glass. It was what she had asked for. "Take us to the dressing room," she had told Renel. "So I can show her my beautiful clothes." But it hadn't been because of the clothes that she wanted to take Lyn there. It was because of the mirrors. That way she could see Lyn reflected in 360-degree glory.

She felt emboldened, now that they were alone. She reached out her hand to touch Lyn, and Lyn did the same. But a barrier, a little spark of electricity, kept them a hair's breadth away from each other.

Lyn blushed. She actually blushed at the thought of a single touch.

She was so modest. And even more beautiful for it.

Eve wondered if this is what it had been like in older times, when a mere glance could have been deemed inappropriate. She had laughed when she was told that men once swooned over the sight of a bare ankle. That women would faint over a lingering glance.

Now she thought there might be something to that. An exquisite agony that could be ignited by the smallest thing.

She wanted to try something. She held up her palm and looked at it. Just a palm. Nothing aggressive, nothing offensive. Then she offered it to Lyn. Lyn reciprocated. But as they got closer and closer, it was as if a magnet held them at a tiny distance apart. She could feel Lyn's hand, but not in the physical sense . . . She could feel the chemistry between them, so solid, like a wall. She could push against it, but she still didn't get closer to Lyn's palm. It sent shivers running up and down her spine, it made her blood run cold and then searing hot again. Could you really be in love with someone you had never been able to touch?

Yes, absolutely yes.

She withdrew her hand and placed it demurely back in her lap.

When she had nothing, what she wouldn't do for a glimpse of Lyn's ankle.

A touch of her palm.

A glance from her eyes.

That, she could have. She looked up, and yes—there it was.

There was a knock at the door, and Renel entered. Eve looked at him coolly. "I told you I did not want to be interrupted."

"I know, my Princess—"

"How dare you disobey me? After what happened last time?"

"I know—"

"Are you still interrupting me? Leave, you horrid man!"

But he did not.

Eve felt an anger building inside her, and she could see fear rise in Renel's face. Good! Let him feel fear! He should fear her wrath. He should obey her. She would not appear weak in front of Lyn.

The mirror behind Renel's head cracked, and with it one of the reflected images of Lyn. "Look what you have done!" Eve shrieked.

Renel did not turn and leave as she expected, but instead ran toward her. "Evelyn, you must calm down."

"Get off me! What are you doing?" He had her by the shoulders, and it hurt.

"You're losing control!"

"I am not! You're the one doing this!"

The mirrors all around the room kept on breaking, a million shards falling onto the floor, raining glass and silver onto the stone pavings. Searing heat coursed through her body, sending waves of power through her fingertips. Did Lyn like this display? she wondered. Was she impressed?

Maybe she could do more.

She gathered the sense of heat in her palms. One clap of her hands and she could send earthquakes cracking through the floors, she could break the barriers that separated her and Lyn. But then Renel covered her mouth with a cloth, and she swooned. The last thing she did was stare into Lyn's eyes and think, *I love you.*

Chapter Twenty-Five

Samantha

WE RIDE FOR ALMOST FOUR HOURS straight, pulling up eventually at a decrepit-looking hotel on the outskirts of a small village. We have been heading steadily north, according to Kirsty, and the air around us is definitely colder by a few degrees. Kirsty bangs on the door until a sleepy-looking man opens up. He reluctantly agrees to rent us a room, but when he shows it to us I get the distinct impression no one has stayed there for years. Decades maybe. There are huge cobwebs everywhere—but then the spiders in Bharat are probably big enough to spin webs that size every night without breaking a sweat. It sends an involuntary shiver down my spine.

But hey, at least the Wi-Fi works.

Once I'm online, I call my parents to fill them in on the news. Kirsty reminds me not to mention any details of where we are. I also decide to leave out the part about Emilia, but it turns out we aren't the only team to have had trouble. Kirsty and I haven't had a chance to catch up on the casts yet, so Dad fills me in.

"Everyone knows you're back in now—a girl posted a picture of you at the airport on TalentChat. Then there were cameras in Bharat following Anita and Arjun and they spotted you leaving the airport and getting into their car—although they couldn't get good shots of your faces. But they lost you thanks to some pretty crazy driving. I thought Kirsty was supposed to be keeping you safe?"

My stomach drops. So Kirsty had been right. The media had been trailing Anita and Arjun. That meant it wouldn't have been too difficult for Emilia to find us. "What are they saying about me?"

"They say you're . . . flying under the radar at the moment."

"So they think I don't have a hope." The thought fills me with disappointment, even though I know it shouldn't. Kirsty would say it's a good thing. And if Emilia is coming after us herself, then she thinks we're a threat. That gives me a strange sense of satisfaction.

"What about the other teams?" I ask.

"Two of the Participants have dropped out," says Dad. "Not ZA," he adds, anticipating my next question. "Their stashes of merpearl powder were stolen in separate raids. One of the alchemists was the CEO of a small synth firm just starting out, and their lab burned down. Arson, apparently."

"That's beginning to seem like Emilia's signature," I mumble.

"What was that?" Concern appears on my mum's face. "Did Emilia do something to you? That's the rumor, but no one has found any evidence yet to point to her."

"No, Mum, I'm okay," I say, hating myself for every lie.

"The CEO is trying to claim compensation from the royals, being really vocal about it, but apparently it's in the risks of the hunt."

"All I can say is thank goodness you and the Patels can look out for one another," says Mum. "Maybe it's best if you come back . . ."

"I can't, Mum." My voice breaks as I relay why we've split from Arjun and Anita, and niggling doubt begins to gnaw at the back of my mind.

Mum clearly disapproves but is trying hard to let me figure out how to resolve my mistakes by myself. The overwhelming desire for them to be with me, here, in Bharat, hits me so strongly I don't have time to stop the tears. Mum's face is immediately concerned again. I wipe the tears away hastily. "Any news on the princess?" I ask, breaking the silence.

"No, but they're not letting the press near her. There was a freak lightning storm last night, which they think might have come from her. There's even talk about evacuating some of old Kingstown," says Mum.

"Sounds dangerous. Now it's your turn to be careful," I say.

"You concentrate on you. What's your plan now?" says Dad.

"Tomorrow we're going to head out to find the eluvian ivy."

"We'll be in and out of the jungle in an hour, tops," says Kirsty from the other end of the bed, where she is studying some maps.

Suddenly there's a loud pounding on our door. Kirsty jumps up to open it. I can see Mum and Dad craning their necks, as if that would help them see beyond the confines of the screen. "Okay, Mum, Dad, gotta go—talk as soon as we have the luvy." Kirsty turns back to grin at me; I'm even speaking like a Finder now, using their slang for eluvian ivy.

I blow some air kisses their way, which they return, and then snap the lid of my laptop shut.

I raise an eyebrow at Kirsty, who shrugs and opens the door.

It's a man—another guest, it looks like. His face is red and puffy with sweat and exertion. "Are you the Kemi team?" He whips out a notebook, and that's when it dawns on us both: He's a journalist.

"Get out of here," Kirsty says, and slams the door shut.

He knocks again, but we ignore it.

"How did he find us?" I ask.

Kirsty waves her hands frantically. "I have no idea."

His knocking becomes more urgent.

"Go away!" shouts Kirsty.

"Please!" says the man through the door. "I swear I didn't track you here—this is just luck. My media team was ambushed outside the jungle by that crazy exiled woman. She took everything: my money, my equipment, my ID . . ."

"Not our problem!"

"She knocked me out, and when I woke up I was all alone. Luckily she didn't find my van or else I would have been trapped, but I've run out of petrol . . ."

"Still not our problem!"

"Please. Have you heard what they're saying about you on the casts? They're calling you weak. They're trying to discredit you. I can tell your story."

Kirsty and I exchange a look. "He's got a point," she says. "Better to have someone on our side. We need to take control of this media circus before it takes over us. Who do you work for?" she says, more loudly so that the journo can hear.

"The *Novaen Times*."

"Talented or ordinary?"

"Ordinary!"

Kirsty opens the door again. "Fine. Look, we're running from an Emilia attack too. We're still in the hunt."

He looks relieved that he's managed to get some kind

of statement, and now that he's calmed down, I can see that he's a lot younger than I thought he was. If he wasn't breathing like he'd run a marathon, he might even be attractive.

"Now that you've got your quote, how about a beer? Off the record, of course," says Kirsty, who sounds like she's just come to the same conclusion I did.

"Sounds like a plan."

"Sam, you coming downstairs?"

I shake my head. "I'm going to hit the hay . . . or the cobwebs, as it were."

"No problem." Kirsty shuts the door behind her, taking the journalist far away. Thankfully.

As I flick off the light and am about to jump into bed, my phone goes off, the vibrations bringing scraps of paint from the ceiling down onto my head. I snatch it from the bedside table, but don't recognize the number of the text. Fear shoots through me as I wonder if the media have found my private number, but it's not a journo.

It's Zain.

Hey, reads the text.

My heart beats rapidly even as I read that one little word—and I'm appalled by my incredibly pathetic emotional response, even if I can't seem to control it or stop it.

I'm running through the best way to reply when it buzzes again.

Are you in Bharat? I saw you on a cast, you were
in the airport. Sorry for taking you off Connect. My
dad found out and threw a bit of a fit.

Now the excited butterflies turn a little sour. Is he just
texting me to find out where I am? And to tell me his
dad hates me (not that that's a surprise)?

I haven't even typed anything, and the phone goes off
one more time.

Oh god, that came out wrong. My dad is threatened by you. Actually so am I, but not for the reasons you think. Do you hate me now?

I can't help but laugh. Not only because it's like Zain
has a window into my brain, but because he actually
seems nervous. His bumbling texts seem more like something I would write.

I finally write a reply.

Don't hate you. I'll show your dad in the end.

A few seconds later, it buzzes.

Don't doubt it for a second.

I fall asleep, dreaming of boys with jet-black hair and
bright blue eyes.

Chapter Twenty-Six

Samantha

I WAKE UP AND SIT BOLT UPRIGHT. KIRSTY is still not in the room. It's not inconceivable that she simply got up earlier than me—but as I wipe the sleep from my eyes I can tell that nothing in the room has been touched since I fell asleep. My stomach lurches and visions of Emilia abducting Kirsty swim through my brain. That'd be one way to get me out of the hunt.

I throw on the same cargo pants and vest top as yesterday. There's no time to worry about my image out here.

As I lace my boots up, I itch to be in the lab. Exhaustion threatens to beat my mental faculties into submission, but I won't let it. Still, this whole hunt is confirming to me what I already knew: that I am a lab rat, a potions mixer, a researcher, not a Finder. Kirsty's life—of zero attachments, far-flung adventures, avoiding danger at every turn—isn't for me. I like the idea of adventure, but not every day. Not at this pace. I want time to think, and at this rate, I feel like I'm in danger of missing something really vital.

My phone buzzes, and my heart jumps, but it's not Zain this time. It's Kirsty. I send up a quick prayer that she's okay.

Meet downstairs for breakfast? Bring the bags.

I look down at our two massive backpacks and groan.

Kirsty sits at a table in the lounge of the hotel, the owner and the journalist across from her laughing at one of her jokes. I marvel for a moment at her ability to charm just about anybody.

"There you are! Sam, this is Daniel—the writer who has taken such an interest in your story. And Raj, our host. Quick, grab some breakfast and then we'll make a move. We need to get to that eluvian ivy ASAP. At least it's the two of us now."

I grimace at the reminder of what I did to Anita and Arjun, and distract myself by looking over the breakfast options. There's not much choice, so I grab a banana to be safe. That's one tip I was taught by my dad. When in doubt, choose peelable fruit. Raj offers me coffee, which I gladly accept. But this coffee is different—it's thick, gloopy almost, and spiced with cinnamon, cumin, and other spices I can't place. It's a bit of a shock first thing in the morning, but I decide that I like it.

I long for a triple-syrup-shot vanilla bean latte from Coffee Magic—which, although ubiquitous on Kingstown streets, probably won't be found deep in the Bharat jungle. Once, I'd even taken a cup back to the lab to make sure it wasn't laced with some kind of magic substance, but no—sometimes the best potions are the simplest: just delicious coffee beans, ground to smooth, filtered with water and mixed with velvety milk and several pumps of sugar. Turns out it doesn't take much to perk someone up—but to make them fall deeply in love?

Now that's a bit more complicated.

Kirsty lets me drain my coffee, and then: "Let's go. We're going to take Dan's van instead of the bike."

"He's coming with us?"

"I am," Dan says. "You'll move faster in my van."

"Raj has fuel we can buy." Kirsty stands up and grabs our bags. I take that as a cue and follow her, swiftly slipping into the back of the van. Kirsty hops into the driver's seat, even as Dan comes and stands by the door. He hesitates for a second, then chucks the keys through the open window and into her lap. She grins.

Well, he must have some kind of brain if he's smart enough to let Kirsty take the lead.

The back of the truck is filled with mud-stained ropes, and there is a bucketful of carabiners. Climbing must be involved somehow. Oh joy.

"Sounds to me like I should have followed you from

the beginning. You've had a bit of action," says Dan, flipping open his notebook as Kirsty drives.

"Too much action for my liking."

"Emilia Thoth has been waiting for her moment to bring the royal family down. Maybe she thinks this is it."

My eyes open wide. "Would she really want her niece to die?"

"For a chance at the crown, who knows how far she'll go?" he says. "She's managed to stay one step ahead of the royals so far. They've apparently sent the secret service out looking for her. And none of the cameras have been able to capture a glimpse of her. She's playing a game of cat and mouse with the media. She wants to be feared but not reviled. She knows how to keep the public on their toes."

"Well, when Sam saves the princess, they won't have anything to worry about," says Kirsty. "Seriously, I don't know what stars aligned, but the Kemi genes have collected in this girl and come out stronger. The royals are lucky to have her on this hunt. Even over her grandfather. He is the most irritating, stubborn old man you could ever meet."

"Hey!" I say.

"We are talking about Ostanes Kemi, right?" Dan sucks on the end of his pen. "The same Ostanes who, as a twelve-year-old apprentice, saved the Queen Mother from certain death when she contracted whooping cough? Who then at fourteen developed a potion vaccine that rid Nova of ebula pox?"

I shoot Dan a look. I'd forgotten that Granddad had once saved the Queen Mother's life. No wonder she stopped to say hello to me at the palace.

Kirsty raises her eyebrow. "You've done your homework, I see."

"Ostanes Kemi is a genius. Well, I guess that was all before the last Wilde Hunt," he finishes. "And the synths took over."

"And that's why I will never mix for a synth. And why I'll win this hunt and take back the pride in the Kemi name."

"An admirable goal," he says.

For some reason I keep expecting to see a cliff face, a mountain, or some large boulder to use the climbing equipment on, but everywhere I look is just trees, trees and more trees. Did I mention the trees?

The van slows to a crawl.

"Okay," Kirsty finally says. "Everybody out."

"Hey, I'm not leaving my van here," says Dan.

She throws him a look, and he capitulates. I really ought to get some tips from Kirsty one of these days.

We plod through the dense brush, me sandwiched between Kirsty and Dan.

"Keep an eye out for luvy," she whispers.

"How?" says Dan.

"Just guard your thoughts. Luvy latches on to emotions—and you don't want to get caught up."

I crane my neck to take in the majesty of the forest. There's no one around apart from us, and I feel like I'm in a sacred place—a natural cathedral, a living library, an organic lab.

It's beautiful—haunting, even—but it gives me the creeps all the same. It's not the wildlife or the amazing flora. It's the fact that I keep expecting tongues of fire to leap out at me, winding a searing hot cord of destruction through the trees. Will Emilia only be happy when she has completely and utterly annihilated us?

Then I remember. We are a threat. It fills me with a warm glow of pride, and I lift my chin up further. She thinks we can win. An immense love for my family swirls through me. The Kemi mixing gene might have skipped my dad, but he is still my idol, and I miss his comforting hugs. He would have advised me better on the Patel situation. My mum, who is the lifeblood of the family. She gave up her Talented heritage to be with my dad, and despite her flighty ways she is the glue that keeps us together.

Then there is my grandfather, the fount of knowledge in my universe. Obstinate, old-fashioned, gruff, and the person who understands me most in the world, even if I don't understand him all the time. And lastly my sister. Dear, sweet, Talented Molly. I'm so protective of her . . .

I feel like I'm drifting, floating out of control with

love for my family. The feeling encompasses me like a blanket, reassuring me that nothing is ever going to go wrong. Nothing can go wrong. It's a weightless feeling, like flying on a cloud of their support. It's the best feeling in the entire world.

A distant voice breaks my happy stupor. A male voice. Only a vague flicker of recognition registers, but I feel my body recoil from it. I wrap myself further into the cocoon of my family's love. It's warm here. There's another voice, female.

"Shh, don't let her hear you. Wake her too quickly and she'll panic."

I recognize that voice, but I still don't release myself from my protective thoughts. I feel myself withdraw further from them, and I hear the female voice swear.

Suddenly, I remember something about luvy. Instinctively, I struggle. Bonds that have wrapped themselves around me tighten, enclosing me further within the cocoon. But this is no cocoon of love. This is entrapment. This is the ivy, feeding on my love, taking my emotions for its own. What an idiot I am.

Luckily, Kirsty's voice manages to reach me.

"Keep still, Sam! I've almost got you."

I try to calm myself, but I can't stop the fear—as the new emotion surges, the luvy grips my neck and tightens. I can't open my eyes. It's like tiny hands are holding my eyelids down, and no matter how hard I try, I can't see.

I try to raise my arms to claw at whatever is holding my eyes shut. But I can't move them either. They're glued to my sides, and when I try to spread my limbs wide, it pulls me inward. The ivy has surrounded me completely.

There's a tug on my foot—and then a searing pain as something rough tightens around my ankle and tries to pull me down. All thoughts of my family are out of my head as I focus on the pain.

The luvy's grip loosens. My eyes snap open.

But I wish they hadn't.

I'm high up. The luvy has dragged me up amongst the jungle trees, so high I can barely see the ground, just the branches and leaves and a long, long drop . . .

Oh, dragons. I fight the urge to close my eyes again, to return to that place of love where I felt safe and grounded, and far less scared.

I hear my name.

My ankle hurts again. The luvy loosens.

I drop. I scream.

I think of my mum and the luvy tightens. Safe. Safety.

"Sam," the voice comes again, more urgent. I turn my head to the sound, even as I feel the luvy creep up my neck and prepare to cover my face again. Finally, I spot Kirsty. She's hanging on to one of the nearby tree trunks, a thin spiral of rope wrapped around the tree. The climbing equipment. So that's what that was for.

"Sam," she says evenly. "If you go beyond the canopy, I

won't be able to reach you. The trees around here won't be able to hold my weight."

As she says that, my brain—stupid, stupid organ that it is—jumps to thoughts of safety, of love, and the luvy responds. It pulls me upward, higher into the tops of the trees.

Then I remember something else about luvy. Something amazing. Something that might make this ordeal worthwhile.

I turn to look at Kirsty one last time, and in that split second, she reads my mind. Instant panic shows on her face. She opens her mouth to shout at me.

But I'm being pulled up too fast now for her to do anything about it. Instead, she gestures frantically to her ankle. I look down at mine, where the pain was, and I see it—a piece of rope hooked around my leg.

It's too late to pay it much attention now, because the luvy has lost patience with me, and its tendrils gallop upward. It's not going to let me escape this time.

When it breaks through the treetops, I'm blinded by the brightness of the sun. Down on the jungle floor, the light had been mottled, filtered through the leaves, but above the canopy is pure, unadulterated daylight. I can't let it distract me from my purpose though, and I blink furiously to clear the spots from my eyes.

Strangely, being above the canopy is less scary than being just below it. The tops of the trees look solid, like another level of ground. I imagine if I fell here, I would drop onto the leaves and bounce, like falling on a green mattress. But my brain knows that is far from the truth.

The luvy is like a carpet laid over the canopy floor. It sits on top of the leaves of the trees, a symbiotic entity, waiting for the right animal—or, in this case, human—to come by. For a moment, I think how lucky we are to have found it amidst the acres and acres and acres of jungle that surrounds us. The leaves are delicate five-pointed stars, absolutely stunning in their intricacy. Little white veins stretch and wend their way through the dark green of the leaves. They suck up emotion— and their favorite is happiness. It's the flower of the luvy that I'm looking for. It's not part of the potion, but it could still change everything. A huge white blossom so valuable and rare that I've only ever seen a drawing of it; we've never had one in the store.

My Finder instincts leave a lot to be desired, but I read about the luvy flower in an old textbook, fascinated because even the synths haven't been able to replicate the effect of the luvy flower with chemical mixes. It's used in very few potions, but the ones that contain it are astronomically expensive. If I can get it . . . well, I could do with someone paying me an astronomical sum right about now.

Gazing out over the canopy, all I can see is green. For a moment I think I've taken this risk for nothing. But then, finally, I spot a white petal, swaying slightly in the breeze. At the same time, though, a vine of luvy tugs at the bottom of my lip. It wants to consume me.

I start to—for lack of a better description—swim toward the white flower. I pull at the ivy just as much as it pulls at me. It's wrapped tightly around my body, but as I reach out with my arms it moves with me. More vines start to lift and creep around my head, poking at my ears, my mouth, my nose; one even tries to get into my eyelid. I thought I'd be more terrified, but my mind is crystal clear: get to the luvy flower, or the luvy will get you. Simple as that. And in this battle for my survival, I'm going to do everything I can to win.

I reach it, finally, and the luvy vines are in my hair, around my neck. But the luvy has grown complacent. Left undisturbed for so long, it's forgotten how to guard its most precious treasure: its own flower. Thin stems of green wend their way around my body, pinning my arms to my sides. When I'm finally close enough to the flower, I have no choice in how to grab at it. I lunge forward, throwing my body weight into the movement, and bite over the precious petals, down the stem, trapping it in between my teeth and ripping.

I think I hear the luvy scream. Except, it's not a scream, it's a screech of vines unraveling themselves from around me. The leaves expel this slippery substance, an oil, which makes the vines slick—too slick to grab hold of, too slick to keep hold of me. It hates me; it wants me out. It's wounded and I'm the cause.

And now I'm falling. The effort of keeping the luvy flower in my mouth works to keep me ridiculously calm, considering the circumstances. Why did I think I could go up there, with only a rope around my ankle for safety? At this rate, if the rope catches, my leg will likely be yanked from its socket before it saves me. That's going to be fun.

The canopy rushes past me, a reversal from a few moments earlier, as if I'm rewinding my life. Leaves, twigs, branches batter the back of my head, my back, but the luvy flower remains in my teeth as I try hard to resist the urge to swallow.

Maybe this is what death is like. My life flashing before me in reverse.

My muscles relax. I feel content with my decision.

Then there are no longer leaves beneath me, just open air. I'm through the canopy and now, with no resistance, I'm falling faster. Finally, I feel fear. My heart stops beating, literally.

There's a painful moment. I smack against a slightly flexible material and bounce. There's screaming around me, loud shouts. I bounce again, starting to roll off what I now realize is a net. I see Kirsty gesturing frantically at Dan, trying to lift the net up to capture me, but it's too late. I'm almost off the edge. But I reach out with a hand, making frantic grabbing gestures until I catch one of the holes in the net. The rest of my body is flung over the side, and my wrist sears with pain as the rope burns it. But it holds. I'm there, dangling. I'm alive, still terrifyingly high above the forest floor.

The net dips again as Kirsty scrambles over. She throws down a rope to me. "Clip this to your belt."

I do exactly as she says. Once I've safely clipped the carabiner onto my waist, she nods grimly, then pulls me up onto the relative safety of the netting. On the other side, I can see Dan, his face white with shock and his forehead damp. Kirsty rolls her eyes at him. "I told him to keep the net slack, not pull it taut, useless idiot." Then, she pulls me into a huge hug. "You're a crazy girl, you know that?"

I don't answer. She pats me on the back, then gestures across the net and toward the tree trunk. From there, we are able to rappel down the trunk and back to the rainforest floor.

I almost fall to my knees and kiss the ground. I've never been so happy to see it.

"Well," Kirsty says. "I don't know about you, but at least I managed to grab at some luvy while you were being sucked away." She holds out three strands of the evil substance. "It's not much, but it should be enough for the potion. I can't believe it . . . all that work, and that's all we come away with."

I take her hand and hold it palm upward. Then I open

my mouth. Out drops the luvy flower, glistening with my saliva.

Both Dan and Kirsty stare at it, their mouths dropping open too.

Then Kirsty pulls me into another massive hug. "Sam, you're a genius."

I finally allow myself to grin, before my body gives up and collapses onto the forest floor.

Chapter Twenty-Seven

Samantha

KIRSTY AND DAN TAKE TURNS DRIVING the van, and it's late evening by the time we check ourselves into the most extravagant hotel Kirsty can find in Loga, with views overlooking the Red Palace. It's so luxurious it even has its own transport lift from the lobby to the penthouse suites. The best thing, though, is that they've got a separate entrance so we can avoid running into the paparazzi—and avoid alerting Emilia to our location.

I gaze up at the intricate gold filigree that covers the ceiling, sparkling against cold white marble. In a way, it reminds me of the luvy, but from this distance I can admire it rather than fear it. Any closer and I might change my mind.

Kirsty is closing the transaction on the sale of the luvy flower. She sold it through one of her rare goods agents, not having the contacts herself to find the right buyer for such an ingredient. The amount we get is enough to pay for the next leg of our journey, this hotel room—an extravagance that Kirsty insists upon—and still have some left over.

Dan writes up my experience in the jungle and posts it on the *Novaen Times* blog as "The Hunt Heats Up for Sam Kemi." Kirsty ensures he obscures any references to the actual ingredients and our location, in case any of the other Participants read it.

Because of the time difference, it hits Nova just as the morning news is breaking. And then it's like the internet explodes before our eyes. Before I know it, the blog has received thousands of hits and shares on Connect, TalentChat, and every other social media on the planet. My in-box is flooded with email.

Almost instantly, articles are posted in response, some calling me a hero for risking my life to save the princess, others claiming that I'm just in it for the free publicity for the store and I have no hope against the likes of the superior ZA Corp. Obviously the hunt is even bigger news than we realized. I can't stop scrolling through my phone to read all the messages, which thrill and sicken me in equal measure.

In the end, Kirsty has to confiscate my phone and laptop just to make sure I get a good night's rest.

The next morning, refreshed after a night in one of the comfiest beds ever, I deliberately avoid the internet except to send an email to my dad saying that we'll pay for him to come here. He's bringing along several key pieces of equipment and ingredients so I can start mixing the potion. And, after all that I've been through, a hug from my dad wouldn't go amiss.

To get here quickly enough, he's going to have to transport. At first, he balks at the suggestion. He's never transported before, and this is the longest distance he could possibly make. He suggests flying instead, but we don't have the time.

Finally, I convince him. We can pay for the very best Talented porters in Loga to pull him through, along with all the safeguards money can buy, so there's no chance of him falling. I watch through the screen as he steps into the Summons. It's a pretty incredible thing to see, and I'm so proud of my dad. He barely flinches throughout the journey, even though the world must be flying past him at unprecedented speeds.

Only fifteen minutes later he's with us in the hotel lobby. When he lands, I rush forward and throw my arms around him. He squeezes me tightly back.

We opt for the stairs; my dad doesn't feel like porting even a few floors up after his journey. When we reach the hotel room door, I finally feel myself relax.

The door opens out into our suite. I spy Kirsty's ponytail draped over the arm of the sofa. She's completely conked out. Still asleep. I smile. I don't think she's really slept for ages, especially not since my narrow escape with the luvy, and I'm glad that for a little while, she can get some rest. Plus, for where we're going next, she's going to need all the energy she can get.

And there's the fact I get to have my dad to myself for a little moment longer.

I put my finger to my lips and point at Kirsty. Dad nods, picking up the bag again, and I direct him into the office room (yeah, this hotel room is so big it has its own office), which we've completely checked over for bugs. Dan made us paranoid about that—after he logged onto his email and saw that yet another team had dropped out because of Emilia's interference, we realized we couldn't take any risks.

In the office, the luvy rests inside a wicker basket, the wood keeping it contained. Even looking at it turns my stomach, as if it might multiply under my gaze until it's big enough to consume me again. Kirsty assures me there is no way it can get to me in the other rooms, and I'm grateful that she doesn't make fun of me for thinking that a mere clipping might morph into the monstrous plant we encountered in the jungle.

Dad unpacks his bag, carefully removing each piece of equipment. There is a small ceramic pot, a portable heater, a mortar and pestle, the glass jar filled with merpearl. The last item is a bulbous jar filled with a dusky-pink liquid: the patented Kemi rosewater potion base.

"So, what's first?" Dad asks, once he's finished laying everything out.

I let out a short, sharp breath. This is the real deal. Not

apprentice level. This is alchemy master level stuff. "This kind of fresh luvy can't be left out for too long, or else it will dry up." I think of the vial of synthetic luvy powder I have. Another reason why synths gained prominence: The powders aren't nearly so temperamental. "You have to mix it into a paste first."

Luvy is best mixed with rosewater. But how will that apply to a love potion? How can I draw out the secure, safe, comforting aspects of love, which the eluvian ivy feeds on, and use it in this potion? I feel sure that it is a key ingredient, but something is missing. I open my diary up, laying it flat to the love potion page.

"To make the paste I'll mix it with the rosewater base and then add the pearl," I continue. "I think some people might save the pearl until the end, but if we do it this way around, the luvy will have the chance to absorb some of the beauty from the Aphroditas pearl. They will enhance each other."

"Trust your instincts, sweetheart."

A small smile appears on my face, but then my brow furrows. I remove the stopper from the jar containing the pearl and pour a little of the fine powder into the bottom of the mortar. I then eye the wicker basket and swallow. "Dad? Do you think you could cut the luvy up for me? It needs to be in about inch-long strips, just to release the oils. But I don't want to touch it."

Dad doesn't know the details of what happened in

the jungle—but even on video chat my parents could see the scratches on my face, neck, and arms from where the vines had gripped my bare skin. And the fact that I had a luvy flower can only mean I put myself in danger. He knows better than to ask me about it now, but I'm sure that when the hunt is over, I will hear a proper lecture about managing my risk . . .

While I mash tiny drops of rosewater into the pearl with the pestle, Dad cuts up the luvy, dropping the strips into my mixture one by one. As he adds the luvy, more and more of it takes up the color of the pearl, softening into a gentle pink-white. I grind and grind, encouraging the ingredients to form a thick paste.

When the paste is ready, I scoop it out of the mortar and scrape it into a glass jar. I then seal down the lid and hand it to my dad.

"Are you worried about not having the jasmine?" Dad asks.

"Mixing the jasmine will come in toward the end, I think. But for the same reason that I wouldn't ever use anything but fresh luvy, I want to know exactly where the jasmine is sourced from, how it was grown, before we buy it."

My stomach lurches as I think about everything Emilia destroyed—not only a place of great religious significance for the Patels and the other villagers, but also the perfect ingredient to use in a love potion. The Daharama legend told that pink jasmine has a great propensity toward love. Whatever we buy will never be able to replace that potential, and that bothers me more than I realize.

"That paste will be stable for a few days, but might need to be stirred every so often," I say.

Dad nods, but a frown line appears between his brows. "I have to stay in the hotel for twenty-four hours before I can port again. Can you two not stay a bit longer?"

"Unfortunately not." Kirsty appears at the doorway, fully dressed. I swallow hard, but I know it's true.

Dad smiles at Kirsty, but I know he's worried. "So, do you know where you're going next?"

We both nod. "Up north," I say. "The next ingredient is hair. From an abominable."

His jaw drops. It scares me to see my dad, normally a pillar of strength in my world, look so scared for me. "You're going up into the mountains? That's . . . insanity!"

"It's a Wilde Hunt, John. It was never going to be a walk in the park."

"But Sam's not prepared for this! People train for years to tackle those mountains."

"Dad, it's okay," I say, even though I can hardly believe I'm saying it myself. In a snap, I know Dad would let me come home, forget about the hunt, go back to eating homemade lasagna and mixing prescriptions for the pensioners of Kingstown. He wouldn't judge. "This is my choice. I'll be careful."

"This isn't about being careful anymore. This is about being prepared for dangers you can't even imagine!"

"Sam, we'd better go," says Kirsty.

"At least give me a couple more minutes alone with my daughter before you head off?"

Kirsty holds up two fingers—two minutes—and then spins on her heels.

Dad looks over at me and sighs. "Look, I'm not going to lecture you any more about the mountains. But your mother and I think it's a shame about the Patels. I preferred it when they were around to keep an eye on you. That you guys were looking out for each other."

"I know, Dad, but—"

"Wait, I wasn't finished. We're proud of you, Sam. Really proud. You've already done so much, and the whole family believes you might do this thing. Even Granddad. But it's not just us. The world is behind you now, Sam. Even the press, after seeing the challenges you've overcome so far. You're the underdog, and this time, the underdog is going to win. So let's make sure we see this whole thing through. Kick some synth butt for us, okay?"

I nod, trying not to cry. He pulls me into a bear hug, and eventually pushes me away, but not before a last kiss on the forehead. "I'll get this paste back to the store. It'll be waiting for you. We all are. Stay safe, my heart."

Chapter Twenty-Eight

Samantha

WE LEAVE THROUGH THE KITCHENS OF THE hotel, out into a back alley where a flatbed truck is parked. I cringe when Kirsty makes me hide in a tiny crawlspace between several large boxes on the bed of the truck. She and Dan hide as well, and it gives me a little comfort to know their journey will be as uncomfortable as mine.

She explained the plan to me earlier. There are only a few mountain passes that will be accessible enough for me to climb with zero training. But not only does Kirsty know that—Emilia knows it as well. If abominables are the right ingredient and she knows that's where we might be heading next, we have to cover our tracks as much as possible. She would expect us to transport to the mountains, or fly, so we're taking the long route. When I'm finally able to escape from the back of the truck and stretch my aching limbs, we've arrived at a bus station.

And I'm so glad we choose the long way. By the time

we arrive in the bustling town of Pahara at the base of the mountains, there's a high wind blowing, so strong that the airport and main transport portal are both closed. The wind buffets the bus, but the driver navigates the climbing, twisting roads with ease. Maybe a little too easily. I huddle into my down jacket and grip the arm-rest, praying the bus doesn't skid around the next mountainous bend and just tumble off the side completely. No matter how unsafe I feel, the seats and aisle are so packed full of people and bags—I swear I even saw a chicken—that there's nowhere to escape even if I wanted to.

It felt really odd to be buying thick winter clothing in Loga, where the temperatures hovered between hot and boiling, but now, as I look outside, I see how necessary it was. Snow covers the ground, and delicate fingers of frost spread across the base of the windows. Locals we pass on the road are wrapped up in fur-trimmed hoods. And we haven't even reached the start of our trek yet.

Kirsty has already called ahead and lined up our very own Sherpa who will lead us up the mountain. He won't take us directly to where an abominable might live, though. Kirsty and I are agreed that meeting an actual abominable is not on the agenda. Though naturally reclusive, they're fearsome creatures. Sightings are rare, and often end in a gruesome manner. Recently there's been a spate of attacks, as it becomes more and more popular to climb the mountains. Talenteds checking "adventures" off their bucket lists.

No, all we need is a patch of their fur, and for that, we need to find a cave or a rock where an abominable might have stopped for a scratch. This is the beginning of summer, so the abominables should be shedding. If they're not, we're in trouble.

Despite the precautions we've taken to cover our route, I wonder if any of the other teams will be here. Kirsty seems to think I'm the only one who has a feel for the ingredients, but putting the combination together wasn't so hard. Arjun and Anita know about the abominable— maybe I will see them here too? My heart aches with guilt, although it's mixed with the tiniest spark of hope. Hope that they will forgive me. And the Zs have all those researchers working for them. Surely one of them will have figured it out.

Kirsty's done this trek before. She's known for it; it's her signature. So for once, I feel totally confident in the fact that we're going to get this ingredient without much trouble. The bus pulls up to its first stop at a village half-way up the mountain. Thankfully, the majority of people get off here. Just beyond is the official entrance to the Wilds, and we have to show our passes.

Kirsty puts her legs up on the now-empty seat between us. "Not long now," she says. She tosses a bottle of water to me, and another to Dan. "Drink up. You need to stay hydrated up here. You've had a slow adjustment to the altitude—yet another reason why we chose the bus instead of flying. Anyone who flies—or worse, ports—up here gets the most terrible altitude sickness, especially if they go out on a trek right away. At least we've had a slow build. Ideally, we'd spend a couple of nights in this village, but we don't have that luxury."

A gust of wind rattles the bus on its (probably) rusty axles, and Kirsty grins. "Well, hopefully this weather means that some of our competition has been stranded. The next bus up isn't for another twenty-four hours, and hopefully we'll have the fur and be back down the mountain by then."

"How close do you think you are to the cure?" Dan has been interviewing me on-and-off on the way up. "After the abominable, what's next?"

This is the question I've been asking myself. I spend every spare moment writing in my diary, working through my suspicions about ingredients and my own gut feelings. The physical act of writing, of putting pen to paper, helps me solve problems my brain can't work out on its own. But formula after formula has flowed out of the pen and onto the page, and none of them feel right. I can't put my finger on the next thing. "I'm not sure. We're close, but not there yet."

Kirsty tells me to cut myself some slack. "You'll need all your energy for the climb," she says. "Save your brain and get as much rest as you can."

But by the time the bus pulls up to the lodge where we're going to launch our expedition, it's clear our efforts to be alone have failed. Zol stands outside, red in the face and yelling at some poor Sherpa.

The bus doors open, and his screams jump in volume. "We paid good money, and we're going up the mountain tonight! Do you see these passes? Do you see them? It's not our fault that the ports closed just before our guide arrived."

I grab my bag down from the rack above my head. By the time I look back out the window again, the shouting has stopped. But still, my heart catches in my mouth. If Zol is here, that must mean Zain is too. That's when I see him: He's wrapped in a snug-fitting bright red jacket, trying hard to calm his dad down.

At that moment he looks up at the bus and sees me staring. A blush immediately rises to my face and I turn away.

I shuffle off the bus, lagging behind Kirsty. I'm hit with a blast of cold air, and I'm thankful for it if it gives me an excuse for the redness in my cheeks. The Sherpa who Zol is arguing with sees Kirsty and races over to her, bowing deeply. She bows back. Then they embrace.

"Jedda!"

"Kirsty, miss, it is our honor to have you back here again."

Kirsty smiles warmly. "No, no, the honor is mine." She

raises an eyebrow at Zol. He's obviously not feeling the cold—in fact, it looks as if steam is going to pour out of his ears.

Jedda shakes his head slowly. "He wants to trek in the mountains, but even with his pass I cannot let him through without a guide."

Fearless as ever, Kirsty laughs while looking at Zol. "Are you serious? You're thinking of going up there without a Sherpa? That's madness."

Zol crosses his arms. "Our guide couldn't make it up through the storm. But my son and I have enough Talent between us that we don't need help in these mountains."

"Talent only goes so far up here. Altitude does crazy things to magic. I'd be more cautious if I were you. Why not take another?"

"Because there is no other Sherpa, you blasted woman. For some reason this godforsaken place only has one at the moment."

Dan stands directly behind Kirsty, taking notes on a pad and paper.

"Who is that?" Zol asks.

"That's Dan. He's a journalist from the *Novaen Times*."

"You brought a journalist up here? Are you mad? As soon as he posts anything online, that insane woman Emilia will know where we are."

"We thought it better to have someone along to tell

our side of the story. And don't worry, he's not stupid enough to geotag his posts up here."

"That's still a ridiculous risk!" splutters Zol, but Kirsty ignores him.

"Jedda, about the other Sherpas?" she asks.

The man shrugs. "It is Summer Festival. Most have gone home to celebrate with their families. One is currently up at base camp. I am only here because you reserved me, Kirsty miss. Abominable season doesn't start for another two weeks. It is still very dangerous on Hallah."

Hallah. The great mountain, and the first in an immense range that stretches across the northern border of Bharat. A good potential home for the elusive abominable. I look up for the first time and really take it in. The little lodge is perched at the bottom of one of the main routes up. The mountain looks far away from here, and I can hardly believe I will be walking up there soon. The thought is enough to take my breath away.

"I told Master Zol that he could wait two days for the other Sherpas to come down, but he does not want to. And, if I may say, it would be best for all of you if you went as a group together. It is safest that way."

"No!" I shout, before I can even think. But my protest is almost drowned out by Zol's own.

Kirsty is silent, though. Then she nods. "Fine, yes. It is safer that way."

"What are you talking about?" I say to Kirsty. "You don't want to cooperate with the Patels, but now it's okay to team with ZA?"

"You don't know what it's like up there, Sam. The mountain can turn on you in an instant. It is so much safer in a bigger group." She looks past me, at Zol and Zain. "Look, no one likes this arrangement, but we'll go up to base camp together. Then we can go our separate ways, and ZA can use the Sherpa who is up there. Deal?" She extends a hand to Zol.

He doesn't take it. "Fine," he says. "But the journalist stays behind."

Chapter Twenty-Nine

Samantha

WE'RE LEAVING AT FIRST LIGHT TOMORROW, so we have one night in the mountain lodge.

The window in the dining room on the second floor offers the most amazing view of Mount Hallah. The peak here rises dramatically out of the earth, the first of a series of mountains that stretch beyond my range of vision, rising and falling like waves frozen in time. A blanket of white covers the top third of the mountain's visible surface—crisp and unbroken.

As if fulfilling a wish I hadn't made yet, a gentle drift of snow begins to fall outside the window. I watch it as the sun goes down, bathing the mountainside in a pink glow. It is a peaceful scene.

I shiver and look down into my hot mug of cocoa. I think my bones know the words "mountain" and "peaceful" don't really go well together.

Chocolate—so many uses it's stupid to list them all, even in my head.

I'm alone now. Zol didn't come down to dinner at all, thankfully. Zain did, but he kept his distance while Kirsty and Dan were around. I overheard him talking on the phone to their team of lab techs back at ZA headquarters. I think back to my dad arriving at our hotel room in Loga and taking home the paste. I wonder how things would be different if I had the resources of a full mixing lab. Or even if Granddad had agreed to come. He's the only person I know who must feel the same rush that I do when I think about the mix. And I keep returning to Dan's awe-filled words. I sometimes forget that my granddad was younger than me when he made some of his most important mixes.

Zain catches my eye a couple of times during dinner, but I successfully avoid holding his gaze. Still, my stomach can't stop fluttering, making it difficult to eat. Stupid, treacherous tummy.

I spin around at the sound of an awkward cough. He's standing in the doorway, dressed in the most casual clothes I've seen him in: a hoodie, faded blue and worn at the wrists, ripped jeans, and a knitted beanie covering all his hair except the most unruly strands.

He's never looked so hot. I am in similarly relaxed clothes, but while he manages effortless cool, I manage . . . just plain slob.

"Any chance of a hot drink around here?"

I slowly place the mug in my lap and swallow the mouthful I'd been drinking in a big gulp. "I finished the last of the cocoa, so there's only instant coffee. And black, I'm afraid. The milk's gone off."

"Right now, I think I'd take lukewarm instant over a steaming hot shot of espresso any day."

I laugh. "Yeah, so much better than an extra-large vanilla bean latte."

"Completely." He drops two heaped teaspoons of instant into a mug and moves toward the flask of hot water.

"I'd add sugar to that," I pipe up. "Helps take away the dishwater taste."

"Wise. Not only good at potions mixing, huh? You've got barista skills too?"

"I'm a girl of many talents."

"Got that right." He smiles. "I'm glad you're still in the hunt. I wasn't sure if I'd see you again, what with Emilia doing everything possible to stop us."

I wish I hadn't finished my drink so quickly. Now I have nothing to do but hold my mug and look at him. Luckily, he keeps talking and doesn't notice my awkward, fidgeting hands. "Everyone seems to forget that at the center of this is just a girl. Things are getting really bad for Evelyn, you know? They've had to restrain her . . . but it could make things worse. Evelyn is so insanely strong."

"You're really worried about her, huh?"

"I'm worried that none of us are going to be able to save her. If we can't . . . I don't want to know what that will mean for her. For the whole of Nova. And this Wilde Hunt—we think we're collecting the right ingredients, but who knows? She's been working on her potion for years. What if we miss something? What if no one gets it right?"

"I guess it's why the hunt was called, to get the best of the best on the case . . ."

"But we're risking Evelyn's life." He pauses. "And the hunt also called Emilia, who is only thinking about the power—she doesn't want Evelyn to be cured." He pounds his fist on the table. "The worst thing is, I can't actually believe Evelyn hid the potion from me this whole time. If she'd been so desperate for help, I would've done something. I mean, we were friends. The best of, or so I thought."

This sounds like a rant he's needed to have for a long time, so I let him finish. After a few moments of silence, I say, "Zain?"

"Yeah."

"Do you think it was meant for you?"

"What?"

I don't answer, just tap the rim of my empty mug.

"The love potion?" He sighs. "Yeah. It looks like."

"Then she put us all at risk first. For you."

We sit in silence. Staying here any longer feels more dangerous than the hike up the mountain. "I better get some sleep," I say. "See you tomorrow?"

He nods. "Night."

"Night." I jump off the window ledge. I only get the chance to take a few steps before Zain calls me back. "Sam?"

I turn around, hesitant. If I look at him, I might not be able to tear my eyes away again.

"Look . . ." He fumbles his coffee mug, sloshing liquid over the side. He cries out in pain so I leap for some paper towels, and before I know it I'm dabbing hot coffee from the back of his hand. He laughs. "Well, that was smooth. What I meant to say was, you never answered me before, when I asked if I could see you after this is all over?"

I concentrate hard on dabbing, but he moves his other hand over mine. I let him hold it there for a second before I pull away. I remember who this is. This is Zain Aster. "Um, I don't know . . ."

"Okay, don't answer now. When this is over?"

I bite my lip and nod, then continue back to my room.

Kirsty isn't there. I lie on the bed, listening to my heart racing in my chest. All I want now is to call up Anita and tell her how crazy my life is right now. I wonder if she's up in some other mountain lodge somewhere, thinking about me. She probably hates me.

I hug a pillow tight to my chest. Dissecting Zain's actions will need to wait until after I'm back from the mountain. And then I can think about how unfair it is that the guy I have a huge crush on, who has just asked me out, who I want to go out with, is my biggest competition.

Chapter Thirty

Samantha

I THOUGHT I WAS PRETTY FIT, BUT CLIMBING this mountain—even just to the base camp—is steadily killing me. We left so early we watched the sunrise over the range, and I don't think I've experienced anything more breathtaking—quite literally. The sky now is such a clear, crisp blue that it makes any other blue sky I've ever seen feel gray and smog-ridden by comparison. Ahead, the snow blankets the ground, blazingly bright as far as the eye can see. Every now and then a shrub bursts through the frozen ground and there are white flowers, as pretty as snowflakes, growing in bunches. I scoop up a handful and put them in my pack.

Mountain sweet petals—for schizophrenia and delusions. Also a potent cure for insomnia.

They're lovely, and would be perfect in our stockroom. Maybe I do have Finding instincts in my blood after all.

"Come on, keep up."

Kirsty stands a few feet away with her thumbs looped behind the straps of her backpack. I roll my eyes at her and don't bother replying. She's been grumpy ever since we had to leave Dan back at the hotel. But I concentrate. I can do this.

The first sign of flags fluttering over the crest of the hill is an incredibly welcome sight. I take another bite of an energy bar to keep going. It seems to help, because all of a sudden I've caught up with the rest of the group. They are staring down at the cabin that marks the base camp. A line of flags stand tall on the roof of the cabin, signifying the nationalities of people who have climbed the mountain.

"Something wrong?" Kirsty says to Jedda. He's about five foot five—a good five inches shorter than me—but he's made a giant by the immensity of his backpack. He's carrying the ZA supplies—tents, sleeping bags, food, potion equipment, everything. Kirsty and I have shared out our belongings between us.

Jedda sucks on his bottom lip. "There should be smoke coming from that cabin, but there is nothing."

"Oh, don't tell me that you lied to us," said Zol, throwing up his arms in exasperation. "There's no one up here, is there?"

"Have some respect," says Kirsty, throwing Zol a dirty look as Jedda bounds down the mountain path toward the cabin. We follow close behind, his speed worrying me. There's a curious electricity in the air up here, and I wonder if it's because we're so deep into the Wilds—it's so fresh it almost makes my skin sting. But there's another sensation underneath that, something that feels wrong—and it's probably being driven by Jedda's nervousness. He's now walking up to the cabin trying to appear relaxed, but I can see the whites of his knuckles as he grips the backpack.

Kirsty overtakes him and reaches the cabin first. She knocks. Like something out of a horror flick, the door swings open at her touch. That's not a good thing. Up here, in this cold, with this weather . . . I can't imagine anyone leaving a door open by accident.

She steps inside, quickly followed by Jedda and the rest of us. The cabin is completely deserted. Papers are strewn everywhere, cupboard doors open, one of them a pile of splintering wood on the ground. The cupboards are completely bare. Somehow, I don't think this is what base camp is supposed to look like.

It's not very big, with only one main room and a bathroom, and it's empty of people. There are no other Sherpas up here, and no sign of any other teams from the hunt either. Well, except for the fact that it's been ransacked.

I look at Kirsty. She's thinking the same thing.

Emilia.

Jedda reaches into his pack and pulls out a radio. He

tries to radio down to the village, but he only gets static. He frowns. "Normally, we get signal up here, even though we are so high," he says. I wonder about the electric crackle I felt outside, whether that has anything to do with it.

"We should go back," Jedda says.

"No!" we all say in unison, then look at each other nervously.

I say the words we've all been too cagey to mention yet. "We're both here for abominable fur, right?" I wait, and then Zain nods. "Well, let's find it together and then get out of here."

Zol looks like he's about to burst with fury, but his anger and power hold no sway up here in the mountains. Or maybe he looks so red-faced because he's even more out of shape than me. He takes a blisterpack from his coat and pops out a red pill.

"What is that?" Kirsty asks.

"Zolorantium. Helps with the altitude sickness."

"Yeah right," she scoffs.

"It's been highly praised by many great Finders, hikers, and skiers."

"All of whom probably travel with their own stash of coca leaves." Kirsty holds out a few leaves in her hand to me, and I take them. "Best to chew them," she says as I look down at the leaves dubiously. Then, in a generous gesture for Kirsty, she offers them to Zol.

He turns his nose up at the leaves, predictably, and

takes two of the red pills instead. "Right, then," he says. "Let's get going, shall we? No point messing around in here while clearly someone is trying to prevent us from finding the abominable."

For once, I agree with Zol. I don't want to stay in this empty cabin, up this terrifying mountain, for any longer than I have to.

"What if it's Emilia?" I ask.

"Then I'd like to see that woman come after me," Zol says, puffing out his chest. "She should have remained in exile."

"Hey, look at this."

Zain kneels in the debris. There's a broken picture frame in his hand. He waves me over and passes the picture to me. I run my fingers gently over the image, carefully avoiding the broken glass. It's a photo of a young woman, her crimson lips the only splash of color in an otherwise black-and-white still. Her hair is tied in a bun at the nape of her neck, and she's wearing a military-style jacket with a high collar. While the expression in her round face is solemn, there's a twinkle in her eye that I recognize. I think.

"Cleopatra Maria Kemi," Zain says, looking down at a little gold plaque that has also been ripped from the wall. "Looks like she was here over a century ago—the first woman to conquer the mountain. Relative of yours?"

"My great-grandmother," I say in barely a whisper.

"Seriously?" He raises an eyebrow. "That's epic."

I swallow and nod. Pride grips my heart. This is what I've known all along. The Kemi legacy. Great-grandma Cleo was a pioneer. Maybe I can be a pioneer too. I want to take the picture with me, but she belongs here. I hang her back up on the wall, adjusting the frame until it sits perfectly straight.

We gather outside, and the wind has picked up considerably. Jedda points to a pass leading further up the mountain. "The last abominable to be seen was up that way. Do you want to start there?"

Kirsty and Zol nod. After a quick check of supplies, we begin the climb. Now I appreciate having the heavy boots. The climb is much steeper here than it was before, and I need the grip against the icy slopes.

Dotted up the mountainside, I can see the yawning black entrances of caves, home to the abominables. The cave system is so extensive that there could be an abominable looking down on us right now and we would never know.

Every now and again, Kirsty stops and looks through her binoculars. She gazes across the mountains in broad sweeps, focusing on the caves but also on the seemingly flat expanses of white snow. What might look like flat ground because of the sheer, shadowless white is actually steep mountainside.

I unwind the scarf from around my neck. Despite

the temperature, I'm warm from the exercise and being under the sun. Kirsty looks over at me, then passes me the binoculars.

"What am I looking for?" I ask.

"Tracks," she says. "Abominables themselves are pretty hard to spot. But look for deep tracks in the snow, and then for any rocks nearby. Rocks—bare, not-yet-covered-in-snow rocks—are going to be the only way for us to find any fur. Trees maybe, but we're moving pretty high beyond the treeline now, so any shrubs you see are gonna get more and more sparse."

I do a slow, steady panorama of the nearest mountainside, but can't see anything. I pass the binoculars back to Kirsty. "Never mind," she says. "Our luck would have to take a pretty sharp turn for us to find it straightaway. I'd expect at least one night on the mountain."

Zol scoffs loudly. "I'm not spending a night on this bloody mountain if I can help it."

"And I suppose you have some abominable tracking device—"

"Actually, I do," he says. "This is why you ordinary Finders are nothing more than unemployed hippies. Talenteds have ways of dealing with this—satellite imagery, heat detection, access to recent sightings—all accessible using our objects. I don't need to bother with scanning the entire mountain range with a pair of hardware-store binoculars."

I expect Kirsty to explode with rage, but she laughs. "You don't think there's a reason most Finders are ordinary, and if they're Talented then they don't use their magic? Don't think you can replace instincts, honed through experience, with synthetic ones, like you've done with potions and their ingredients."

Zol isn't listening. He's removed his ring from around his neck, and it glows gently in his palm. I dig into my pocket and find my phone. Predictably, there's no signal up here. I look over at his ring. If he is able to access his satellite imagery and whatnot via magic, that would help us out a lot. Speed up the process. So despite what Kirsty says, I pray that it works.

Something works. After a few of his whispered words, a map of the mountain range flashes up before us, lit in eerie green glowing light. Zain pipes up: "Look, there we are." He points to a flashing blue dot.

"All right, see? Now, I'll find out if there are any large animals around that could be abominables . . . it's not likely to be anything else, right?" He looks over at Jedda, who is staring wide-eyed at the map and slowly backing away. I wonder if he's ever seen magic like this before. But Kirsty is backing up too. She tilts her head urgently, signaling for me to move. I frown.

Suddenly there's a whoosh like air being sucked up by a vacuum, and I'm blinded by green light. I scream and drop to the ground. As my vision returns, I see Zol, his face soot-black. He's coughing and covering his eyes. The map is gone; his ring is smoking. I look down and see that I'm covered in the same black stuff that Zol is. Magic soot.

"My ring!" Zol's face is white with panic. "What am I to do without it? We have to turn back. We *must* turn back." He turns and walks in the other direction.

Kirsty laughs. She's untouched by the black residue. "Can't you survive without that object just for one day?"

"No," says Zol. "Not a single moment. I've . . . I've never been without it." He looks like a baby that's just lost its blanket. I forget how reliant Talenteds are on their objects.

"We can't go back now. It's the altitude," says Kirsty. "It messes with your magic. Especially in the Wilds. That's why most of us 'Finder hippies' are ordinary. I told you magic is unpredictable in these parts."

"Well, at least one good thing came out of this," Zain says, trying to calm his father. "At least we know where to find an abominable. I saw it before the map exploded. It's close. Just on the other side of that mountain pass."

Chapter Thirty-One

Samantha

I COULD HAVE THROWN MY ARMS AROUND Zain when he said he'd caught sight of the abominable. It is worth even having to clean my face in the freezing snow and hiking with the rest of my clothing covered in black dust. He's found an abominable! That means we can get out of here fast. And good thing too, because as the day progresses, it seems to be getting even colder.

I wrap my scarf more firmly around my neck, trying to contain my warm breath. The problem is that where the air escapes—around my nose and cheekbones—it freezes fast, creating crystals that scratch at my skin. It's still bright, but any warmth that the sun could provide is leeched by the wind.

I'm too cold even to think about Zain. Although when his voice rings out, I lift my head, and am rewarded with another blast of cold air. His words are worth it, though. "Tracks!" he says. "Really close."

Kirsty jogs up to him, and I catch up a few moments later. Ahead of us is a set of deep tracks. We can literally follow in an abominable's footsteps if we change our course.

Jedda does a few calculations, and spends several moments examining the snow. "We can proceed, but it must be with caution. These mountain paths are deceptively narrow, and the snow hides steep drops." Re-energized, our group follows in his footsteps.

A series of caves runs high above our heads, parallel to us. They're a long way up, but they creep me out. They look like dozens of black eyes dotted in the mountain.

While I'm distracted, Jedda cries out. He jumps back, but his leg is rooted to the ground, caught up in a gruesome-looking metal trap. Kirsty steps forward, but Jedda throws his arm out to stop her. She leaps back just as another trap springs up out of the ground. "What the hell?" she cries.

Then a figure rounds the corner of the path up ahead of us.

My stomach almost drops out of my body. It's Emilia Thoth. At her side is someone I assume must be the missing Sherpa, his eyes full of fear. And in her hand is a gun.

"Sam and Kirsty," she says, her voice steady as she points the weapon at us. "I thought I told you to stop hunting? And Zol, I'm surprised you've made it this far. I guess those researchers of yours must be doing a good job."

"Emilia, be reasonable . . . ," says Zol, his voice shaking. He clutches for his ring, but his hand freezes once he remembers.

"I reasonably warned you all to stop searching for this cure. Others—like your friends the Patels—were so much happier to oblige."

My heart screams. "What did you do to them?" I shout.

Emilia continues, ignoring my outburst. "But you disobeyed me, so now is my opportunity to be unreasonable. And how are you going to stop me? Magic doesn't work up here, but I shouldn't worry—I've trained in the ordinary arts as hard as the Talented."

"What are you going to do, shoot us all on the mountain?" I could almost kill Kirsty for how bold she sounds. Emilia looks deranged, her eyes flashing in the sun. She's not a woman to challenge.

"I've already dispatched one team on the mountain that way. How else do you think I found this nice Sherpa to show me the path so I could rig it with traps?" Her voice is ice cold. Colder than the mountain. "No one will save the princess except me. Nova has forgotten what true power is. It is time to remind them."

"Emilia . . . Ms. Thoth . . ." Zol has a simpering, begging tone in his voice.

"It's future Queen Emilia, actually."

"Queen Emilia . . . please, spare me and my son. We can be useful to you. My son is a strong Talent! And I have the power of ZoroAster Corp. to support your realm."

Emilia arches an eyebrow. "It would be a shame to kill such a fine Talented boy, even if he does stink of new magic. You're right, you could be useful. But you," she turns her laser-sharp gaze to me. "You're just ordinary scum getting in my way. Once, I might have respected your profession, studied it, even! But you have let your skills rot and you have outlasted your usefulness. So good-bye, Kemi."

I think of Arjun and Anita.

I think of Princess Evelyn.

I think of my family.

I think of my great-grandmother, the first woman to conquer this mountain. She wouldn't have given up. She wouldn't have backed down.

"No." Now I'm really in shock, because out of nowhere, I've found courage. Maybe the mountain air is making me loopy, but I take a step toward Emilia, ignoring the gun and the fear of the traps.

"Don't test me, Kemi!"

"Sam, no!" Kirsty shouts.

My heart fills with fear, but I keep walking, picking up into a run. My vision blurs and I can't see Emilia clearly, but I can sense her. I can sense her outstretched arm. Her gun pointed at my chest.

"You're done," she says. Her finger squeezes the trigger.

For a second, I don't notice the snow shift beneath my feet. My heavy boots lose purchase, my ankle twists, and underneath the path there isn't solid ground at all but air . . . air and a steep drop.

It all happens so fast. The crumbling ground forces Emilia back a few steps. Kirsty rushes at Emilia, tackling her to the ground. All the while, I continue to fall.

The gun goes off. The sound of it echoes off the face of the mountain. I seem to hear it again. *Bang. Bang.* Is it an echo? Or is Emilia shooting the rest of our group, one by one?

Zain shouts my name. At least, I think he does. He's alive. But his voice gets fainter and fainter as I tumble in the snow, down the slope. I try to throw my arms out to grab hold of something, anything, but nothing catches. I'm helpless against the fall and soon I can't tell up from down.

A large rock stops my progress, my back colliding against the hard stone. A jolt of pain shoots up my spine and I groan in agony. Gritting my teeth, I open my eyes to watch as Kirsty wrestles with Emilia; Kirsty's going to be overwhelmed. And Zain rushes down the slope toward me, half-sliding, half-scrambling. His father shouts above him.

Far more disturbing is the rumbling, which seems to be coming from deep within the mountain itself. But I know better, because facing back up the mountain, I can see the movement above their heads. It almost looks pretty, like the heavens descending on us, rapidly gaining speed.

Avalanche.

Jedda can sense it now, and he's screaming, his leg still clamped in the trap. Everyone can feel the ground shaking. The panic is clear on their faces. Emilia shoves Kirsty back, then disappears down the mountainside in the direction she came from—dragging the poor other Sherpa in tow. Kirsty helps Jedda with his leg, pulling the jaws of the trap apart so he can drag himself out. She starts toward me, but Jedda pulls her away, sideways across the mountain.

I am immobile in the face of the wave of snow.

Except Zain. Zain keeps coming. Zain reaches me.

"Are you—"

His words are lost in the roar. He yanks my arm, not concerned about my pain; only our mutual survival. Frankly, I'm okay with that. We stumble into a run, keeping as horizontal as we can.

The snow rushes over where the others had been standing.

The snow hits my rock. Engulfs it. We run until the snow pulls at our legs. I squeeze Zain's hand and the snow takes me. I immediately cover my mouth with my hand. Avalanche Survival 101.

With my other arm, I cling to Zain until the force of the snow drags us apart. Having my hand over my mouth creates a little air pocket, so when I finally stop moving, I am able to take a ragged breath. Then I start swimming. I front-crawl through the snow, trying desperately to make my way out. I thank the heavens for the blue sky, because if it had been gray out, I could have been swimming deeper, rather than swimming out.

Zain and I break the surface at the same time. His face is a mess. His sunglasses have cracked and broken against his nose, creating a deep scratch, which bleeds like crazy. But he's okay. Well, from the neck up. The rest of us is buried deep in snow.

I look around, trying to see any sign of the others. But the snow has carried us far away from where we were, and there's no sign of them anywhere.

We may be the only ones left alive.

Chapter Thirty-Two

Samantha

I'M GOING TO DIE ON A MOUNTAIN. THAT'S fact right about now. Pain throbs in the base of my spine and I don't know how much further I can go on. We manage to create a path through the snow out of the avalanche's wake, so we can walk on more solid ground. But the avalanche also turned around our sense of direction so completely we can't tell which way we came from.

I let out a groan, and it must sound more primal, more agony-filled than before, because Zain stops and turns around, concern etched on his face.

"You okay?"

"My back . . ."

He reaches over and lifts one of the straps of my pack, then gestures for me to twist my way out of the bag. "Let me take this for a while."

"But you've already got a pack . . ."

"Just for a while. Until we find somewhere to stop for the night."

He's right. Already purple and red streaks adorn the sky, signs that darkness is coming.

"What do you have in here?"

"My tent, sleeping bag, a few rations . . . and my potions supplies. Kirsty has most of the food. And all the other survival stuff—ropes, carabiners, cooking stove."

"You replaced your food with a potions-mixing kit?"

"I didn't think I'd be separated from Kirsty!"

"Typical alchemist," he says. I grimace, and he softens his tone. "Well, you have a tent, which is better than me." He frowns. "I don't even have my compass, because I thought I could pull up directions using my wand."

I shrug. "I don't have a compass either. Kirsty carries that. But don't feel too bad; the mountains can mess with magnetic stuff too. So it's not just Talenteds that have a problem."

"That makes me feel only marginally less dumb."

We keep trudging, hoping to find somewhere before dark where we can pitch our tent without fearing being blown off a cliff or taken by another avalanche.

"Look, over there!" Zain points at a flat ledge above us. "That looks like a pretty good spot."

I nod. I don't want to argue; I don't even want to

have any part in making the decisions. I only want to stop moving, be rescued, and go home.

Zain walks ahead of me. It's clear that we'll have to actually climb a small but sheer rock face to make it up to the ledge. With my back hurting the way it is, I don't know if I will make it.

Zain is full of confidence, though. He throws the packs up first, so I guess now we are forced to go up there, or be outside without our stuff. If I were feeling stronger, I'd punch him.

He manages to haul himself up using only a couple of holds. He looks down at me from the top. "We can spend the night up here. There's even . . . well, you'll see. Think you can make it?"

I look up at him and grit my teeth. I reach up the wall, my back screaming. I bring my knee up high to my chest, resting my foot on the flattest bit of rock I can find, trying to use the strength in my legs as much as possible.

"Grab my hand," Zain says.

My arms tremble, my fingers turn blue, my thighs burn. I swallow hard, and I focus on his hand. What choice do I have?

I launch myself up with an enormous push. He catches my wrist, and I catch his. At that moment, my feet slip from the freezing wall, but Zain has me. He lifts with all his strength, dragging me up and over the edge, and then we are lying there in the snow together. His arms wrap around me, and I sense his relief that I've made it up. We're in this together. "Thank god you're tall," he says with a laugh.

"Lots of reach," I reply.

Then I look up. Looming behind us is the mouth of an enormous cave.

"We're not going to sleep in there, are we?"

"It might be safest."

I shudder.

He pulls his arms tighter around me. "Yeah, I know; I'm freaked out too. Okay, pros and cons: If we go in the cave, it might be warmer and drier, but no one will be able to spot us if we're in there. So we'll set up the tent as close to the cave as possible, but not in it. Plan?"

"Plan."

We set up the tent. Well, Zain does most of it. I help slide the poles together, wishing we had one of those expensive tents that spring up at the pull of a ripcord. I want to do more, but my back won't let me. Instead, I sit by the cave and breathe until the pain passes, watching him. He looks like a bear in his huge coat, with its fur-lined trim. His legs are encased in snow trousers and his face is still streaked with dried blood. "Come here," I say. He walks over to me. I wipe his face with my mittened hand, until most of the blood is gone.

The cut could use a seaweed strip or at least a plaster, but we have nothing.

"Thanks," he says, and his face is so close to mine. He's still the most beautiful boy I've ever seen, despite it all. He goes back to setting up the tent.

My stomach rumbles. I struggle to my feet. It's not fair that I sit there while Zain does all the work. "I'm going to see if I find something to start a fire with . . . then maybe we can have something to eat." I gesture toward the cave.

He brushes some hair away from his face, tucking it under his beanie. "Fine, but don't go too far."

"I don't think I could. I'll stay within sight."

I wander into the cave. Immediately it's warmer, and my eyes have trouble adjusting to the dark after the brightness of outside.

Only a few steps in and the ceiling of the cave expands, growing tall. Rocks and debris scatter the ground, and— lo and behold—a few dead shrubs too. Enough to use for some kind of kindling. I collect them up.

There's a low, yawning sound from deep inside the cave, one that makes me drop my twigs. I stare into the darkness, my heart pounding. One beat, two beats. But there's nothing there. Nothing moves that I can see, and the sound doesn't come again. I snatch my twigs from the ground and rush to the entrance.

Zain is finished with the tent.

"I found a few twigs." I show him my pitiful supply. "Probably not enough to make a decent fire. I also heard something . . . in the cave."

Zain looks into the darkness of the cave's mouth. "It was likely the wind. Maybe come in the tent and we can get warm in there?"

I scramble into the tent and take off my boots in the little awning in the front. "I suppose we could just pee into bottles and sleep with them to get warm," I say.

"That's gross," Zain says, wrinkling his nose.

"It's better than your toes falling off."

Now that my boots are off, my feet feel free—lighter than air, almost. I continue my crawl to the back of the tent and curl up into my sleeping bag, bringing it up to my chin. Zain follows me in. Under the bright orange plastic of the tent, his skin glows. He pulls his own boots off and removes his coat. The skintight undershirt he's wearing hugs the muscles of his arms, and I can see the outline of his tattoos underneath.

Once he's in, the tent zipped up, his presence feels enormous. He stretches out, his head by the door of the tent, and even though I'm curled up as small as possible at the back, his feet end up close to mine. He must sense my toes curl away from his, but he doesn't move them away. In fact, he brings them toward mine, until our feet are touching in their respective covers. I try not to recoil again and let myself relax.

"Cozy, isn't it?" he says with a grin.

"They . . . they are going to find us, aren't they?" And then suddenly I can't help it. Tears are streaming down my face. I can't help thinking that we're out here, lost in the mountains, out in the Wilds, with no magic or ordinary communication devices. It's a long shot that we will ever be found. At least, it feels like it, in the dead of the night, in this tiny tent.

Immediately, Zain is with me. He wraps his arms around my shaking shoulders and hugs me tight into his chest. He holds me as I cry.

"In the morning, we'll get out of here," he says. "You will be back home in a couple of days. Safe and sound. You and I, we'll find a way back."

"Together?"

"Together." He finds my hand under the sleeping bag and laces his fingers through mine.

The wind outside picks up, buffeting the tent. One strong gust sends a tent pole down and one of our guy ropes is lifted from the ground and lashes against the tent. The noise is scarier than the event, and we both jump, which makes us laugh. I wipe my eyes. I've done enough crying on this mountain.

Zain passes me an energy bar. "It's not a juicy steak and mashed potato, but it will work."

"I'd do anything for Mum's shepherd's pie right about now."

"Don't think about it," he says.

I unwrap the energy bar, which is half-frozen and hard to chew. At least it will make the experience of eating last longer.

"Do you think Princess Evelyn knew it would come to this?" I regret asking the question almost immediately, as he shifts his body weight away from me.

"Do I think she knew it'd come to her crazed aunt threatening people with guns, and two people trapped on the side of a mountain?" He shakes his head. "No. But Evelyn wasn't exactly known for thinking about long-term consequences . . ." He pauses. "That's unfair. I think she was just desperate to find someone she trusted to share her power with."

"Well, with each ingredient I feel more and more impressed that she actually managed to create a real love potion."

"She's so smart, Sam. I think you would like her a lot."

I scoff. "If she's anything like you other Talenteds . . ." Then I wince. "Sorry, but you know what I mean."

"I do. And she's not. But then, she probably would be weird with you as she's likely never met an ordinary person in her life. Oh, maybe shook one's hand at a party or something, but never actually spent any time with one. They keep her so sheltered. Imagine if you've never been wrong in your whole life. How would you deal with it when things did start to fall apart?"

I nod, but I don't feel like I understand, not really. "You sound like a good friend, though."

He laughs, and it sounds hollow. "She did try to potion me, so not sure what that makes us." He looks at me. "You're going to fix her, aren't you? Find the love potion? ZA could find the ingredients, but finding the right mix, getting the potion right . . . you have the best chance at that."

"Yeah sure—with your researchers and big fancy labs . . ."

"It takes more than that to be a good alchemist, and you know it." He stares at my eyes, looking from one pupil to the other. "I've never known anyone who's been able to mix potions as well as you."

"Well, what good does it do me when everyone uses synths now anyway?"

"Come and work for ZA. We need people like you there."

"And betray the Kemi legacy and disappoint my grandfather? I don't think so. I know my place, and it's in our store. Nowhere else. That might be hard for you to understand—"

"I know more about disappointing people than you think."

I roll my eyes. "Whatever."

"You don't think I'm the biggest disappointment to my father? I turned down the princess. I turned down the chance to be royal. I never told him that she'd asked me, but he suspected. Now he knows for sure.

"And now I have to save her. Because I'm the one that put her life in danger—heck, I put the whole country in danger, if the succession goes to Emilia Thoth!" He sighs. "Even if that means admitting ZA can't create the potion and making sure you do."

"Why don't you think ZA can do it? You've got all the money and the Talent and your dad is some great mixer and you're his apprentice and you're top in your class in everything, studying at the best university . . ."

He looks up at me from beneath his dark brown eyebrows. He takes his hand away from mine, and I instantly feel colder. I wish I was brave enough to reach out and take it back. "Because while the researchers can help us find the ingredients, my father and I have to be the ones to make the mix. And both my father and I are frauds."

I gasp, but the dam holding back Zain's thoughts has burst now and he doesn't stop. "My father's no great mixer. My grandfather was the one with the brains, the big ideas, but he had too little Talent to be of note and too much Talent to be a great alchemist. He had this idea that ingredients could be made synthetic-ally, so that it didn't matter if you were Talented or ordinary—you could still learn to mix. He wanted to level the playing field."

"He didn't level the playing field—he destroyed it and flipped it in the whole other direction," I interrupt, unable to keep the bitterness from my voice.

"But that's just it—he didn't do it. Have you ever heard the story of how our company was founded?"

"What, about how your grandfather, the great Zoro Aster, cheated his way to winning the hunt and used the prize power to set up the company? Yeah, I've heard it."

Zain has the good graces to blush, at least. "I've been wanting to talk to you, to tell you the real story for so long. But even when we went to school together, there never seemed to be a good moment. You always avoided me whenever I was around."

"Yes, but—"

"I get it, I'm the enemy. But I don't have to be. And I don't think I am. Because a few years ago, on my grandfather's deathbed, he told the real story—that he and your great-grandmother worked together on the last Wilde Hunt. There was one ingredient no one could find to save Queen Valeri II—a centaur's eye. When it looked like they wouldn't be able to develop the cure naturally, Zoro told Cleo about his idea for synthetic ingredients. And she came up with the synth version of the eye."

"No." I shake my head, his words hardly computing. "What?"

"You're lying. Granddad told me that Cleo created the potion, but Zoro stole it and passed it off as his own. He told everyone he'd used his new-fangled synth ingredients in making the potion. That's how he won. He cheated."

Zain's blush turns into the bright red of shame. "My grandfather did a lot of things wrong, but he wasn't a thief. Your great-grandmother didn't want to use the synth version of the potion, so Zoro submitted it. And the horn turned gold. He used his winnings to set up ZoroAster Corp., and he felt threatened by your family, so he cut the Kemis out. That was wrong. But I'm saying this because I know there's no way my grandfather created that first potion on his own. They worked together—and I can prove it to you. He said your great-grandmother's diary had a lock embedded with an amber stone. It was very unusual and caught his eye. How would I know that if my granddad hadn't worked with her?"

"Her diary is lost! You could have made up anything."

"I'm not making it up, Sam. Please, I need you to believe me. There's no way my father and I are going to produce the right potion. But I can help you get there."

"So you can steal it from me? I think all this mountain air has gone to your head. I'd leave, but there's nowhere else for me to go."

"No, but I have money, resources . . ."

"But your dad . . ."

"Screw my dad! This is bigger than petty rivalries. We don't have to be our parents, our grandparents. This is about saving Evie's life."

"I have to get out of here," I say. I don't know what I'm doing, but before I know it my boots are back on, I throw my jacket over my thermals and jump out of the tent. I walk a few steps away, knowing I'm trapped on the ledge but needing a breather.

"What are you doing? Are you crazy?" shouts Zain.

Outside, I take deep gulps of the freezing mountain air. I look up and stare at the sky. I've only had a few moments, when Zain appears beside me. "You're shivering," he says. "Come back inside."

But I'm not shivering, I'm stupefied. Out here, the night sky is as clear as I've ever seen it, and it's so full of stars—I never imagined the universe to be so crowded. And so colorful. There are pinks and greens mixed with the bright points of light. A shooting star wends its way across the sky, thrilling me. "I dreamed of seeing a sky like this," I say. I think back to the stickers on my bedroom ceiling. "I never thought I would."

"I think there's a lot you'll achieve, if you put your mind to it," replies Zain.

I am cold now, and I let him lead me back inside the tent. My heart is screaming *lies, lies, lies* at Zain's words. My head is asking, Why would he lie? Why does my grandfather hate synths, with a passion that borders on manic? Why does he hate the Wilde Hunts? He always says that the alchemists belong in the lab. But my great-grandmother conquered this mountain. She was an adventurer. I look at Zain and try to talk, but my voice only comes out as a whisper. "I still don't know why I should trust you."

"Because I'm telling you the truth. This is the real me. I'll prove it to you." He takes his wand out, turns it so that it faces him, and whispers a spell too quietly for me to hear.

"What are you doing?" I'm angry at him, so angry I want to storm off the mountainside, but I don't want him to hurt himself by casting a spell, especially after what happened with his father's ring. But what happens surprises me so much, I forget about my worries.

The glamours slowly slip from him, so skillfully applied I'd always thought he shunned that touch of vanity—apart from his tattoos. His jet-black hair—his signature—pales to a caramel brown, the light from the oil lamp giving it an almost golden sheen. The tattoos fade too, disappearing, and even his eyebrows shift slightly, losing their manicured edge and instead becoming something wilder, less tamed. He smiles at my wide-eyed stare, and I see that even his teeth have lost their perfect lines—one tooth now overlaps another, ever so slightly. But his eyes don't change. They're the same dazzling blue they've always been.

What can I say? He's still beautiful.

His smiles wavers a touch, and I realize how nervous he is.

"I don't want to work against you, Sam."

I don't let him say much more, because before I think myself out of it, I lean forward and kiss him. Then I pull away, and he smiles.

I can't look at him, but the sound of the wind outside is replaced by the beating of my heart, and the beating of his heart, which seems exponentially louder.

His fingers trace the contour of my neck, until they reach the base of my ear and embed themselves in my hair. He pulls me toward him and his kiss takes on a deeper urgency.

But then his nose brushes my cheek, and it's an icy shock. The temperature has dropped considerably. When we pull away from the kiss, I can see his breath, warming the air between us.

I can't help it; I have to laugh.

"What's so funny?"

"Oh, I don't know . . . My first time kissing Zain Aster"—he grimaces as I fake-swoon over his name— "and we're stranded halfway up a mountain with the threat of imminent death hanging over our heads. Not quite how I imagined it."

"Hmm, I suppose I did think I would need to take you for dinner and a movie first."

"Well, if we ever get down from here, then you owe me."

He smiles, showing off his slightly crooked teeth. "Definitely."

Chapter Thirty-Three

Samantha

WE SPEND THE REST OF THE NIGHT shivering, huddled into each other, but only for warmth. Survival trumps romance. I know today is going to be another long day of hiking through the snow and my body is already protesting. By first light I want to get it over with. I can't stay cooped up in the tent any longer.

My stirring wakes Zain. He looks over at me, and my eyes widen. It's still strange seeing him without his glamours, and in the orange light of the tent it looks even stranger. He half-smiles and grabs his beanie, pulling it down over his hair self-consciously.

"Okay," he says, rubbing the sleep from his eyes. "Let's pack up quickly and then I'll use one magic spell to try to find the way home. I think it's worth ruining a wand for that."

I'm already stuffing my sleeping bag into its sack,

and then burying it deep in my backpack. We debate abandoning the tent; the loose guy rope ripped the outer sheet as it whipped around so ferociously in the wind. But there's the unspoken reality that we might need it again—another night on the mountain.

I lace up my boots and exit the tent. The view stops me in my tracks. All around me, as far as the eye can see, the sun is rising over the magnificent peaks of the mountain range, casting pink, orange and yellow light on the snow. And in the furthest distance, I can see the tallest mountain in the world: Mount Oberon, dominating the skyline even here, in a skyline of giants. It's rough, craggy, a jagged beauty.

Zain is packing up the tent behind me. "Sam, did you check through this cave yesterday?"

"Well, not exactly . . . ," I say, not taking my eyes off the view. I want to drink it all in, as it might be the last chance I get.

"Maybe there's some abominable fur in there."

I shiver, despite myself. "If you want to check, go ahead."

He comes over and puts both hands on my shoulders. I look up at him. "I will be no more than five minutes, okay? A quick check, just so that this doesn't become a complete waste of search-and-rescue, and then we'll start heading for home. No more detours. Deal?"

"Deal."

Even now, looking at the cave entrance, I have to turn my back on it. I remember the yawning noise I heard yesterday, and it unsettles me. What if it was more than just the wind?

I prepare both of our backpacks, so that we can put them on and move the second Zain's ready. I feel a little dizzy, light-headed. It's most likely my body reacting to the altitude. I open the flap at the base of my backpack and pull out the squished red bag of potion supplies from the bottom. I need to chew a couple of coca leaves, as Kirsty suggested.

I'm about to put the red bag back when a movement from the side of the ledge captures my attention. It's the snow. It's crumbling over the edge.

"Zain?" I say over my shoulder. My first thought is that the ledge is disintegrating. But then something happens to change my mind. The reality is even more terrifying. "Zain?!" I hiss louder.

"Sam? What is it?" I hear his footsteps echoing in the cave, pounding toward me.

But it's going to be too late.

Because now I can really see what's happening. An enormous hand—gnarled black fingers topped with long, razor-sharp nails—is creeping its way across the ledge. The fingers bury themselves into the snow, finding purchase.

Zain skids to a halt beside me. "What is it?"

I don't answer, because as soon as he finishes

speaking, he sees it too. He throws his arm in front of me, and we both take several steps backward. I don't know how he thinks that arm is going to help. If what's coming up in front of us is what I think it is, then we're dead already.

Zain takes out his wand from where he holsters it, just underneath his arm. I hope he's smart enough to remember he's probably only got one shot in that thing, and then it's spent. If he messes it up . . . did I mention already that it's all over?

Another arm appears, and it is so long it appears almost double-jointed, twisted at unnatural angles. The snow clings to its fur, coating it like a jacket.

Then the head appears. No—not the head, a hump, a great length of shoulder that towers up above the body. Its eyes, when they do appear, are dark, small and round like marbles. The abominable sees us, and for a moment it looks as if it's about to run away and leave us be.

Zain thinks the lump is the head. He thrusts his wand at the abominable, and before I can scream at him to stop, he's blasted. The creature cries out in pain, but it doesn't come out like a normal scream. It's a screech as loud as a banshee, and I throw my hands over my ears.

The normally solitary abominable is a creature that would run from mankind if it had the choice—but now Zain's just made it angry. He runs to the edge, but as we feared—it's too far to jump without breaking our legs or our necks or both.

The abominable's already clambering onto our ledge. Its face is completely black and the hump smoulders where Zain hit it. It's twice the size of Zain. Zain tries—in vain—to use his wand again, but his wand smokes, combusting from the inside. There's no performing magic with that again.

I grab his hand. "Come on!" There's only one place that we can go. Back—back into the cave. Find somewhere to hide from it, wait until it gets bored, figure out some kind of plan.

We run into the cave. The abominable stops by our backpacks—maybe it thinks they are also a threat, just lying there like other humans—and takes them up in its great hands, ripping them apart and shredding them with its fingernails. It tears into our tent, sending strips of orange plastic into the air. It then dives in with its teeth, but that's when I know we've lost our small advantage. Nothing in those packs is going to taste nice. It tosses them off the side.

"This way." Zain pulls my arm. He's chosen a path where the tunnel twists through a narrow channel. The abominable has spotted us, though. It comes toward us at a canter, and the entire cave shakes with its movement. Stalactites shake from their posts and fall on the monster, shattering off its back. No wonder Zain's spell had no effect. Its hide must be extremely tough, if ancient stalactites that would easily have killed us can barely make an impact.

In the seconds it takes for the creature to reach the entrance of the narrow tunnel, we already know that it's a dead end. We slam up against sheer rock, and I spin around. If I'm going to meet my end, I'm going to do it bravely.

Zain scrambles against the wall, trying to find something, anything that might help us break through or fight back. But there's nothing.

The only blessing is that the abominable can't get through to us. It thrusts its arm down the narrow tunnel, the claws, those nails, coming so insanely close that I scream and scream and scream. Zain grabs me, pinning me to the rock as closely as possible, even as the abominable screeches its frustration. Eventually those claws retreat, and maybe it realizes we have no place to go, because it sits down right outside the entrance of our tunnel. I grab a pebble from the floor and mark a line in our little alcove. That's how far the abominable's claws will go. We don't pass that line. Zain looks at me and nods.

Then he holds his head in his hands. "Wh-what do we do?" he stutters. "Oh god, we're never getting out of here. We're going to die here."

He's right. We could die here. It's scary seeing him

break down like this. I would be acting the same, if I didn't have a plan.

In his panic, Zain throws down his smoking wand, and it crosses our line. The abominable jams its arm back down the tunnel, trying to reach the evil piece of wood that hurt it earlier. But I need that wand. I jump down and grab at it too.

The abominable's nails rake my hand. I cry out in anguish. Zain pulls me back. "What are you doing?" he yells.

I clutch my hand to my chest. Blood gushes from the wounds, and I can't look at it or else I might pass out. Zain takes his scarf and wraps it tightly around my hand. The muscles in my arm are trembling. I keep it tight against my body.

"What did you do that for?" he hisses.

"I have a plan, but it needs your wand."

"Well, you could have said something . . ."

"I didn't have time! If you could just keep your head!" Tears blind my eyes. My hand stings like crazy. I'm lucky that abominables don't have poisonous claws. At least, I think they don't.

"I'm sorry." He hugs my shoulders, careful not to press on my hand. "Right, a plan? That's more than I've got. Can I help?"

"I think you're going to have to now. The only thing I was holding onto when the creature attacked is this."

I point to the bag of ingredients that I dropped on the ground. "I think I have something in there that might help us."

Zain picks up the red bag. He opens up the drawstring and peers inside. "Oh god, Sam, I could kiss you."

"Let's not start that again. The plan hasn't worked yet. And honestly, I'm not sure that it will at this distance. At least . . . not with the abominable so awake. We might have to wait for a bit."

Zain shrugs. "I don't think we're going anywhere."

"True."

"What do you need the wand for?"

"It's burning. Look at it." The wand still glows red. Still smokes. I blow on it, and its embers glow. It's slightly magical fire, of course.

We settle down at the back of the cave, waiting for the abominable to show any signs of tiring. After an hour, the abominable has finally calmed down, and stopped clawing the edges of the tunnel. But its beady black eyes still stare at us with a glint of anger. It's in this for the long haul.

"Okay," I say. "Shake out some of the petals from the bag, and put them around the wand." It's the mountain sweet I collected earlier. A heavy sedative—which only affects abominables. Nature often keeps its remedies close by. I'm just lucky my instincts struck me on the journey up here.

The petals need to smoke, or else it won't work. But they won't stay on top of the wand.

"The drawstring," I say. Zain nods, and unthreads the drawstring from the bag. Then he ties the petals to the wand. Immediately the smoke, which had been black, turns a light blue color. It's working. I stand behind the smoky concoction, which we place right by the line. Then I start waving it down the tunnel.

The abominable shuts one of its eyes. It might be because of my concoction, we just can't tell. "We're going to have to get closer to it."

"But . . . is it working?"

"I don't know. If we're lucky, it's getting sleepy already. But we don't have much mountain sweet petal left."

He takes my hand, my good hand. "I'm going ahead of you, okay? This is my wand. My choice."

"It's my idea, though!"

"And you've already been hurt for it. But you promise me something. If anything happens, and I mean anything, you run for it. You run as fast as you can, and don't look back."

"We're doing this together. I won't leave you."

"Don't be stubborn!"

"I'm not being stubborn. I'm just saying. We're both going to get out of this, or neither of us are. This works, or it doesn't."

He studies my eyes, but he's not going to see any hint of weakness.

Finally, he capitulates. He doesn't have much choice. "Ready?"

"Ready."

We step over the line together. Then we both stop, our breath caught in our throats. I don't even think my heart is beating. The abominable doesn't move. Maybe some of the sedating smoke did reach it.

We take another step. Zain tries to pull ahead of me despite our agreement, but I catch up with him. We stand shoulder to shoulder, and take another step. Still no movement. Another step. Zain pushes in front as the tunnel narrows. Then there is movement. The abominable grunts, shifts its position. Zain holds the wand, with the petals still smoking at the end of it, the blue smoke drifting toward the creature. It tries to get up, but we keep moving forward. The smoke gets stronger. I can see the abominable groaning, struggling, its eyes rolling listlessly in its head. This is going to work.

The smoke embroils itself around the monster, drawn to it, attracted to it, settling on the creature's fur, on its eyes. It's managed to stand—it's strong, this one—but as it tries to step forward it slumps down, suddenly drowsy. We're almost in the cave proper. The abominable falls over, so that it's lying on the ground. It opens one eye at me with an effort.

Zain starts running toward the cave entrance,

toward the light, toward freedom and the exit.

For a second, I don't come with him. I stare at the abominable, and it stares back. Zain yells my name.

The smoke starts to disperse. But I can't have come all this way for nothing. I simply can't. I lunge for the abominable, but it has just enough strength to attempt to swat me away. I jump back.

"Run, Sam!" says Zain, and I turn reluctantly from the beast. Then I spot a clump of fur pinned to the ground by a fallen stalactite. I manage to grab a handful, wrenching it from beneath the rock.

Now I run.

I don't look over my shoulder. I can sense the abominable lumbering to its feet, stumbling into the cave wall and causing other spears of stone to fall from the ceiling. I dodge around the falling debris, sheer adrenaline keeping me going. I can see Zain is yelling at me from the cave entrance, silhouetted by the bright light of the outside, but all of a sudden I can't hear him. The beanie on his head is lifted up by a strong wind, and whips away. Then, from behind him rises an enormous helicopter, blades thumping in the cold mountain air.

Zain grabs the railing running down the side of the door and jumps up onto the first step, his other arm reaching back to me. I run to his open hand, and he pulls me up.

I'm inside the chopper, a seat belt being strapped

around me. Back on the ledge, the abominable is nowhere to be seen. It won't come near this terrifying flying beast. But as we pull away from the mountain, back toward safety, and home, I swear that I hear a mournful cry, almost human, from the depths of the cave.

Chapter Thirty-Four

Samantha

"IF THEY WEREN'T READY TO BEFORE, YOUR parents are going to absolutely murder me," says Kirsty. "I swear, being a Finder isn't normally this exciting."

"Oh really? I'm disappointed," I reply with a small half-smile. We're back in Pahara, in a small but cozy hotel. Kirsty filled me in on how she, Jedda, and Zol struggled to get back down to base camp, and how Emilia escaped yet again, back down the other side of the mountain with her Sherpa. The others didn't want to leave the mountain but knew they couldn't find us on their own. Jedda's leg needed urgent medical care, but he was now recovering. I don't know what Zol must have paid to get a helicopter up to us. He probably could have bought the mountain with that amount of money.

It was Zain's attack on the abominable—his useless attempt to use the wand—that helped us in the end. The spell worked like a flare. That, and the abominable scattering pieces of our orange tent to the wind. Of course, when Kirsty spotted the first sign of a ripped-up tent, her mind jumped to the worst conclusion. In her head, we were as shredded as that tent. Luckily, though, for his sins, Zol refused to believe that his son wouldn't make it down from the mountain alive.

As for my parents—they were beside themselves, but there was no point in them coming out to Bharat when I was going to be on the next flight home. (After my near-death ordeal, they weren't going to let me port anywhere—and there was no way I'd have the concentration anyway.) Other people did make the journey—namely, the media. There was no hiding from them this time, no reflective material to ward them off. Cameras flashed in Zain's and my faces as we descended from the helicopter, and we rushed into the hotel to sounds of their shouting:

"Zain! Zain! How close are you to curing the princess?"

"Sam, what does your family think of you allying with ZA Corp.?"

"Are you together now?"

We're not allies, I don't think Zain and I are together, but thanks to me, we both have the ingredient.

Yes, I shared the fur. Of course I shared. Even though my pride won't let me entertain Zain's idea of working with him toward a cure, I wasn't going to thwart his attempts. Someone has to win the hunt—and we can't let it be Emilia Thoth.

Admittedly, that's not the reaction I get when I speak to Dan and Kirsty that night.

"You gave ZA half the abominable fur?" says Dan. His voice is laced with scepticism. He's taking notes for his big piece, but I don't care how I come across.

"Of course I did. Zain helped save my life. Twice, in fact—once from Emilia, once in the cave."

"It sounds to me more like you saved his life," says Kirsty, her arms folded across her chest.

She's right about that. All Zain can go on about is how I saved him on the mountain with my impromptu mix of mountain sweet and wand fire. To the press, to his parents, to everyone, Zain's been insisting that I'm the hero.

I can't get his story out of my brain. Hearing it has filled in pieces of a puzzle I hadn't realized was incomplete. Great-grandma Cleo's missing diary. Granddad's outright refusal to entertain even the idea of synths. His virulent hatred of the Wilde Hunts.

But without Cleo's diary, I fear I'll never know the truth.

I always thought that the Kemi legacy was to be stuck in the past, rooted to our ways. Bound to our traditions like eluvian ivy around our hearts. But what if that wasn't true? What if being a Kemi meant being known for progress, for innovation? I think back to that picture on the wall of the Mount Hallah base camp. My great-grandmother made it all the way up that mountain over a hundred years ago, without all our modern supplies and gear. She was an adventurer, a hero.

"Well, it doesn't matter now. I gave it to him, so it's done," I say.

"Of course it does," says Dan. "Especially now that only you and the Zs are the only real Participants left in the competition."

My face drains of color. "There's really no one else? What happened to Arjun and Anita?" I ask, dreading the answer.

"The reports say everyone is fine."

I breathe a sigh of relief.

"It was a close call," continues Dan. "A spell was delivered by courier to their lab. Luckily, Mr. Patel had been called away and wasn't caught in the explosion."

I drop my head in my hands. "That's awful. Wait, please, I have to call Anita."

I dial her number but she doesn't pick up, and neither does Arjun. I email, Connect, text, and basically bombard them with messages, to no avail. I don't blame them. I can't imagine what they must be going through.

I just thank my lucky stars they're safe and unharmed.

"I hate Emilia," I say when I look up from my devices. My whole body is shaking with rage. "We have to stop her."

"No one has caught her in the act yet," says Dan. "I've heard that some people are even starting to take her side. Saying that we are all scapegoating Emilia because of her past and that she deserves another chance . . ."

"After what she did to us on the mountain? She almost killed us!"

"But no one saw it."

"Of course they didn't, we've been hiding from the media, remember!"

"Hey, don't shoot the messenger."

Kirsty nudges Dan. "That's enough for tonight. Sam, you should hit the sack. You'll be back home tomorrow, and then we can tackle the next ingredient."

The next ingredient. Now the pressure is on.

I ready myself for bed, taking extra care over everything that has previously seemed routine—brushing my teeth, for example, and putting on my favorite polka-dot pajamas.

Every moment feels like a luxury, but especially climbing into a proper bed and snuggling under a duvet. I make a resolution for tomorrow. The second thing I'm going to do when I get home (after the first: give my entire family big hugs) is go over to the Patels' house and apologize. Profusely. Grovel, if I have to.

Despite my tiredness, I can't shut my mind off. I pick up my diary, thinking of Granddad. I think he would be proud of my trick with the mountain sweet. I scribble down a few notes on a separate page:

Abominables. Characteristics: lonely, stubborn, reclusive, slow to anger—but long to hold grudges. Deep sleep can be triggered by fumes from mountain sweet. Abominable hair (coarse, brittle, 10 cm long) can be used in love potions.

Once I finally flick off the bedside light, there's a gentle tap at my door. I wonder if Kirsty has forgotten something. I turn the light back on again and walk over to the door.

It's Zain.

"Hey," he says. His glamours—the normal ones—are back on. I feel a tinge of disappointment, and it makes me even more self-conscious in my pj's.

"Hey," is all I can manage back.

"Can I . . . ?"

"Oh, sure, yeah." I shuffle backward, bumping into the furniture. We perch awkwardly on the end of my bed.

"How are you doing?"

"Better now. I still . . ." I close my eyes, just for a moment, but behind them is the abominable and its claws. The scratch marks are almost healed now, magicked away with a potion they have here. I made a mental note of the ingredients, of course. Witch hazel— for scarring. Millefolium—for blood clotting. But the memory is still there. I shudder, despite myself.

"You were amazing yesterday. Honestly—I thought I was going to have a complete freak-out when we got to that dead end . . . but you kept your head."

"Your smoking wand gave me the idea."

Zain turns red with shame. "I keep thinking about what my dad said on the mountain. It was awful."

I put my hand on his. "Your father said whatever he thought he needed to say to save your life. He was just trying to protect you. He was desperate."

"It was pathetic."

"You know what? I don't blame him. It's less stupid than walking up to someone with a gun."

A smile tugs at his lips. "Yeah, I guess so."

"Lucky I picked that mountain sweet when I did."

"Well, you saved my life." He holds my hand tighter. "Seriously, you are one amazing girl."

"Stop it," I say.

He lets go and looks a little hurt. "Sam, I mean it . . ."

"No, I heard what you said yesterday. You don't like me. You like this idea of me. You've been waiting for the right moment to talk to me because you think that since I belong to this ancient family, I'm somehow special. Let me break it to you, Zain: I'm not special. Evelyn is special. She's a princess. I'm just me. So either I need you to like me for me, or you need to leave me alone."

"It is you I like, Sam."

"You don't even know me," I throw back.

"Okay, fine. You're right. My grandfather was obsessed with you Kemis and it made me want to meet you. He thought you had some kind of mystical powers, some source of alchemical knowledge. But now I know the truth. You're just smart, Sam. So smart.

"That's why I like you. And I want to get to know you, if you'll let me."

I stare down at the pattern on the duvet, unable to look up at him. He's said everything I want to hear, and I can't help my treacherous heart from swelling. He reaches out and touches my cheek.

"And plus, you saved my life."

I look up at him, and he winks. I laugh; I can't help myself.

"We saved each other," I say.

"Exactly. You're the only person in the whole world who knows what we've been through. Really knows." He takes his hand away, and my face burns from where he touched it.

"It was kind of a crazy first date," I say.

"A story to tell the grandkids." He grins and looks awkward. "I've got to transport back to Nova in a couple of hours. My father—"

I don't want to hear this, but even before I can let it sink in, there's a big bang as the shutters of my hotel window are thrown against the glass by the wind. It makes us both jump. Ordinarily I would have laughed, but I'm too tense after the abominable.

"Can you stay with me till I fall asleep?" I ask, hating

how small my voice sounds. But he's the only person in the world I want to be with right now.

"Of course."

I head back into bed, resting my head on Zain's chest, listening to his heartbeat pound beneath my ear. I close my eyes and drift into a deep sleep.

When I wake up, there's a cup of coffee on the side table that he's enchanted to keep warm. I mutter something about Talented flirting techniques, but I have to admit: His tactics are pretty good. As I sip the coffee, warmth spreads from my mouth down to my toes. I catch sight of something on the cup—words, glamoured to appear just underneath the coffee line:

You are special to me, Samantha Kemi.

Chapter Thirty-Five

Princess Evelyn

"WHAT'S HAPPENING . . . WHERE AM I?" She opened her eyes, a sweet dream of Lyn fluttering away. There was someone in the room with her. But it was not Lyn, as her heart so desperately wished—it was another. Zain.

His face was etched with concern, deep frown lines criss-crossing his forehead. He had a scar between his eyes she couldn't remember seeing before. *It doesn't suit him*, she thought, and she chuckled to herself. "Tell me how you did it, Evie," he whispered. "Please . . ."

He looked strange, too. And then she realized it was because he had a weird tan around his eyes. Had he gone on a ski trip without her? How unfair. Then she thought of Lyn. Maybe Lyn didn't like skiing. That would explain why she hadn't gone too. "I don't know what you're talking about," she said.

Zain walked over and placed his hand on her head.

She shook it off. He looked at her, his eyes wide. "How are you? I heard about the incident with the mirrors . . ."

"I was just sleeping," she began, but as she said it, something about the statement immediately struck her as false. "Oh God . . . oh God, Zain, I am so sorry!"

"Shh, shh," he said. "It's okay."

"Okay? No it's not! I tried to give you a love potion! Wait . . . you're not here because you love me now, right?" Suddenly her stomach filled with dread. What if that was the reason Lyn wasn't here?

"No, no," Zain reassured her. "The love potion . . . didn't affect me."

"Well then, I know someone you just have to meet. She's the love of my life, Zain. She's amazing. Lyn? Where are you, Lyn?" Her voice got higher as she gazed round the bare room. There were dark squares in the wallpaper, where something had once hung, although Eve couldn't remember what.

"Calm down." Zain kept his voice soft but she could hear its urgency and sensed movement beyond the walls, someone ready to come in. "I need to know what the ingredients of your potion are. Please, Evie . . ."

"Don't call me that!" she screamed. "Only Lyn can call me that! What have you done to her? Where is she? She should be in here with me!" Her skin crackled, and that's when she realized that her wrists were shackled to the bed. "Did you do this?" she said to Zain, who backed away, shaking his head furiously. "You did, didn't you? To keep us apart? How dare you!"

"No, no, Evie . . . Evelyn—you know I would never do that. I'm trying to help you."

"Help? I don't need any help!"

The shackles disintegrated as if they were nothing. Her parents, Renel, Zain—they thought they could contain her, but nothing could. Not when they were standing in the way of her true love.

"She's breaking loose!" Zain was shouting. The room was shaking. Someone slammed through the walls— Renel—and now he was shouting too.

"I told you this wouldn't work!" he thundered.

But she didn't care. She was floating now, floating high above the bed. She could feel the magic in the atmosphere, and she brought it toward her, sending sparks of it out like lightning bolts into the walls. She was going to find Lyn, wherever she was. She would break apart the palace to find her, if that's what it took.

The brick crumbled, and the beautiful tile mosaic that had been on the ceiling rained down on Zain's head— but he had stood in the way of her and her love, so she didn't care what happened to him.

She pushed her magic out even further. She felt Renel, felt her mother, felt her father, felt her grandmother's magic pushing back against her, but she could be stronger than all of them—didn't they realize that?

She was so hurt that they would do this to her. It was their fault. All they needed to do was reunite her with Lyn, and then she would be happy again.

There was another deep crack, as if an earthquake was beneath the room, but how could that be, since the palace wasn't on the ground?

Lyn, Lyn, I will find you. Wait for me. Wait for me.

She felt a tap on her foot, so gentle she could have imagined it. She looked down, and saw that somehow Zain had managed to crawl toward her. Renel was screaming at Zain, something that sounded like "Stop!"

Yes, you should stop, Zain. We might have been friends once, but that won't stop me if you get in my way.

Then she saw what he had in his hands. It was his watch. Or rather, it was the reverse side of his watch, which was mirrored. And in it, she caught a tiny glimpse of Lyn.

Immediately she felt her power, her magic, concentrated on that one tiny spot. Lyn, the one I love. She came back down to earth. Then there was a stab of pain in her neck, and she collapsed into Zain's arms.

"Is she out?" asked Renel.

She wanted to scream "No!" but her lips, her vocal chords, wouldn't respond. Whatever they'd done to her, she couldn't move or speak.

"I think so," said Zain. He placed her gently on her bed, stroked her hair. She wished he would get away from her. She wanted no touch but Lyn's.

There was an oscillation of power in the air, and her parents strode through the walls and into the room. "What happened?" asked the king. "The ceiling of our throne room almost collapsed on my head. The chandelier almost killed the queen."

Good, she thought. *Serves you right for sedating your own daughter.*

"It's the princess, sire. The potion is breaking down her mind; she's losing control of her magic. We've given her a stronger sedative, but it won't hold her forever."

The king turned on Zain. "How close is your father to finishing the potion?"

"I . . . I don't know, Your Highness."

"Well, work faster!"

Ah, so that was their plan. They wanted to hurt her by taking away the one person she had only ever truly loved.

Renel spoke next, his tone tentative. "Sire, the physicians are saying we might only have a few days before she goes past the point of no return. The government is asking us to take her to an underground bunker they've prepared. If the magic floods her system completely . . ."

"We can't think about that. But she can't be moved far from the horn. When the right potion is found, we will need to administer it immediately."

She wondered if the sedative had reached her heart

then, because it appeared to stop for a moment. Was her love for Lyn really causing so much harm? Her whole life, her parents had encouraged her to marry. Now that she had chosen, they wanted to punish her for it. It was just as her aunt had said.

"As you say, sir. They might start evacuating some of the city. You will be putting lives in danger."

"That is what this blasted Wilde Hunt is for! Someone will find a cure."

"And if it's your sister?"

"If Emilia wins—then magic save us all."

Her aunt was in on this? Emilia was the only person on the planet who knew what it was like to have her life ruined by the royal family of Nova. And now she was working to keep Eve from Lyn? It didn't make sense.

"You should have got rid of that woman when you had the chance!" said the queen.

Of course you'd want that, you cold and vicious woman. All you care about is your position in life. I didn't even know I had an aunt. Not until her letters came. How she got them into the palace, I still don't know. But I relished every word. She understood the pressures I was under.

No one else even tried to understand.

"We can't destroy a Novaen heir."

"Then you should have locked her up in a dungeon from which she could never escape instead of letting her gallivant off—"

Her aunt had inspired her. Inspired her to take her future into her own hands.

"This isn't the middle ages, Richeline! We can't put her in a dungeon anymore. We have better mixers than her and someone will cure Evelyn. Watch her," her father said to Renel, as if she were a rabid dog rather than his beloved daughter. He swept out of the room.

She needed to throw them off, somehow. She couldn't let them take Lyn away.

"Love," she said, forcing the word up and out past her paralysis.

"What?" Zain swooped down, his ear close to her lips. "What did you say, Evelyn?" Her eyes were still closed, but she knew he had heard her. She cursed him for being so slow.

"Be in love and . . . ," she said. Then her body gave up fighting and let the sedative take her away into a deep and powerless sleep.

Chapter Thirty-Six

Samantha

MY DREAMS ON THE FLIGHT HOME ARE DARK and strange. Aphroditas dances in front of my eyes, her body twisting and spinning. Wrapped around her wrists are dark green bracelets of luvy that beckon me to join in, winding up Aphroditas's arms. Yet when I look up at her again, she's the mercrone, all mottled skin and rotting teeth. In the dream I cry out, but it's the mournful cry of the abominable. A bright white light interrupts us, so pure I have the urge to bow in its presence. I'm on my hands and knees, praying to the light. Something soft and gentle caresses my face. I lift up my head and it's snowing petals of pink jasmine.

Kirsty shakes me awake. "Hey, earth to Samantha." I blink back sleep from my eyes and find my legs are cramped up against the seat in front of me. Kirsty didn't want to spring for better seats—the luvy money won't last forever and we have more ingredients to find—but then she isn't as tall as me. "You're kicking the people in front."

"Sorry, weird dreams," I say, hoping to stay awake till we get home.

We land back in Kingstown and I'm accosted by my mum, who jumps past crowds and security to get through to me and holds me tight.

My dad stands a little bit off to the side, holding Molly's hand. Mum hug-walks me over to them, and then lets me go just a fraction to let them in too. "I . . . am . . . so . . . glad . . . to . . . see . . . you," says Mum, between kisses on the forehead. I envisage my face, covered in her bright pink lipstick. I'd like to tattoo it there, that symbol of family love.

They've hired a car to take me home, and I've never been so glad to pull up on Kemi Street and see the front of our store. A few things have changed, though. The sign is new. It's been done in the old style, with our family coat of arms carved into a beautiful piece of dark wood, but it glints with new paint. There's something different about the glass in the window too. The square panes appear artfully frosted rather than caked with a potent mixture of dirt, grime, and dust.

"We spent some of the luvy money on doing up the storefront," Dad says, taking in my expression and reading it perfectly. "There were so many media here, journalists, photographers, cameras—they all want a piece of you."

Dad beams with happiness. I know I should too, but instead I feel the mounting pressure. They've had a taste of the life we could live, and they like it. This is what I wanted, but now it's up to me to make it happen.

I put on a smile, even if it doesn't reach my eyes. It's better than nothing.

Once I'm inside the kitchen, it's nice and familiar. Nothing has changed here. "I'm going to find Granddad," I say. All the questions that have been sitting in the back of my mind bubble up to the front. I push through the kitchen to the lab, where he's at his desk, just like always.

"Well, you've had quite the adventure, young lady."

"What happened in the last Wilde Hunt?" I try to keep my voice calm, but my heart is pounding in my ears. Granddad stops working, placing both his palms on the table. He removes his half-moon glasses and rubs his eyes.

"I've told you this story. The royals broke the rules and let a synth win, and your great-grandmother lost her livelihood because of it."

"You never told me she went to Mount Hallah."

"I didn't know."

"How could you not know? You were her apprentice!"

He levels me with a stare. "Masters don't share all their secrets with their apprentices."

"Then did she tell you she created the first synth?"

Granddad slams his hands on the table, and I flinch. "Lies! Who told you that?" He shakes with fierce rage, but it dissipates almost as quickly as it rose up. He slumps in his chair, his fingers tracing one of the knots in the wooden table. "She wouldn't let me come with her on the final leg of the hunt. The last ingredient was mystifying us all—eye of a centaur—and we couldn't find it anywhere. Can you imagine asking a centaur for its eye? They protect the bodies of their dead more fiercely than any creature on this earth. No, there was no procuring that ingredient.

"We had an argument. She sent me home from the hunt. I knew she was up to something, creating something . . . but without her diary, I will never know what it was. And then the next thing I knew, that fool Zoro Aster had won the hunt and Cleo had lost her potions diary. She was never the same after that. Within the year, she died. Her diary was never found. In one fell swoop, I lost everything."

I reach out and put my hand over his. "You were sixteen. There wasn't anything you could have done."

"There is so much I could have done. I shouldn't have left. But that is all in the past now." He rubs his long beard. "There is something you can do," he says. "Trust your instincts."

Granddad turns back to his desk and resumes scribbling in his journal. It's a dismissal, but a kind one. He's shared more with me in the past ten minutes than he has in my entire life.

That's when it hits me. Maybe it's not my instincts I need to trust. Maybe it's my dreams. I spin around abruptly, bumping into the table and sending the glass jars tinkling on the surface. Luckily nothing breaks.

Dad pops his head into the lab. "Everything okay in here?"

I rush toward the kitchen. "Is Kirsty back yet?"

"She just arrived."

"Good, because I think I know what the next ingredient is."

I take a deep breath before I begin. If I'm right, the next ingredient requires highly specialized skill to find. Plus, it's an ingredient that's well-protected to the point of being almost illegal—you need to jump through innumerable hoops and get pages of government permissions to acquire it through the normal channels. I wonder how Princess Evelyn did it without alerting anyone. Did she get it by herself? Did she pay some extortionate sum for it? Maybe she has one in the palace backyard, and we don't even know it. Somehow, I doubt it.

I follow Dad into the kitchen, where Mum, Molly, and Kirsty are waiting for me, all looking at me with expectation in their eyes.

"Unicorn tail."

There's a group intake of breath.

"Whoa," Molly says, her eyes opening wide. "I've always wanted to see a unicorn." Molly's favorite toy is a stuffed unicorn with a sparkly horn that she received on her sixth birthday. They're by far her favorite creature.

Kirsty drops her head into her hands. "Unicorn! That's a problem for us." Unicorns can only be approached by virgins. Let's just say that puts Kirsty at a disadvantage.

"Why? I can get it," I say.

"Can you?" Kirsty raises an eyebrow.

"What?" I squeak. I can't believe Kirsty's just asked that in front of my parents.

"I saw Zain leaving your room last night."

"No! We didn't . . ." The blood rushes to my face.

She holds up her hand. "Don't freak out. That's not what I'm asking. The whole unicorns only appearing to virgins thing is a common misconception," she says.

"But nothing . . . I can't believe you think that . . . I am still . . ." My face gets warmer and warmer, and I turn an unhealthy shade of beetroot.

Kirsty laughs. "Do you need me to get you some water?"

I stick my tongue out and relax when I realize no one is actually judging me. "What do you mean, then? Why can't I get it? I thought that's why most of the specialized Finders for unicorns come from that religious order that follow vows of complete chastity."

"It's not about virginity in the physical sense. The

ancient word for love can actually be translated in many ways, only one of which implies the physical. It's a juicier myth that way, isn't it?" Kirsty wiggles her eyebrows. "But turns out, unicorns are even pickier than that. So I have to ask, Sam . . . have you ever fallen in love?"

"No!" But then my heart spikes. Is that true anymore? I hesitate. "At least . . . I don't know. I'm not sure."

"That's not going to fool the unicorns."

"Oh, Sam—I didn't know! Do you have a boyfriend?" my mum asks.

I bite my lip. "Well, over the past few weeks, Zain and I have got a lot closer. Then last night we talked . . ."

Now my dad gets angry. He narrows his eyes. "He knew."

My face drains of color at Dad's statement. Mum turns to him, worry in her voice. "John . . ."

"Well of course he did! That snake, he must have planned it. He makes Sam believe she's in love just before she has to meet a unicorn? You don't find that a bit suspicious?"

"He didn't 'make' me anything—I suppose you think he planned the whole night on the mountain and the abominable too?" I snap. "Anyway, it's none of your business." Tears burn my eyes. "Zain cares about me. We care about each other. He wanted to work with us on finding the cure, not against us." I face my dad, who thankfully has the decency to look ashamed by his outburst. I can see him reach out, wanting to apologize, to take back what he said, but I'm far too angry to let him. "We'll find a way; we'll pay someone . . ."

Kirsty begins, "I'll call the Sisters and get a quote—" but then another voice cuts in. "I'll do it," Molly says. "I'll go to get the unicorn."

"No," my parents and I say in unison.

Now it's Molly's turn to be hurt. She stands up, the tips of her dark brown braids quivering. "You never let me help! I'm strong too, and I've never been in love. I can do this."

"No, it's far too dangerous for you, Molly," I say.

"I'm part of this family. This is our hunt."

I stare at her. She suddenly seems so much older than twelve in that moment. Kirsty is staring at her too.

But Dad shakes his head. "Molly, it's absolutely out of the question. We will hire a specialized Finder, that way both of you can stay safe. And let's not forget that Emilia is still out there. Who knows what she'll do."

"That's so unfair. You let Sam do whatever she wants, but you never let me do anything." She runs out of the room, and I hear her take the stairs two at a time to her room, slamming the door.

I stand up from the table. I can't even look at Dad, or Mum, and definitely not at Kirsty. I'm angry, but I'm also ashamed, which only makes me angrier at them for making me feel shame. Do I love Zain? I'm not even sure. But I know things have changed between us, and that this fire in my chest is new and uncomfortable. To be honest,

I still can't really believe he knows my name. Let alone, that we might be . . . well, special to each other . . . after what we've been through. I don't even dare put it into words in my head. Can you put a jinx on something just by thinking about it? Can you ruin something before it's even begun, with the pressure of expectation? Of course you can, and that's why I say nothing. Not even to myself.

He didn't know—couldn't have known—about the next ingredient. He could have figured it out, I suppose. And now I'm doubting him, doubting me, and that makes me feel worse.

"I need to take a walk." When I leave the house, there's no word of protestation from anyone, no "Be back by ten" or "Where do you think you're going?" They just let me leave. They'll be busy trying to find a specialized Finder, anyway.

A sick feeling turns my stomach, gnawing at my insides, as the cool air blasts my skin. What if they're right? What if he just used me last night? Was I an idiot for believing that there might actually be something between us?

I don't really care where I'm going, I just let my feet take me away from my home. But they have a mind of their own, and soon it's pretty obvious that I'm heading toward the one place I might find an answer. Or, if not an answer, then maybe a big hug. If I can get her to forgive me, that is.

Anita.

I turn my walk into a jog, getting rained on by a light

drizzle. I careen around the corner, flying through the Patels' front gate until I almost collapse against their front door, and try to regain my composure. Suddenly I'm scared. I need Anita like I need air, but there's every chance that she won't forgive me.

What I did was pretty bad, after all.

Even though I didn't knock, I must have caused enough of a ruckus, as I can hear locks shifting in the door. I push back from the frame and run my hands over my hair, trying to make myself look presentable.

Anita's mum answers the door. She's obviously surprised, but smoothes her reaction into a gentle smile. I've always loved Mrs. Patel. Her cooking introduced me to curries and naan bread, and she's never raised her voice, even when Anita and I stole her henna kit and spilled black goo over her handmade carpet.

"Come in, Sam, dear."

"What are you doing here?" says a voice laced with daggers.

I stop on the threshold and look into the house, where Anita is standing at the top of the stairs. I shuffle in a bit as Mrs. Patel shuts the door behind me; she shoots a look I can't see at Anita, who rolls her eyes. Then Mrs. Patel disappears into the living room, leaving me in the hallway, feeling only a few inches tall.

Anita folds her arms over her chest. "Shouldn't you be off Finding somewhere?"

"I'm here to say sorry . . ."

"Well, you've said it. See you around." She spins on her heels.

"Wait, Anita." She hesitates, which is enough encouragement for me. I jump up the first couple of stairs, so familiar with this house it might as well be my own. "I am sorry. Really sorry. What happened in Bharat—it wasn't me. I wasn't thinking."

Her shoulders slump a little. I climb one more stair. "I . . . I got swept away in this whole hunt thing. I can't believe I hurt you like that."

"You really did hurt me."

"I know—"

"We would have helped you, supported you, right until the end, even if it wasn't us who made the potion . . ."

"I know."

"And Arjun is totally crushed too." She spins around now, to face me. "You owe him an apology."

I cringe. "Of course. Of course."

She opens her arms, and I rush up the stairs two at a time and fall into them. Immediately, we both burst into tears.

"I am so stupid," I say through sobs.

"Yeah, you are," she replies, but there's laughter in her voice now. Our tears have made ridiculous figures of us both, clutching each other on the landing. Still clinging to each other, we sidestep along the hallway toward her room, collapsing on her bed.

"So, what happened?" she asks, finally.

"What do you mean?"

"Well, you look like you've just run through a bramble bush backward—did you run here? Something must have happened. . . . Was it Zain?"

My eyes open wide. "How did you know about that?"

"The rescue was all over the casts, and you two looked pretty cozy in all the pictures after the mountain rescue."

I blush, but then words tumble out of my mouth before I can stop them. "We went through so much on the mountain. And then we had this crazy talk back at the hotel and I just felt so close to him. I think he feels the same way about me. Wow, I haven't really admitted that out loud before! But then I figured out that the next ingredient is unicorn tail."

"No way, really?" Anita asks, her eyes wide.

"Apparently the rumors about unicorns aren't true—it's not about being a virgin, it's about never being in love at all . . . and because of my feelings for Zain, Kirsty and Dad are convinced he's used me to prevent us from getting the ingredient. They think he duped me for the sake of the hunt, but that's crazy, because I know he isn't like that."

"Isn't he, Sam?" She looks at me.

"Look, I know you don't know him very well, but we really bonded. I mean, we saved each other's lives, but he also really understands me. He's got the same kind of pressures at home that I do. And I know he always came across like a bit of a stuck-up jerk in school, but when you talk to him he's not like that at all . . ." I keep babbling, but she remains quiet. It even starts to annoy me slightly.

She sees it in my face, though, because she responds. "Sam . . . have you heard from Zain since you got back?"

I check my phone, even though I know there are no messages from him on it. I flick it on and log in to Connect. Nothing there either. He's not even added me again as a friend.

I want to keep my heart, my hope, above water, but he's making it damn hard. So is the look of—is that pity?—on Anita's face. "It hasn't been that long since we got back from the mountain," I say defensively. But even in my mouth, the words seem hollow.

Anita leans over me and grabs a remote control off the bedside table. "You haven't seen any casts since you've been home, have you?"

I shake my head, suddenly filled with trepidation.

She puts her hand on my arm and squeezes it. "Sam, you're my best friend. I'm not going to pull any punches with you, okay? Just know that I love you and that essentially, boys suck."

A vice tightens around my heart. I'm not sure that I can breathe. I don't know where Anita is going with this, but it can't be good. I opened up to Zain, against my better judgment. *Please don't tell me my better judgment was right,* I plead to the television.

She taps the top button on the remote, and the TV jumps to life. It's already showing the main newscast, the breaking story about an earthquake in a far corner of the globe.

"And now, in national news . . . after last night's devastating breakdown at the palace, Princess Evelyn appears to have taken a turn for the worse. We are told now the government is considering evacuating Kingstown Hill, and with the hunt suffering several setbacks, insiders fear that time is running out for our nation's sweetheart."

"Oh no," I say. "What happened to Evelyn?"

Anita shushes me with her hands. I shut up and keep my eyes glued to the screen. I couldn't stop watching anyway, not after the presenter's next words hit my ears:

"Son of ZoroAster's CEO and friend of the princess, Zain Aster, visited her earlier today, and came out making a shocking announcement."

"I spoke with Princess Evelyn and I can confirm that the poison she took was a love potion meant for me," Zain says, to the snap and fizzle of flashbulbs, and the furious shouting of reporters.

"Zain, Zain, tell me, why did the princess feel the need to use a love potion? Do you not feel the same way?"

I can see Zain's brow furrow, his face the picture of concern. "I don't know why Evie chose to use a love potion." His voice chokes up as he speaks, and the tip of the knife slides into my heart. "I've always loved

302

Princess Evelyn. I love her now. And I will do anything to get her back. The ZA team are doing everything we can to win the hunt, and we are confident that we will have the cure—before it's too late." He doesn't sound like himself. He sounds older, more serious. He leaves the screen, descending the stairs of the palace to cries of his name.

The news presenter comes on again and looks like she's almost holding back tears herself. "We here at News 21 wish Zain the best in bringing back the princess from her love sickness. We know that these two are meant to be."

There's a click as Anita changes the channel. Another newscast takes over, but this time it's a panel show with four commentators all debating the hunt. One of them is Dan, but his rounded shoulders and pale face tell me he's losing whatever side of the debate he's on. A woman so tanned she glows bright orange mentions my name. "That Sam Kemi," she says, "is clearly just out to seduce Zain so he won't have a chance at saving the princess."

"That's not true," refutes Dan. "She—"

But the woman cuts him off. "You weren't on the mountain, so we can't rely on your 'on the scene' reports anymore, Dan. I'll tell that ordinary girl one thing: True love conquers all, missy, so you might as well back down."

Anita rushes to turn the TV off. She takes my hand in hers, but I barely even feel it. I've gone numb all over. I try to make it compute in my mind. Everything Zain said about Evelyn, and how he felt about her, and how he felt about me . . . Was it all lies? Every word of it?

I can hardly believe that I let myself fall for him.

What an absolute fool. And now the media have turned on me too. But I don't care about them. All I can think about is Zain.

My parents were right. He must have found out what the last ingredient was when we were in the hotel, and then decided to make sure I could never get the ingredient myself. He's slick. He knew how to get me to fall for him. And I fell. But this time there's no safety net. Only a hard, painful crash.

I collapse onto Anita's bed and she strokes my hair gently. "I'm so sorry, hon."

I curse myself for ever daring to take our friendship for granted. I just want to curl up in a ball and let my emotions wash over me like a pebble on a beach.

"Look at what the hunt has done to us. Dad is devastated about the lab," Anita says, her long hair tickling my cheek. "He doesn't think it's worth repairing. I guess he'll have to retire early or find another job or . . ."

I sit up. "It'll be okay."

She smiles, holding back her tears. "It'll only be okay if it was worth it. You have to win. How is the hunt going apart from the unicorn?"

"I'm constantly feeling one step behind. I don't know if the unicorn tail is the last thing, or if there's more . . . It feels like we're close, but we still don't have the jasmine."

Anita's eyes light up. "Come with me," she says, lifting my chin up and grabbing hold of my hands. "I have something to show you that might help."

"What is it?" I can't think of anything that will help in this situation. Unless it's some kind of tonic for selective memory loss.

We head back downstairs, through the kitchen where the sweet smell of chai tea wafts in the air. "Would you girls like a cup?" Anita's mum asks.

"Not yet, Mum," Anita replies for the both of us, heading out to the garden.

Tucked to one side is a little greenhouse. "In there," she says.

I lift the latch on the door and a wave of heat hits me first, followed quickly by the humidity. All around me are lush plants, their leaves green and healthy. And in the corner is a flash of bright pink.

Pink jasmine.

I spin around as Anita squeezes into the greenhouse beside me. "What? How?"

"Ah, so you spotted it."

"How could I miss it? I thought Emilia had burned it all?"

"She had. But, as I would have told you if you hadn't been in such a hurry to get on that motorcycle, she hadn't burned it completely down to the roots. I managed to salvage a root and regrow it here. I was carrying it to show you when you left."

A memory hits me. Anita's dark handprints on my backpack. Dark because she had been burrowing in the ashes and soot, looking for the root.

Anita shrugs. "Like I said. It's okay. I forgive you, and you're going to need it to complete the potion, now that we don't stand a chance. And you need to beat Zain more than ever now. So, it's yours."

My eyes well up with tears again. I reach forward and pull her into a hug. "Thank you so much. I'll let everyone know how you've helped me. Now we have to wait to see if my parents can commission a Finder for the unicorn tail."

Just then, like a curse, my phone vibrates. I take it out of my pocket, and my heart sinks. It's not him, calling to apologize like I thought he might, or to offer some kind of explanation. Because I mean nothing to him, nothing at all, not when he's declared to the whole world who he's really been waiting for this entire time.

The call is from my mum.

I debate not answering. But I can't be mad at them too long. Not when they were right.

I pick up. "Sam, oh, Sam, thank goodness." Her voice is filled with fear.

"What is it?" I say. I reach out and grab Anita's hand. Anita looks at me quizzically.

"It's Kirsty. She's gone, and she's taken Molly with her."

"What?" I screech.

"They've taken your Wilds pass, so we can't even follow her out there. Oh, Sam, what are we going to do? It's so dangerous!"

"Don't worry." My mind is racing, my words reassuring her, but in reality I have no clue how we're going to get to Molly. Mum's right. Where she's going, where the unicorns are . . . it's more dangerous than anywhere I've been yet, including the mountain. "Don't worry, I'll figure something out. I'll be right there. I'll get Mr. Patel to drive me home."

I click off the phone and feel the blood drain from my face.

"What is it, Sam?" says Anita.

"Kirsty's taken Molly to Zambi." I race out of the hot, sticky greenhouse and into the fresh air outside. I pace in her garden. "What am I going to do? Kirsty is so reckless . . . she just wants to get the ingredient no matter what."

"We'll go," says a voice from the back door of the house.

I look up and see Arjun standing there. "We'll go," he repeats. "We still have two Wilds passes for the hunt. If you and I leave now, we can catch them."

I run at him, almost tackling him into a hug. He pats my back awkwardly. "I'm so sorry, Arjun."

"Don't even think about it. Pay me back later."

"Deal."

"Come on, then, guys. I'll drive you—Dad let me borrow the keys earlier today," says Anita. "Mum? We're—"

Mrs. Patel nods before Anita has finished speaking. "You go and get your sister," she says, but not before pulling me toward her and giving me a big kiss on my forehead. She does the same to Anita and Arjun before waving us off.

We run through the hallway and all pile into the car.

This feels right, the three of us together again. And we're going to get Molly back.

Chapter Thirty-Seven

Samantha

"I'M SORRY, BUT I CAN'T DISCOUNT THESE prices," says Joan, a dippy brunette hostess with bright red glamoured lips, from behind the desk at the Kingstown Transport Terminal. "It's twenty thousand crowns to transport to Zambi this evening. We're very busy. Haven't you heard about the evacuation? Everyone is getting out in case these earthquakes get worse."

"But we need to get there! It's for the hunt! You don't want to be responsible for the death of the princess, do you?" I don't care about hiding my comings and goings anymore.

She narrows her eyes at me slightly, as if trying to remember my face. "Wait—you're that Kemi girl, right? I saw you on TV last night. What are you up to now? Who knows what you'll do to stop that poor boy, Zain." She looks over at Arjun. "Are you some other poor sap she's suckered into helping her?"

I let out a muffled cry of frustration.

"Do you honestly believe everything the casts tell you?" Anita snaps.

Joan purses her lips and taps her keyboard. "There's nothing I can do. There's a flight to Zambi leaving from the airport in four hours. You have to stop over in Ellara, but you'll be there by tomorrow evening."

"We don't have until tomorrow evening!" I cry, and slam my hands down on the desk.

"Now, calm down, young lady, or I'll have to call security." Joan looks alarmed, her hand reaching for a phone.

"Now, now, now, what's this fuss? Let an old man through."

I recognize that voice. I spin around. "Granddad, what are you doing here?"

"Sam, I've come to take you home. Arjun, Anita, you should go too."

"What? But Molly . . ."

"Thank you, sir," says Joan, who drops any pretense of being nice to us. "Your granddaughter is out of control."

Granddad stands so close to the counter, he's practically leaning on it. He reaches over to pat her hand. "I'm so sorry they inconvenienced you," he says, tutting. "Youth nowadays." But then he grips her wrist tightly. She squirms, looking uncomfortable, but Granddad is the picture of frailty and he starts to cough. The cough builds into a hack, until his entire body is shaking.

"Granddad!" I try to comfort him, but he waves me

away with his free hand. He delves into his pocket and pulls out a handkerchief. He faces Joan, flips open the hankie and blows a cloud of dust into her face. It settles over her like a sprinkling of icing sugar, then disappears.

Granddad's coughing stops immediately. "So, two tickets to Zambi?" he asks Joan with a sly smile.

"Right away, sir. Here you go, sir. Transport safely."

Granddad needs to usher Arjun and me away from the desk, as we're both slack-jawed with awe.

"Quick, the potion won't last much longer."

"What did you do to her?" Arjun asks.

Granddad winks at me.

"Charm powder!" I release a long breath. "And it worked so well!" Another banned potion, incredibly difficult to make. He hasn't lost his touch one bit. "But what about when she recovers?"

"She won't know a thing is wrong. I'm not a Kemi for nothing," he says. "Now get moving."

I give both him and Anita a quick hug, then dash through the portal zone to get to the security area and beyond to the launch screens.

I turn to Arjun, who has little beads of sweat appearing on his forehead. "You okay?"

"I haven't done this yet . . ."

"Oh wow, I forgot." I'm not sure how, my first experience was terrifying. "Honestly, it's fine. Just remember the rules. Especially about maintaining eye contact."

He nods. "I guess I better get used to it if I want to be a proper Finder. Let's go. If I think about this for too long, it's going to get the better of me."

"You go first. I'll follow right behind you. I just have to make one phone call first."

When I land, the area is in chaos. Arjun is shivering violently, and guards suround him with reflective blankets.

"He's going into transporting shock," one of the medics says.

"Don't you have a potion for that?" I say.

Crushed silver meteorite, mixed with essence of shepherd's purse and threads of glow worm, to bring him out of the streams of magic and tie him to the earthly ground, where he belongs.

A mix that would help. Not that I have it. I wish I could turn my brain off.

The medic pulls out a blister pack of pills, the logo ZA imprinted on them. "Here, these will help. I'll get some water."

"I'm already feeling better," says Arjun. "I . . . I'll be fine."

The medic shrugs. "These will make you feel way more normal. Otherwise"—he turns to me—"make sure he stays warm and rested, if you don't want him to experience any long-term damage."

"Fair enough," I say. I take the pills from him anyway.

As soon as we step out of the terminal, the heat is extreme, but in a different way to Bharat—it's so dry. I wonder briefly why we live in the land of drizzle and constant gray clouds when there are other places in the world with much better climates.

I open my phone—immediately accruing roaming charges, but what are you going to do—and see that Anita has sent us the details for our rental car into the Wilds. Despite the fact that Zambi isn't particularly well-developed, they are much stricter about their Wilds laws than almost anywhere else in the world. It's a dangerous, unpredictable place. They say that the source of all Talented magic is in Zambi. If the magic over Nova flows in streams, here it flows like a waterfall. Magic pounds at the earth, and even as an ordinary I feel like I can reach out and grab it with my hands.

We pick up the keys to the car and thankfully it starts without any trouble. Since we've come in via portal, this is probably the most affluent area of Zambi. Everything is well manicured, rhododendron trees lining the streets in neat, evenly spaced lines, and there's even an arrangement of luscious fountains, which seems particularly ostentatious considering the fact that over 80 percent of the Zambi Wilds are in drought.

"Are you okay to drive?" I ask Arjun. He sways slightly, his eyes unfocused.

"I think I just need some rest."

"Okay, you rest. I'll drive. You can help navigate." I help him into the side door, and he slumps against the window. He still doesn't want to take the pills, and all I have to offer him instead is water. I press a bottle into his hand and force him to take a few sips.

"Seriously, I'm fine. I just feel a bit woozy, that's all."

Once we're out of the portal station, the driving takes on an altogether different sort of challenge. It's not nearly as bad as Bharat, but I'm trying to concentrate on navigating our route and the road ahead of me as well. I wish we'd borrowed Mr. Patel's satnav.

The Wilds of Zambi. I can hardly believe that this is going to be my first time here—this rushed, crazed trip. On a hunt for unicorn tail. But this isn't just about getting the ingredient. I need to rescue Molly.

The Wilds of Zambi intrude on almost all of their big cities, and so it doesn't take us long until we reach a border. Once I saw on a nature documentary cast that a sabre-tooth lion stalked through the streets of Jambo, causing a city-wide panic. In the rich neighborhoods, they have to put barbed wire at ground level to stop the double-tailed crocs from taking a swim in their pools.

The border is just a small hut with a thatched roof and a sleepy-looking guard. I drive up and hand over our passes.

"Everything should be in order, sir," I say in my politest tone possible, even though I feel like bursting and telling him to hurry up.

"Stay here; I can't let you through." He stands up, stretches, and starts to walk away from the car toward another small building marked WILDS GUARD. Without thinking, I get out of the car and walk after him. "Wait—sir, can we have our passes back?"

"No, I have to pass these to my manager to examine."

"Please . . ."

Then I remember something. Something Kirsty once told me about Wilds guards, the crap job they have, forced to guard a border that not many people really want to cross. "I know you want to check with your manager, but maybe this will help speed things up?" I flash him a twenty-crown note. He pockets the bill and hands back the passes in exchange.

"You can go through."

I walk back to the car, my hands shaking.

"Did you just bribe that guy?" Arjun asks, his head leaning against the window.

"I think I did."

"Samantha Kemi, you're a bit of a badass."

I grin at him and rev the engine. The car jumps forward, and we're into the Wilds.

Something akin to elation—maybe it's the adrenaline—finally takes over me. We're here. We've done it. And only a few hours have elapsed since we found out that Kirsty had taken Molly. Maybe there's actually a chance of catching up with them out here, before anyone gets hurt.

I take out my phone, about to text my parents the good news.

"Crap."

"What is it?" Arjun says weakly.

"No signal."

"Seriously?" He pulls himself more upright and digs his phone out of his pocket. "Same here. That's weird. I took a course on communication in the Wilds last semester. Zambi was one of the first Wilds areas to be completely overlaid with signal because the risks are so high. Rescue teams need to be able to get out here fast."

"I say again—crap."

"Something—someone—must be jamming the signal."

I slap my hands against the wheel. Three guesses who that must be. "Emilia." I don't dare take my eyes off the road, which is becoming less like a road and more like arbitrary lanes, winding through the tall grass in the savannah. "What do you think we should do?"

"We keep going."

"But, where?"

He places his thumb and forefinger on the inner corner of each eye, and squeezes. It's what he does whenever he's trying to remember something. I don't know how many times I've seen him do it in exams. Whatever it is, it works.

"Unicorns . . . Okay. We almost never have to cover this stuff, you know? First year Finder training consists of the basic stuff. And this is not basic."

I swerve to avoid the branches of a huge baobab tree hanging over the road. "Come on, Arjun. I know you go above and beyond your training at every moment. You must have read something . . ."

"Yes, hang on. Okay. Okay."

I pull to a stop in the huge open savannah. How are we ever going to find them out here? Grass, plains, and trees as far as the eye can see—but no sign of another car. No sign of any other life. What if they went into the Wilds and turned left instead of straight on? Turned right? We could be searching the savannah for days and not have any clue where they are.

I try not to wonder if we're going to run into Zain and the ZA team. It's over. I keep reminding myself of that.

Suddenly there's a screech overhead, and hundreds of thick black silhouettes fill the sky, casting a shadow over the sun. I scream, despite the fact that we're inside the jeep. Arjun takes out his phone, opens an app, and points it at the sky.

"What are those things?" I cry.

He shows me the screen. There's a picture of the creatures on it, and a little whirling white circle indicating that the phone is working. "The Finders app helps us identify species out in the Wilds, like a Finding database which anyone can tap into." The screen flashes up with a picture of a vicious-looking bat, the tips of its wings curved into cruel-looking claws. Under the picture are the words *Zambiera desmodus*.

"Vampire bats?" I ask.

"No, these are like vampire bats 2.0. Look at their wings! They're vicious, and a huge pack like this . . ." He pauses. "We have to follow them. Follow the bats, Sam!"

"What, why?"

"Their favorite blood is human. If someone is injured, they'll be drawn to the scent."

I put my foot down flat on the pedal, swinging the wheel in the direction of the bats.

Arjun braces himself against the dashboard. "It could be the ZA team that's in trouble . . ."

"Or it could be Molly." I'm in a race now. A race to find Molly, against these evil beasts in the sky. I grit my teeth as the steering wheel judders in my hands, the tires bouncing over the rough terrain.

"Left! Angle left!"

The bats are still flying straight, but I give Arjun the benefit of the doubt.

"Okay, straighten up!"

I can see what he's spotted now. A jeep, up ahead. It's parked in front of a thick clump of trees, the thickest I've seen in the savannah so far.

"It's a gallery forest!" Arjun says. "According to the database, that's where unicorns like to hide out because it means there's water nearby, but also cover. Maybe that's where they are. The bats should circle for a bit, but when they descend on the forest, they'll be everywhere, okay? You don't have long."

I jump out of our vehicle as we come level with the jeep. I peer inside, but I don't recognize anything. It could belong to Molly and Kirsty. It could be ZA. It could be Emilia. I just have to pray that it's Molly.

Arjun slumps in his seat. I can see the ashen determination on his face. When I find Molly, I will drive us all back to safety, and home. But this part, I'm going to have to do alone. No Finder to help me.

"I'll be back," I say to him. I grab his phone and punch in a number. "The moment there's a signal, you dial this."

"If you're not here in half an hour, I'm coming in."

"Okay. Or, you know, if you hear any screaming."

He smiles. I run toward the forest.

It's deathly quiet inside. The trees absorb all the sound, the wind, the birds and the bats that had seemed so loud outside now snuffed out, replaced by a claustrophobic silence. I make my way through the thick trunks, deeper into the forest.

Then, I spot it: a flash of unnaturally bright orange in the trees. I pick up my pace. I want to shout, but something about the silence of this place makes me keep my mouth shut.

I break through into a clearing. Kirsty is there, clear as day, a reflective orange jacket over her normal uniform.

She does not look surprised to see me at all. In fact, she looks like she is expecting me. She holds up a hand, and I freeze on the spot.

"Sam!" cries Molly. My head snaps up toward the sound. She's in one of the trees, suspended in a battered cage made from strips of lacquered wood. She looks so small in there, she could probably fit through the bars if she tried. But it's too high off the ground for her to jump down safely.

Then a unicorn bursts into the clearing, into the space beneath the cage.

I almost fall to the ground. I've never seen a creature more beautiful in my entire life. I want to throw myself at its hooves and pray for forgiveness. I want to bury myself in the earth and tear my eyes from their sockets; they don't deserve its majesty. It's a creature that appears born of light itself, light and beauty and—at the moment—great and terrible rage.

Almost twice her height, it leaps past Kirsty, who in turn leaps to the side, rolling to a stop, barely moments after the creature's horn slices through the space where her head was. It gallops in circles around the clearing, pawing at the tree, pounding its muscular body against the trunk and making the entire forest shake.

It's like a horse, but it's more than that. It appears to have more muscles, to be made of more than just blood and skin and sinew but also of steel and strength and sunlight and the universe itself. Its horn is its most incredible feature. It stretches out in a dagger-straight line, but it's made up of curves and coils, somehow still menacing, dangerous. When it stops under the cage again, it rears up, but to no avail. Whoever placed that cage up there did so with the utmost precision. The tip of its horn is inches away from the bottom, but it cannot reach. Every time the unicorn rears, Molly draws herself further into the fetal position she's adopted in a corner of the cage. But for some reason I don't think the beast wants to hurt Molly. It wants to save her.

Tears stream down my face. I can't help it. There's something about seeing the unicorn so angry, raging at us for keeping from it the one thing that it wants. But I won't let it get Molly. My eyes dart from side to side, looking for a way through to the tree.

"Stay back, Sam," Kirsty says. "I've never seen a unicorn act this way!"

"You don't understand," I shout back. "We think Emilia's jamming the phone signals. And there's a swarm of crazy Zambian vampire bats heading this way! They'll be here any minute."

At that, Kirsty's face turns gray.

The beat of wings confirms my statement, and Kirsty looks up at the sky, her eyes narrow.

She darts out into the clearing again, taunting the great beast. It stands beneath the cage, raking the ground with a diamond-hard hoof.

My mind races at a million miles a minute. If I can make it to the tree, if Kirsty somehow gets the unicorn to move, if Molly can break free, if, if, if, then what?

Kirsty is wide-eyed with panic, and fear grips my heart. She must have had a plan. Clearly she meant to lure the unicorn here with Molly's youth and innocence. But she hadn't taken into account Emilia, although she should have done. She should have known that Emilia wouldn't stop until we were all dead, including the princess.

The unicorn lowers its horn.

Kirsty stands there, her arms spread wide, holding open her jacket, trying to make herself seem like a huge, imposing target.

Then it charges.

At that moment, I charge too, springing forward from my position behind a tree, and I run to the tree in the center of the clearing.

It's not the easiest to climb, by any means. But I recognize exactly what kind of tree this is from one of my obscure potions books. I take out a knife from the bag at my side and slash at the trunk. Immediately, the cuts fill with sticky sap.

Amber laticifer tree. The thick resin from its bark can be used in the creation of funeral pendants, as it is ideal for binding and storing memories.

I dip my hands in it, coating them in the thick, shiny, light gold substance.

Kirsty turns and runs into the woods, the unicorn following swiftly behind. But the sound of beating wings is getting closer, louder, and I know I don't have much time.

I rub my hands together, the heat of the reaction making the sap sticky. Then I slam my right hand hard against the trunk as I jump up as high as possible. It catches, and I throw my other hand up as well, my feet scrambling for purchase against the bark, struggling to find a good foothold.

The sap starts peeling away almost immediately, so I have to keep moving, throwing one hand higher than the other. My shoulders burn with the effort, but it's only four more swings and I've reached the first branch. From here, now it will be easier.

I jump up onto the next branch.

"I'm coming, Molly!"

"Hurry!" She sounds so scared, her voice a high-pitched squeal.

There's a branch just underneath the cage. If I can remove the thick stake of wood that's holding the cage door closed, Molly will be able to swing over to me, and I'll be able to grab her. That must have been how Kirsty got Molly in the cage in the first place. From here, I'd be able to lift Molly up into it.

The problem is, the first bat lands on the branch at the same time that I do.

"Shoo!" I say, feeling utterly ridiculous. As if a vampire bat is going to shoo? It bares its teeth at me—they're incredibly sharp and long, more like needles than fangs, perfect for injecting venom and removing blood. It squawks, mocking me. Then it stretches out its wings and hisses like a snake.

I take the closest thing I have to hand—my torch—and throw it at the bat. It hits it square on, and the bat screeches at me, then flies off.

"Molly, I'm here!"

I stand on the branch and reach out. I yank the end of the stake several times, trying to pull it out of the lock.

But then the first bat lands on the cage. Its handlike little claws wrap around the bars, its wings beating ferociously against the bowing wood. The force of it sends the cage swinging, but only for a moment. Then it's like a rainstorm of black as the bats swarm over the cage, covering it completely, layering two, three, four deep, attacking and biting each other in their desperation to get to the precious blood inside. The blood that belongs to my Molly.

I can't even hear her screaming anymore. They've completely blocked my view of her, and even more are landing all the time on my branch. I don't have time to make a decision. I stretch out on the branch, and I jump toward the cage.

I don't even get close. A bat slams into my back, its

claws wrenching into my skin, its wings beating against my arms and head. The force of it sends my jump off balance, more like a fall than anything. I throw my arms up, and the sticky sap on my hands helps me cling to the branch. I swing myself toward the trunk, the bat still raging in my hair. I swing my legs around the tree, then peel my hands away from the bark and focus on pulling at the bat. I wrench it away from me, but not before its fangs leave deep scratches along my neck. My hand snaps off a twig from the branch, and as soon as I feel the slightest bit of leeway, I slash at the bat's wing. It falls away.

I'm scrambling now to try to get back up to the cage, and suddenly I see movement. The bottom drops from it; a compartment, a false floor. And Molly, she drops too. The creatures don't notice. But she's falling, and it's way too high.

"Molly!" I scream, as if my words could create some kind of cushion that will protect her. There is no time for me to react. There's nothing I can do. I can only watch her fall.

From the woods, the unicorn bursts out of the foliage. A vision of Molly skewered on the unicorn's horn plagues my mind, but it dips its head at the last minute and instead she falls like a ragdoll onto its body. Her arms instinctively grip its neck, and it carries her off into the forest. A stream of bats follow them, descending from the cage and sky.

I scuttle down the tree, beating off the last remaining bats as they swoop down on me, but the majority of their attention has been diverted.

I stagger off in the direction of the unicorn, running as fast as my weak legs can carry me. Someone calls my name, and I turn my head to see Kirsty stumbling out of the other side of the woods, her face caked with blood, her hand gripping a wound at her shoulder.

"Kirsty, it took her, it took Molly."

Kirsty purses her lips, sheer determination on her face. And as much as I hate her, and I hate her so much in this moment, she is the only one who's going to be able to make this better.

She breaks into a run, and seeing her do that with her bleeding shoulder means I can run too.

There's a loud whinny from deep within the forest.

I can barely breathe; I don't want to know what's going on.

We reach another clearing, where there's a growth of rock, covered in moss. Molly is there, and she's still sitting astride the unicorn's back, her eyes closed, her hands outstretched. She's got a scratch on her cheek that is dripping blood, and she's wearing a pair of silk gloves.

"No, Molly, stop!" I scream. She's using magic in the most dangerous part of the Wilds.

The bats swoop and swarm around her, but they're unable to attack. They're being repelled by some kind of force field that is being generated by my sister's gloved hands. Her brown hair streams out behind her, even though there's barely a breath of wind in the forest, and even when the unicorn rears up, Molly holds on with her thighs, moving with the creature as effortlessly as if she'd been riding her entire life.

Kirsty grabs my arm. "Get down!" she says.

"But the magic?"

"She'll be fine, trust me."

I drop to the mossy, muddy ground. And just in time, as Molly claps her hands together. Her force field spreads outwards, upward, and in an instant the bats are cast aside. Those closest to the blast fall like rain around us, while the others are sent swirling into the sky, far away from this girl and her powerful magic.

The power sweeps over Kirsty and me; I feel the residue of it crackle like electricity over my back, sending waves of goosebumps over my skin, every hair raised.

Molly collapses with a slump on the unicorn's back. It dips its legs, letting her slide to the ground. Then it lies down next to her and they both appear to fall into a deep sleep, one of Molly's arms draped around the unicorn's neck.

Slowly, Kirsty and I stand up. She grips her shoulder. "Be careful. The unicorn will be protecting Molly. But there could still be excess magic that you aren't protected from."

I grimace. No magical danger will keep me from my sister in this moment. "Molly?" I whisper. I can see the gentle rise and fall of her chest, her brow smooth, and she looks so peaceful. But I know after expending all that energy that she must be close to drained, and she will need medical attention quickly.

We approach cautiously.

"I've never been so close to a unicorn before," says Kirsty, tears in her eyes. "I mean, at least not for long enough to really examine it properly."

I know what she means. When the unicorn was raging in the clearing, it had been moving too fast for us to truly appreciate its beauty. But lying here, so powerful yet gentle in sleep, it's possible to really appreciate it. It appears white, but every individual strand of its fur seems translucent, like diamonds stretched out into strands. Its horn isn't pearlescent, as I would have expected, but more like a spear—a twisted sheet of precious metal—like silver, but even stronger. It looks slightly damaged at the tip, and streaked with drying blood, which is quickly turning from crimson to dark brown.

I wonder briefly where that blood has come from, but now I can guess what happened to Kirsty's shoulder.

"Careful," says Kirsty as I move closer to the two sleeping figures. I reach out and touch Molly's arm. She shifts, and the unicorn shifts beside her.

"Mols?" I whisper.

She groans in response, but at least it's a response. I gradually lift her arm, moving ever closer to her, extricating her from the unicorn's side. I lift her up in my arms, and she feels light as a feather; lighter than normal.

"Wait," she says, through slightly damp lips. Her eyes flutter open.

"What is it, my love?"

"Did you get the ingredient?"

"Don't worry about that, Mols," I whisper into her hair, gripping her tighter.

"No, it's okay. I asked."

"You . . ." It is almost too unreal for me to ask for an explanation. I move her so she's close enough to reach the unicorn's tail, and she gently breaks off a single strand. Kirsty stands back at a respectful distance. Maybe putting my little sister in so much danger has had an effect on her too. There aren't very many people who've met Molly, who then didn't want to protect her.

But then, it's obvious that Molly doesn't need as much protection as I think. She escaped from those bats herself. She didn't need me. She came out here to get the ingredient, she chose to be brave, despite the barriers that we put up around her ever since we found out she was Talented. She could have become insular; spoiled. But instead, she grew strong.

I'm so proud of her, even looking at her now as she falls asleep in my arms.

I turn back to look at the unicorn one last time, but it's gone—melted back into the woods—the space where it had lain to rest empty.

Lights begin flashing through the trees, and I realize that it must be Arjun, waiting in the jeep. We can finally leave this nightmare . . . and get back home.

Chapter Thirty-Eight

Samantha

JUST ON THE EDGE OF THE FOREST, A metallic stench reaches my nostrils. I recognize it even before she speaks, and this time, I'm expecting it. I close my eyes, take a breath, before turning around to face her.

"Well done, Samantha." Emilia emerges from the trees. Her clothes are singed and dirty, her wand smoking in her hand. She must have been hit by Molly's blast. Good. I can only hope that's stopped her from jamming the phone signal. "To be honest, I'm impressed. You're the last one left in the hunt and you're still standing. Well, sort of."

"The last one?" I'm not able to hide my surprise. Molly is heavy in my arms, and Kirsty leans on me, barely able to stand up straight. I sense her glaring at Emilia, but if she doesn't even have the strength to make a snappy comeback, she's not going to be able to help defend me in any way. The only thing I can do is keep Emilia talking. "What did you do to ZA?"

"Oh, an incident with their transporting might have occurred. To be honest, it's been all too easy." The lights continue to flicker at me, and I wish I could signal back to Arjun in some way. I wonder if he can see Emilia from where he is. "It's simply been a matter of clearing away the competition, one Participant at a time."

"All I want is to save the princess," I say.

"How nice of you. But I think the other Participants had that in mind too, and they're no longer here. And don't worry; the princess will be cured. We both know this potion is nearly done, and each defeated team has handed me the ingredient I need. So long as I am the one to create it, the royals will just have to hand the crown over to me, or risk watching their beloved Evelyn destroy their own kingdom."

"They won't let you!" I say.

"What choice will they have? The royals are desperate. The princess is deteriorating rapidly, the love potion ravishing her mind and sending her power spiraling out of control. She's destroying every room they put her in. If it continues, she will end up levelling Kingstown—even killing her won't stop it now. She needs the cure. And in exchange, the power of the Novaen throne will become mine." The dreamy look leaves her eyes; they flash bright as steel. "Hand over the last ingredient," she says, all business now.

"How do you know it's the last one? What if there's more?"

"Don't play games with me, Kemi."

I don't move. I can't. I'm paralyzed with fear.

"Fine, then I'll take it from you." She storms over and snatches at my bag, pushing Molly.

"Don't touch her!" I scream, my instincts finally awakening. My face is wet with tears. I place Molly, who is mercifully still sleeping, down on the ground. "Take it." I shrug my bag off my shoulder and hold it out.

She grabs it. "Good choice."

"You're nothing but a traitor, Emilia," I spit at her.

"I was going to leave you alive, Kemi," she says, her voice filled with hate. She throws down her smoking wand and pulls out a handgun, pointing it at me. "Who shall I kill first? You?" She moves the gun toward Molly. "Or your sister?"

"Go ahead," I say. "When the world sees what you're doing, you'll never rule Nova."

"What?" She looks up, drawing back the gun.

The air around us fills with the thud of helicopter blades, the wind picking up and whipping around my head. A spotlight dips low over our heads and I can see a man leaning out of the window, a video camera perched on his shoulder. It's Dan. He waves and gives me a thumbs-up.

"Smile, Emilia," I say. "You're on camera, broadcasting to the whole world."

My plan worked. Why fight the media, when I can use them?

Emilia throws her arms up over her face and runs into the forest. The helicopter doors open, and several rope ladders are thrown over the side.

Four men in khaki-colored uniforms with large weapons strapped to their backs climb down the ladders and surround us. "She went back into the forest!" I shout, terrified that she's going to get away again. One of the men shouts an order and the rest run into the trees after her.

Dan is the last man down, and the helicopter swings away. He rushes over to help me with Kirsty.

"You made it!" I smile.

"Thanks for the scoop of the century. I transported straight to Zambi after I got your call, but I was worried when I didn't hear from you about your exact location. When I finally did get the call from Arjun, I thought I might be too late."

"Emilia was jamming the signal right up until Molly saved us from the vampire bats. Did you get it on camera when she pulled the gun on us?"

"Everything. The world will know she's behind the sabotage of the Wilde Hunt now. Plus, I brought reinforcements." He gestures to the men around him.

The man in charge has several gold stripes on his shoulder. A badge on his chest reads PROTECT. SUSTAIN. THRIVE. "I am Colonel James Odoyo of the Zambi Wilds Protection Agency," he says, extending his hand.

"I'm Samantha Kemi. This is my sister Molly Kemi and our Finder Kirsty Donovan. Another friend, Arjun Patel, the one who called you here, is still in our car. Please, we need urgent medical attention."

"We will take you to a hospital. But first, we must search you for illegal unicorn-derived substances on your person."

I nod and they rifle through our bags and pat down our bodies—except for Kirsty, whose shoulder is still streaming blood. Her hand is clamped down tight over the wound, and even the guards can see that removing it would be dangerous. Molly is still passed out on the ground. I keep my head up high. Thanks to Emilia, we have nothing to hide.

Once Colonel Odoyo is satisfied that we have no unicorn parts in our possession, he leads us out of the forest, toward several big trucks that will take us away. I see Arjun already sitting in the back seat of one truck, and I place Molly next to him.

"Not the hospital," Kirsty whispers to me when we're inside the truck. "We need to go straight to the transport terminal."

"But . . ."

"No arguing. Sort it."

I tap the window of the truck. "Colonel Odoyo, can you take us to the Zambi Transport Terminal? I need to get my sister home."

"The hospital is on the way, miss," he replies.

"Please. I know Zambi doesn't follow the Novaen Wilde Hunt tradition, but I must get back. Our princess's life is at stake." I need to tell someone—Renel, the king, anyone—about what Emilia has done and see if we can get the unicorn tail another way.

The man sitting next to Colonel Odoyo turns in his chair, smiling broadly. "We know Princess Evelyn! My wife follows her in all the magazines. She came to Zambi on a visit last year, and I had to line up on the streets with my wife just so she could get a look at her. She said she's much thinner in real life than in the pictures."

"Then you'll help?" I say.

Colonel Odoyo changes the direction of the truck and takes us to the terminal. "You can leave to do what you must. But your friends"—he gestures to Kirsty and Arjun—"will need treatment first."

At the terminal, Colonel Odoyo is proved right—they won't let Arjun or Kirsty through. Neither of them is fit enough to travel. Arjun is still weak from his first transporting experience, and I think he's happy to head back on a plane later on in the day. Kirsty is strangely silent, but she's lost so much blood it's no wonder she can barely argue. They allow Molly and me to use our return tickets though, especially since we're heading home, so Dan volunteers to stay to make sure Kirsty and Arjun are cared for. And he wants to write up his blog as quickly as possible.

Before we head through security, Kirsty calls me over and asks to speak to me privately. The only place we can find is the ladies' bathroom. Classy.

I assume she wants to apologize for kidnapping Molly, so I come in with my arms crossed, immediately on the defensive. What she did was stupid, reckless, dangerous . . .

She pulls me into one of the stalls, shuts the door, then locks it. There's hardly room in here for both of us. "What the heck?" I say, my leg jammed up against the toilet bowl.

She peels off her shirt from her shoulder, wincing as she does it, and reveals a ragged, deep hole from where the unicorn gored her. I cover my mouth with my hand.

"Sam," she says through gritted teeth. "Focus." Then she holds up a pair of tweezers. "The unicorn will have left some splinters of its horn in my shoulder."

"Oh no, I'm not doing that."

"You have to."

"Oh God . . . What for? I don't know if I can."

"We don't have the tail anymore, Sam. But hopefully you can use these as a replacement."

My mind goes blank. "I . . . I . . . I guess it might

work?" I say, the realization that maybe I'm not out of the hunt finally dawning. The horn will have the same properties as the tail, but it's much less commonly used because of the increased difficulty to acquire.

"Good, because I'm not going to have had myself gored for nothing. I was going to sell them on but you need to have them. After all, I wouldn't have been able to get it without . . ."

"Without Molly. Right."

"Sam, she begged me to take her. I know I—" She stops. "Well, anyway, make it quick."

It's not quite an apology, but Kirsty is the toughest Finder—toughest person—I've ever known. She's gone through so much. I feel like being gored by a unicorn is probably punishment enough.

She takes a deep breath. "Okay, I'm ready."

"Okay." I take the tweezers from her hand. I don't give her a count, or build up the anticipation any more than I have to. I dive in, trying to cause as little pain as possible, but I can't see any horn near the surface.

"Are you sure . . . ?"

"It'll be there. Keep looking. Unicorns can't gore things without losing part of their horn. Though normally Finders try to goad them into goring tree trunks—not themselves."

"That would probably make sense."

Finally, after some nasty digging, I see it—a sliver of

silver. I catch the end of it with the tweezers and pull. I drop it into the coin purse of my wallet, which Kirsty is holding open. Then I remove a second one, which I spot glinting in the wound.

"Don't let anyone find them," she says.

Kirsty's wound looks terrible. I bunch up a wad of tissue and press it hard onto her shoulder. "Can I please get you to a doctor now?"

She nods, weakly. "Yes. And then you have to go. Go back and make that love potion, Sam. I'll tell Dan about Emilia's plan. He'll be able to get the word out. But she's going to be moving fast. You have to hurry."

"Just as soon as you're in safe hands," I say. I hold her hand until the medics take over. Before they wheel Arjun away too—he's in a chair now—I give him a hug.

"I'm sorry about the unicorn tail," he says.

"Don't be," I say. "Kirsty found another way." I feel like the slivers of horn are burning a hole in my wallet.

His eyes widen. "No wonder she didn't want anyone to look at that wound. Go on, go," he says. "Kick some potions butt."

I kiss him on the cheek, then Molly and I head through security and over to the transport bays. "You first," I say to her. She nods and steps up to the screen. She pushes her arms through, and because she is Talented—and because she is going back home, a place she knows well, where she has a strong footprint—she doesn't have to have someone pull her through on the other side. It will be a quick, easy journey for her. For that, I'm glad.

Once we're home, I'm quiet. Molly tells Mum and Dad what happened, but when it comes to the part about what she did—the magic she performed—she skips over it. She says she passed out, only to wake up to me rescuing her. She looks over at me, her eyes shining brightly. She thinks I did it. She doesn't realize that it was her all along. I correct her, and she smiles shyly like she doesn't believe it.

"But we got the unicorn tail, didn't we, Sam?" she says, her eyes shining.

"Not exactly." I hesitate to tell them about Emilia, but I don't know why I'm holding back, especially as they've seen it all on the news. It comes out in a flood, and my parents' expressions flicker from horror to anger to relief that we came out of it alive.

Then I get to the part where I performed some minor surgery on Kirsty, and Dad looks like he's about to be sick. I take out my purse and empty the two slivers of horn on the table.

As I'm staring at it, I can sense how it will work with the other ingredients, the process of it swimming before my eyes. Suddenly my hands itch to mix, to crush the fibers up into powder and begin the process of putting the potion together. Still something is missing. "I have to speak to the royals."

I head over to the Summons as my family huddles together to watch. I place my hand on the screen. It takes a few moments, but soon Renel's unwelcoming face appears and my throat closes up. "I had another run-in with Emilia Thoth," I manage to say.

He stops me before I can continue. "It doesn't matter, the princess will be saved. Emilia is no longer a problem."

"What?" My jaw drops.

"ZA have produced the cure."

I'm too stunned to speak. My dad takes over. "They found the recipe for the love potion, and all the ingredients?"

Renel stares down his nose, as if he can barely deign to answer the question. "Zol has had a team of scientists and advanced mixers developing a synth version of the cure at the ZA headquarters since the hunt began. The royal family have agreed that a solution from this very Talented family is the best option for the princess, and that synthetic ingredients have proven to be just as powerful as natural."

"But what about the mirror cure? Won't the horn only accept a natural potion?"

"The Horn will be satisfied once the princess is out of mortal danger. Of course, ZA won't win the hunt exactly, but the princess will be cured—what is the difference? The Wilds passes provided for the hunt will now be rescinded and the royal family requests that all further hunt-related activities cease immediately."

"No!" I cry out. It can't be over, not when we're so close. Not after all we've gone through.

"The royal family asks that you destroy any remnants of a love potion in the making, as it is still an illegal mix. They thank the Kemi family for their participation in the hunt. Good night."

The Summons cuts out. I press on the glass again, and again, but he doesn't return.

My mum puts her hand on my shoulder. "We're sorry, Sam."

Chapter Thirty-Nine

Samantha

I LIE BACK ON MY BED, CURLED UP UNDER the duvet. The hunt had been my distraction, but now I'm out, I can't shut my eyes. Because whenever I shut my eyes, all I can see is Zain Aster and Princess Evelyn. The dark prince, the beautiful princess.

Then there's me. The nerdy, ordinary girl—meant to hide away in the lab with vials of wizard's beard and weird plants for company, not meant for the grand love story. There's no place for me in this formula. I'm a spare ingredient, not meant for the final brew.

My heart aches.

My mind searches for a mix, but there isn't one. There's no potion to cure the way I feel—unless it's the deepest sleep draught I can imagine, one that will whisk me away until my memories of Zain are distant and faded, like photographs left in the sun. But such a potion doesn't exist.

I feel a sudden rush of lunacy, and I want to laugh and laugh and laugh. Instead, I focus on my breathing. I swallow, but my throat feels tight.

I can't imagine why anyone would want a love potion. Why would anyone want to go through this pain? Why would they suffer this voluntarily? Because if there's one thing history has ever taught us about love potions, it's that they always, always end in tragedy and disaster.

The princess will be the exception. She didn't realize that the boy she tried to potion was in love with her all along. She will wake up from her madness—woken by him, if this story is to be written perfectly—and they will realize how lucky they are to have each other. She will realize the error of her ways; she will apologize for being so silly; he will forgive her.

And my moment on the mountain with Zain? A glitch.

She will never know.

I won't tell.

I know where I'll be.

My life won't be like this ever again, out in the Wilds, Finding alongside Kirsty. I've had enough adventure to last a lifetime. Maybe I'll take a night class in business studies, learn how to turn a decent profit—enough to get by—while watching my amazing sister grow into her power. She will go off and do wondrous things, and she'll always know where to find me.

Maybe in time, I'll see Zain and Princess Evelyn again, as I join the throngs crowded against metal railings to witness their big events—their engagement, their wedding, their first baby. I'll be just another face in the crowd. Maybe I'll wear something with a white fur trim, just to see if I can remind him of the abominable, of the mountain—but his eyes will pass me by, glossing over me to whoever is next. He won't want to look at me closely. Because I'll be the only one who knows.

I'll be the one who knows that to be with the person he loves, he trampled over all the ordinary people he saw beneath him. Including me.

My phone buzzes on my bedside table. It's Anita, texting me. *Have you seen the casts?*

I turn on the television but mute the sound. I can read the running news ticker at the bottom: ZA SAVES THE PRINCESS. I groan. This is really what Anita wants to show me? But then there's a second headline: EMILIA THOTH HELD BY POLICE IN ZAMBI. There's an image of Emilia in the type of glamoured handcuffs that can hold a Talented, her face and hands covered in dirt, her hair wild around her face. I feel a jolt of happiness reach through my dark mood. At least something good came from our trip down there. Dan's footage is shown, but we barely get a mention. Our plight is old news already, in light of the ZA cure.

A picture flashes up from an official ZA press release.

It's a glass vial imprinted with the ZA logo. The vial is filled with a dark crimson liquid, thick like blood.

Exactly how you would expect a love potion to look.

I text back to Anita. At least Emilia was wrong. The princess is safe. Good luck to them.

Anita replies almost immediately. You don't need to be brave, lovely. I'll come over as soon as I can.

Her words bring the first hint of tears to my eyes, as I feel grateful to have people who love me. But I'm not being brave. I am glad the princess is safe, even though it means Granddad was right: In the end, the royals did bend the rules to suit themselves. And Zain broke my heart to save her.

The Princess. It's funny that I haven't thought about her all that much through this whole process, even though it's really all about her.

Sitting alone in my room now, I think about what it would be like to be driven to the most desperate of measures. To be so terrified of rejection that you try to prevent it at any cost. I wonder if Princess Evelyn has ever been rejected in her entire life.

It's not rejection that I'm scared of. Lord knows, I've seen enough of it in my time: from school, from the Talenteds. At least if they're rejecting you, they're paying some sort of attention to you.

No, my biggest fear is anonymity. Oblivion. Obscurity. The fear that I will do nothing more with my life than rot away in my family store. The fear I will live my whole life and not do anything to make an impact. The fear that I will find the guy who I want to give my heart to, only for him to ignore me. Forget me.

Zain.

I'm disgusting myself, wallowing here, but I can't help that the image of his face is seared behind my eyelids. I don't need a love potion; I need an antilove cure to ease this pain.

It's as if I've taken one of the dark potions. One that causes pain—another highly illegal mix. Pain potions are idiosyncratic. Personal to the mixer. It requires that the mixer be causing someone immense physical pain during the final moments of creation. The more agonizing the pain, the stronger the potion. With no pain at all, it won't work—except maybe to give the recipient a mild stomachache. Too much pain—if you kill while mixing, for example—then it doesn't work either. The potion will burn itself out and be dead in the pan.

The mixer would have to be a pretty awful person to agree to make one of these potions, and who would want to buy from that person, in case you become the next victim?

And love potions aren't even about love, are they? They're about the illusion of it: the fantasy. They're about the lust, the passion. I've seen real love. My parents have it, for one. There's nothing one-sided about it.

It's about two people agreeing to face the world together, no matter the challenges. It's about respect.

It's personal.

Suddenly, like a fissure caused by an earthquake, a chasm opens deep in my mind. No brain, please not now. But it's not a voice that can be turned off.

A hunch screams that something is wrong.

My mind jumps right back to that moment in the library. The words that stood out to me, in that ancient language. Eluvium was the ivy. Indicum. Indigo. That's the color I would have looked for. Not crimson. It was too obvious.

I shake it out of my head. They won't let the princess drink a faulty love potion. If they can't use the horn to verify the potion's authenticity, they'll rigorously test it. There is no way that ZA will make a mistake. There's too much riding on this. Their reputation. Their business. Not to mention the princess's life.

I sit straight up out of bed. ZA have messed this up.

The love potion they've created is wrong. It's not going to work.

And I'm the only one who can fix it.

Chapter Forty

Samantha

I BARGE THROUGH THE HEAVY WOODEN door that leads into Granddad's lab and breathe a sigh of relief. The lab is neat, unbearably so—exactly as Granddad likes to keep it.

Instead of turning on the overhead light, I head over to the oil burners, lighting them with a long match. It lends the place an eerie glow, the gentle lamplight bouncing off the myriad glass jars and half-formed mixes. I walk over to the long oak table, which runs down the center of the room.

I hear the door swing open, and then I spot a shock of white hair, a wrinkled hand, and the tension disappears from my muscles.

Granddad pops his head around the door and looks at me over his half-moon spectacles. "Everything okay, Sam?"

My eyes well with tears, and I shake my head. "They've got it wrong."

He potters over to the table and places his hand over mine. "I know."

"They won't listen to me if I try to use the Summons. What if she's already taken it?"

"There's only one way to convince them."

I lean my head on his shoulder. "I have to do this, don't I?"

He shifts his shoulder so I'm forced to look up, and then he takes my chin between his fingers. "You never have to do anything. But at this moment, you know the truth. If you want to save her, then you are the only one who will be able to do it."

I nod. Do I want to save her?

Of course I do. She is the one whom Zain loves. I want to give her back to him. He deserves that, even after everything.

I wipe the tears from my eyes.

"Good girl," says Granddad. "You have a strong start here." He walks over to where Dad has stored the potion base I made in Loga. My head feels fuzzy, but I shake it to remove the cobwebs. I lift up the mix of Aphroditas pearl, rosewater, and eluvian ivy, swirling it around in its glass jar.

"It's beautiful," I whisper. I lift the lid off the jar and the air around me is infused with a delicate scent—like roses and the crest of ocean waves and blue sky in a bottle. I almost melt with delight at how good it smells.

"Oh my goodness, they should make this a perfume!"

Granddad winks at me. "Now you know the recipe for Elixir No. 5, the House of Perrod's signature scent."

My eyes widen; that perfume sells in department stores for hundreds of crowns. I run the base through a strainer, collecting any tiny fragments of powder that haven't completely dissolved. When it looks about as clear as I'm ever going to make it, I turn on a blue-flamed burner and set a cast-iron pot on top of it. I pour the liquid into it from a height, watching it flow and steam as it hits the warm edges of the pot. In this light, from this height, it takes on an almost-champagne tinge, a light yellow-gold that sparkles gently. Blink and you'll miss it shimmer.

Granddad observes me, but he doesn't help. All of it must be done by my hand, especially if I would like it to be as strong as it needs to be.

Next I cut the pink jasmine from the pot Anita gave me, its roots still embedded in the soil. That will help with the strength of it too. Somehow, everything has come together as it needed to. This is my potion to make; I know it.

I pound the delicate petals of the jasmine once or twice on the oak table, bruising the blush of the flower, turning pink to almost brown. Then I drop it into the base. Immediately it starts to smoke and thicken, the liquid bubbling ferociously. This is good. This is what I want. Virility.

The abominable fur is next. My hands shake as I unwrap it from the brown paper we stored it in, three thin, incredibly long strands of translucent hair. Laid on top of each other, they create the deep, pure white of the mountain, but separately they look more like crystal. I compare them to the unicorn horn. They are similar in many ways. But there is no shimmer to the abominable. It is cold and matte. One is loneliness. The other is purity.

The abominable hair is brittle, and as I pick up a strand it crumbles in my fingers. I drop the pieces into a large marble mortar, then I pick up the pestle and begin to grind. It's instant stress relief. I twist and twist the strands of abominable, watching them separate out, crush, dance in the bottom of the mortar. Then I start pounding, driving the substance deep into the stone. It's ridiculous how much pleasure this little act of violence gives me.

I scrape the side of the bowl with the side of the pestle, not allowing a single molecule to escape its punishment.

It still needs to be finer, so I tuck the mortar under my arm and continue to grind from a closer angle. When it's done, it's a fine powder. I carefully tip it all into a glass jar that Granddad has labeled in his spindly handwriting. I only need the tiniest touch of the abominable powder, and the rest will go back onto our store shelves. Crushed abominable fur. For use in love potions, for thawing cold shoulders, and alleviating agoraphobia.

I tip a tiny half teaspoonful of the abominable powder into the mix and turn down the heat on the burner. The mixture calms down, resting at a gentle simmer.

"Let's have a cup of tea," Granddad says. "We've got a long night ahead of us still."

I stare back at the mixture wistfully, but nothing is going to happen for the next little while—I must reduce it down by half before we add the unicorn horn.

"Make mine peppermint?" I ask, allowing myself the first small smile in what feels like a long time. I follow him into the kitchen. He fills the kettle up with water and places it on our hot stove. The stove is my favorite part of the kitchen. It's heavy cast iron painted a bright crimson, and it's always on, keeping this part of the house cozy and warm, even if the room is still run down. Looking round at our shabby cupboards and peeling paint, I suddenly think that we might have the money soon to change all that.

"Granddad, why have you never moved the store?"

"Sam, dear, I will never move the store."

"But why? We could be in a much better location with more foot traffic, we could digitize the stock records, track the prescriptions via computer . . . still keeping the traditional elements of our lab and the way we mix. What's the harm in updating if we have the money? We could turn Kemi's Potion Shop into a real business again. Even if this love potion doesn't work . . . we can turn things around. And if anything good is going to come from this whole experience, it's that everyone will be reminded of the name Kemi."

"That's right, which means they know where to find us if they want us."

"But . . ."

"Sam, there is no 'but' about it. This shop is not moving anywhere. You might think that only Talenteds are permitted to access magic, but that couldn't be further from the truth. Magic is a part of our atmosphere, the air we breathe. The secrets in there"—he points to my diary, where I've finished inscribing this stage of the recipe—"are worth protecting. There is more magic in these store shelves than there will be in any other modern building. Magic passed down to us from the generations of Kemi that have lived and worked in this store before us."

The whistle of the kettle interrupts the moment, and I don't have the energy to press on with my questioning. I have a lifetime to learn the store's—and Granddad's—secrets. But first, I have to get the potion right.

After I finish my tea, we head back into the lab. As soon as I open the door, fingers of pale pink smoke slide out into the kitchen. It must be the jasmine. I grab a pair of goggles from a hook before I check on the mixture, and I see that it has dissolved down into a thick, almost gelatinous white substance. It doesn't look anything like a love potion should at the moment, and there aren't many ingredients left to add. I bite my bottom lip, but remind myself that sometimes the right reactions don't happen until everything is in the pot.

I unscrew the lid from the jar containing the unicorn horn and spill the slivers out onto the table. It looks so fragile, but unlike the abominable hair, it doesn't shatter at the first touch. Or at the second. Or when I take a sharp knife to it. It won't break at all.

"Granddad, do you have any ideas?"

He takes up another piece of the unicorn horn. He rolls it around in his palm, testing its strength with his fingers.

"Do you think maybe I should just stir it into the mixture as it is?" I ask doubtfully.

"You must somehow extract the nutrients inside the horn. If you simply use it as is then the other ingredients will only react with the outer casing."

"But I don't think I'll be able to bash it open—I mean, it's not responding to any amount of pressure."

"Well, then maybe you will have to be more subtle than that."

I want to scream at him, *Why won't you just tell me the answer?* But that isn't my granddad's way. He pats my hand and walks out of the lab. That's the boost I need. If he's leaving, he's confident I will figure it out. If only I had the same confidence in myself.

Thick pink smoke billows out of the pot now, so I move one of the lab hoods—almost like a great upside-down beaker—over the top of it. The idea is to catch some of the fumes, as they might be important later. I'm amazed that it's smoking so much, even though the heat is down low on the burner.

Then it strikes me. I can steam out the nutrients from the unicorn horn. I place the shard in an oversize sieve and balance it under the hood and across the cast-iron pot. There I watch as the smoke engulfs it, swirling around it, before the unicorn horn begins to bead and sweat. I can only hope that it will work. Then I watch as one of the beads falls into the mixture. Immediately the white mixture at the base of the pot turns a dark pink where it splashes. Relieved, I leave the horn to sweat out even more.

Instead, now I go over to the desk where my diary is lying open. I pick up Granddad's fountain pen and slowly write out the remaining ingredients, the quantities that I used, and the method of the recipe itself. I think of the princess, working unknowingly with her evil aunt to find the recipe. But Emilia didn't seem to know about the final ingredient. The one that I'd thought of last night. The one I wouldn't have to go out into the Wilds to find. But the one that is just as dangerous as the others, to me.

When I have another thought, it's panic. My head is

on the desk, the pen fallen against my hand and leaking ink onto my palm. I snatch at my watch—five a.m. I've been asleep for four hours.

The potion.

The mix.

I haven't been watching it.

I race over to the table, knocking my chair over in the process. The smoke has died away almost completely, and the shard of unicorn horn is gone. I peer into the cast iron bowl, dreading what I might find there. But instead, it looks remarkably like a liquid again. Floating at the top is the outer casing of the unicorn horn. I take the sieve and fish it out.

Using my gloves, I pick the pot off the burner and turn it off completely. Then I gently pour the liquid into a clear glass beaker. I almost drop it when I see its color. A beautiful rich crimson, exactly like the potion ZA showed on television. It looks exactly how a love potion should look. If I didn't know better, I would say this was perfect.

But I know it isn't. Now is the time for my hunch about the last piece of the puzzle, the true final ingredient in the mix. From the drawer in the far side of the room, I pull out a long-handled, extremely sharp silver knife. I hold it gently between two fingers and walk back to the table.

I place my palm against the glass edge of the beaker.

"Ready?" I say to myself out loud. I hate doing this. My stomach lurches, but I force myself to be calm. It's just a cut. I've been engulfed by eluvian ivy. I've been scratched by an abominable. I've been bitten by a vampire bat. I can handle a little cut.

I slice with the knife.

It barely has to touch my skin before the blood rises in the crevices of my skin. I pull my hand into a fist and watch as a drop of blood falls into the mixture. Where the blood touches it, it turns indigo.

I'm just admiring my handiwork, when the door opens again. I expect it to be Granddad, but it's not, it's Mum. Her hair is disheveled and she's in her dressing gown and slippers.

"Did you hear?"

"Hear what?"

"The synth potion passed all their tests. They're about to administer it to the princess now."

"No!" I shout. "No, they can't!"

"Oh my god, Sam, what happened to your hand?"

I look down and it's gushing blood now. I open it out, and my mum rushes forward, grabbing a tissue from the side table and pressing it onto my palm.

"Mum, you don't understand," I say, barely noticing my hand. "They can't give her that potion. It won't work. It will damage her more. I have the right one."

I spin around and grab the beaker from the table. But

instead of the liquid I expected, the mixture has turned completely to powder, and the color has changed to a dark, deep indigo.

"Are you sure?" Mum says, looking from my face to the powder in my hand.

"I've never been more sure of anything in my entire life."

"Then you'd better hurry."

I race out of the lab, grabbing a bottle of water from the fridge door in the kitchen. I take a moment to measure a teaspoon of the powder and mix it with the water. Then I run to the Summons. If I don't get there in time, the princess is going to be lost, forever.

Once I get to the Summons, I touch the surface tentatively at first, and then harder, until I'm slamming my hand against the glasslike surface.

I scream Renel's name, but if he's there, if he can hear me, he's not listening.

"Renel!" I scream again. "You're making a big mistake! The ZA potion is wrong. You're going to poison her!"

"He's not going to answer," says Granddad. "Come with me."

I have no better option than to follow him, even if I debate whether I can run to the castle from here and scream and shout until I'm let into the palace above. I follow him into his bedroom, which is just as jumbled and full of books and alchemist paraphernalia as the lab.

But there, on the dresser, is a small television screen. Except, as Granddad quickly makes clear, it's not a TV screen at all. It's another Summons.

He places his palm on it, and it immediately jumps to life.

"Ostanes? Is that you?"

The wrinkled face on the other side of the Summons takes my breath away.

It's the Queen Mother.

Chapter Forty-One

Samantha

"TABITHA."

"Ostanes." The look of relief on the Queen Mother's face is apparent. "What have you been waiting for? They're about to administer that vile synth abomination. For a moment I thought you might have failed me." She puts her hand through the Summons, ready to pull me through.

"The Kemi family have never failed you," my granddad says. He keeps his hand firmly on my upper arm, not letting me move. "You failed us."

"Ostanes, please. This is my granddaughter we're talking about."

"And it is my grandchildren that you have endangered by not taking care of your own family."

Fire blazes between the two old titans of the world, and if I know anything about my granddad—and from what little I know about the Queen Mother—this stand-off could go on for a long time. But I don't have a long time. Neither does Evelyn. I tug at my granddad's sleeve. "Whatever is going on here, I don't care. I need to get this to Evelyn."

His mouth doesn't shift from its firm line. But he releases me, and I take the Queen Mother's wrinkled hand. She pulls me from my home straight into her bedroom. My jaw drops as I look around. There's a big crack down one wall, pictures smashed on dark hardwood flooring, glass sprinkled everywhere. One of the posts on her four-poster bed has fallen, bringing down with it a heavy woven tapestry and leaving it in tatters.

It's chaos.

"Quick, child." For someone who can look so frail on the casts, she's fast. I struggle to keep up with her through the twists and turns of the palace corridors.

At one point, she walks straight through a brick wall.

A moment later, she reappears. "I forget you ordinaries have to use doors. How inconvenient." She doesn't magic a door for me to use, though. She simply blasts a hole through the brickwork, leaving me to pick a path through the smoking rubble.

We arrive where Princess Evelyn is being kept. Guards line the corridor on both sides, and an alcove is filled with cameramen and reporters. I'm surprised that they've been let so deep into the palace.

As soon as they spot the Queen Mother and me,

there's a flurry and rush of activity as they turn their cameras on us to get a good shot. It's rare enough to get a video of the Queen Mother under normal circumstances.

"Get out of my way," the Queen Mother says, commanding so much power despite her small stature. Her isolation from the press also means that she suffers none of their nonsense. I find it refreshing.

She passes through the wall of the princess's room, and this time a door appears for me to step through. In the room is Zain—the first person my eyes find. Zol is there too, along with Renel, the queen, and the king.

They all look shocked to see us.

Princess Evelyn is asleep on her bed. Renel has the synth potion in his hands.

Evelyn stirs, fluttering her lashes, letting out a low moan of pain. Zain keeps staring at me, and although my eyes flicker back to him, what I read in his expression is exactly the last thing I ever thought I'd see there. It's relief.

"You're too late." Zol smirks. "Our potion has been administered—"

The hair on my arms stands up on end, shivers running up and down my skin. It's power building, gathering. A smell of roses fills the air, so thick, sweet, and cloying it almost chokes me. Magic, pure and raw and uncontrollable.

A bolt of lightning explodes in the room, sending us

all flying to the ground. I shield my eyes with my hands, and when I look over at Evelyn, I see her floating above the bed, lightning sparking from her fingers.

"It didn't work!" Zain cries out. He leaps to Evelyn's bedside, trying to control her.

A storm gathers inside the room, the ceiling threatening to break away from the walls. The trembling ground sends objects flying around the room; everyone's attention is focused on Evelyn, but mine is focused somewhere else: on Auden's Horn, which has been relocated to the princess's room.

I make a dive for it, the potion in my hand. In what I hope will be a moment of calm, I open the bottle over the horn, but another wave of energy surges from the princess and sends the liquid spraying everywhere.

"No!" I scream.

"Sam, hurry!" says Zain. "I trust you. Administer the potion!"

There is just enough left. I take a running leap toward the princess, and at the same time the earth lifts beneath my feet. A gaping hole opens in the floor, leading into the bright blue sky. I jump onto the princess's bed, grabbing Zain's outstretched arm and pulling myself along, like we're trying to fight against a hurricane. Finally I reach her. She's screaming.

I tip the potion into her mouth. At the same time, her eyes fly open and bore into mine, and then a blast of her magic flings me from the bed, all the way across the room until I land with a crash against the podium, sending Auden's Horn clattering to the ground.

I lie there in a crumpled heap. I can barely move. But I can see the horn. And I can see that it's gold.

The noise, the wind, the lightning, the storm all stop.

"Zain?" I hear Evelyn say.

"Hey, Evie," he whispers back to her, and the tenderness in his voice breaks me. "How are you feeling?" Zain leans down and picks up a shard of broken mirror that has fallen on the ground. We all wait with bated breath, scattered across what's left of the room. If it hasn't worked, it could be the end.

"Oh wow," says Evelyn. "I look dreadful!" She pushes the mirror away, and there's a collective sigh of relief. "Hey, what's going on? What happened in here? Did my eighteenth get a bit out of control?"

Now I know she's safe, the pain hits. Darkness edges at my vision and I feel every lump of broken stone under my back. Someone kneels down beside me and cradles my head in their hands.

"You okay?"

It's Zain.

"Unrequited love," I say, finally able to finish the answer to the question Zol had asked. "That was the missing ingredient."

"You did it, Sam," he says. "You won the hunt."

Chapter Forty-Two

Samantha

I'M STANDING, AWKWARDLY, IN A BEAUTIFUL dress that they had couriered up from one of the most expensive shops in Kingstown. Nothing in my closet was good enough for one's first royal dinner, apparently. I refuse the heels though. I'm already going to be the ordinary in the room, better not to be the ordinary giant.

But before the dinner, I've been asked to wait. My stomach rumbles in anticipation. They've healed my scrapes and broken bones and applied a top-notch glamour to give me color, but they can't use magic on my weary brain. I feel like I could sleep for a year. Renel ushers me into this mirrored receiving room, adjacent to the princess's bedroom. There's an uncomfortable, lion-footed sofa that I try sitting on, but it's so hard and bulbous that I return to standing. I'm also a little bit concerned that I'll ruin my dress.

There's a snap of electricity, and suddenly the princess is in the room with me. I swallow hard. Despite having been close enough to thrust a love potion down her throat, having her awake and looking at me is intimidating. She's so incredibly beautiful up close.

She rushes over to me and takes both of my hands like we are long lost best friends. "Samantha Kemi." She kisses me on both cheeks. Up close, she smells of Elixir No. 5. "So you're the wondrous brain that saved me."

I blush a deep crimson. "I think it was more of a team effort thing . . ."

She waves her hands around dismissively. "Are you kidding me? Do you know how long it took for me to find a recipe for a love potion? Years. I mean, to figure out about the unrequited love." She regards me steadily through her steel-gray irises. "That takes skill."

I bite my lip, considering what to say. The princess stops me with a hand. "You saved my life. And I'm sure it made the potion extra potent for me, that we just so happened to be unrequitedly loving the same person."

Now I don't blush any deeper (because it's not possible), but I want to sink into the ground and have it swallow me up. "And he loves you too," I stammer out. "You didn't need the potion after all."

She laughs. It's completely not the reaction I'm expecting. She reaches out and grabs my wrist. "Oh,

Sam, don't be so silly. He doesn't love me at all—not like that, anyway. He wasn't as smart as you, but you'll find out about that soon enough. And honestly, I'm not sure that I ever loved him in the right way either. You have to understand, Zain is my best friend. Winning his heart—however falsely—was the only path I could see that would lead me to some kind of happiness in the future. You see, the truth is, I don't love anybody. Not yet."

I smile. I'm beginning to warm to Princess Evelyn, despite myself. She must sense it, because she leans in again and kisses me on both cheeks. "Thanks," she says. "Do you have a phone?"

"Umm . . ." I fumble open my tiny handbag, which is also brand-new. I've never had need of a tiny handbag before. "Here," I say, handing it over to her. She taps her number into my contacts.

"There, that way, we can be friends, and you can come to the wedding."

"The wedding?" My eyes open wide.

Evelyn smiles sadly at me. "I tried to cheat my responsibility, and look what happened. I still have to get married. It sucks, but what can you do. I'll see you at dinner?"

"Oh, I'm not sure where I should go . . ."

"Don't worry, I'll send someone up to escort you."

And before I can say anything else, she's gone.

Luckily, this room isn't doorless, or I would have really felt trapped.

I explore the room. This was where it happened, according to the casts. There's a small table by the window, with a couple of glasses on it. A sparkling crystal carafe sits on a little silver tray, but there's no liquid in it.

"I don't trust women who stand by that table," says a voice from the doorway.

I spin around. It's Zain. "What do you want?"

If he's hurt by my curt tone, he doesn't show it. Instead, he bows. "I'm here to escort you to dinner."

"Seriously? You're escorting me? Look, I'd rather just go home than suffer any more humiliation, okay?"

Finally, his expression falters. "Sam—"

"No, you don't get to 'Sam' me. You put me through hell, you know that?"

"I know. My father, he—"

"You can't just blame your dad for this."

"Sam—"

"You think just because the princess has messed with her emotions, that gives you the right to mess with mine in order to save her? There are some things that are just as strong—no—stronger than love potions you know. Like real feelings."

"Sam—"

I can't help it, I am so, so angry at him. "I thought we had something . . . but you couldn't stand up to your father in this? Everything was just one big lie."

"It isn't."

"What?"

"It isn't a lie. I do feel that way about you, everything I said. I thought Evelyn told me that the final ingredient was love. I told my father, and he said that meant the potion had to be made by someone who believed that they were in love with the intended taker."

I fold my arms across my chest. "That's why you did that television interview."

"Exactly. I thought that if I made a public declaration of my love, the potion would work. But my dad was wrong, and so was I. It was unrequited love. And you figured that out, even though you didn't have to. I can't believe that I broke your heart. But listen, in a way, I'm glad that I did."

I narrow my eyes. "And why is that?"

"Because I hope I can spend the rest of the summer trying to make it up to you."

I want to say something, find some witty repartee to come back with, but when I open my mouth absolutely nothing comes out. Treacherous mouth. Then: "Aren't you marrying the princess?"

"What? No."

"But she said . . ." Then I stop. She didn't say she was marrying Zain. Only that she still had to get married.

Zain seizes his opportunity. He reaches out and grabs

my hand. "You're one of a kind, Sam Kemi. Will you let me earn back your trust?"

I allow myself a small smile. "I'll think about it."

He takes my arm. "We're going to be late for dinner."

"Let them wait," I say, and I lift my face to his and kiss him.

Acknowledgments

THIS BOOK HAS POSSESSED ITS OWN special alchemy right from the start: The idea came from a random tweet in 2010, which was then blended with many months spent writing in the darkest hours of the night, and now, with the help of so many people, it is finally ready to be served.

My first thanks must go to Juliet, to whom this book is dedicated, and Sarah—the dream agenting team whom anyone would be lucky to have in their corner. Their hard work means I can keep on doing what I love for a living, and have a lot of fun doing it.

Next up, so many thanks to Elv and Zareen, my editors at S&S UK and US, for your tremendous efforts in helping me whip this book into shape. You have both gone above and beyond the call of duty, and this book would not be the same without you. To Liz at S&S UK, thank you for your awesome marketing and publicity work and for being a cheerleader for this book right from the beginning.

ACKNOWLEDGMENTS

No writer should be without trusted writing friends, and mine are two of the very best. Thank you, Kim and Laura. Without your early thoughts, sound advice, and shoulders to cry on, I wouldn't have survived this journey! I hope there are many more retreats in our future.

To Mum, Dad, and Sophie—thank you for always being the first to read and the first to delight in every milestone I achieve.

And lastly, to Lofty—thank you for not needing a potion to be the love of my life.